CW01507142

STEWART HOME w
the author of twer
into many languages. His works include *69 Things To Do With A Dead Princess*, *She's My Witch*, *The 9 Lives of Ray The Cat Jones* and *Re-Enter The Dragon: Genre Theory, Brucesploitation And The Sleazy Joys Of Lowbrow Cinema*. Home has also worked as an artist (including visual work in the Arts Council England Collection), an art class model, a shop assistant, a typist, a factory labourer and a ventriloquist.

Stewart Home

ART
SCHOOL
ORGY

New Reality Records

6 Poppy Close
Loughborough
LE11 2FA

https://newrealityrecords.bandcamp.com/

A catalogue record for this book is available
from the British Library

ISBN 978-1-7396755-0-9

Printed and bound in Great Britain
by Flexpress Ltd, Leicester.

The fascination of pictures is the fascination of being seduced by a dead object, it is the magic of disappearance, and this particular magic can be found just as easily in pornographic images as in modern art, where the prevailing obsession has been to literally not be viewable, to defy any and all possibilities of visual seduction….

Inasmuch as we have access to neither the beautiful nor the ugly, and are incapable of judging, we are condemned to indifference. Beyond this indifference, however, another kind of fascination emerges, a fascination which replaces aesthetic pleasure. For, once liberated from their respective constraints, the beautiful and the ugly, in a sense, multiply: they become more beautiful than beautiful, more ugly than ugly. Thus painting currently cultivates, if not ugliness exactly which remains an aesthetic value - then the uglier-than-ugly (the 'bad', the 'worse', kitsch), an ugliness raised to the second power because it is liberated from any relationship with its opposite. Once freed from the 'true' Mondrian, we are at liberty to 'out-Mondrian Mondrian'; freed from the true naifs, we can paint in a way that is 'more naif than naif', and so on. And once freed from reality, we can produce the 'realer than real'– hyperrealism. It was in fact with hyperrealism and pop art that everything began, that everyday life was raised to the ironic power of photographic realism. Today this escalation has caught up every form of art, every style; and all, without discrimination, have entered the transaesthetic world of simulation.

Jean Baudrillard, *The Transparency Of Evil*

CHAPTER 1

THE REPUBLICAN COLLEGE OF ART

The Republican College of Art was a moderate-sized art school. There might have been some two or three hundred postgraduates studying there when our rapscallion David Hockney appeared there as a freshman. Of these, unfortunately for the art school, there were a very large proportion of the gentleman-commoners. Enough, in fact, with the other men whom they drew round them, and who lived pretty much as they did, to form the largest and leading set in the college. So the art school was decidedly fast.

The chief characteristic of this set was the most reckless extravagance of every kind. London wine merchants furnished them with liqueurs at a guinea a bottle and wine at five guineas a dozen. London tailors vied with one another in providing them with unheard-of quantities of the most gorgeous clothing. They drove tandems in all directions, scattering their ample grants, which they treated as pocket money, about roadside inns and London taverns with open hand, and "going tick" for everything that could be obtained on the never never. Their cigars cost two guineas a pound, their furniture was the best that could be bought. Pineapples, forced fruit, and the most rare preserves figured at their wine parties. They danced, slept by day, played billiards until the gates closed, and then were ready for vingt-etun, unlimited loo, and hot drink in their own rooms, as long as anyone could be got to sit up and play. The fast set then swamped and set the tone at the art school, of which fact no persons were more astonished and horrified than the authorities of the RCA.

That they of all bodies in the world should be lumbered with a set of reckless young spendthrifts, was indeed a melancholy and unprecedented fact. For the body of fellows of the RCA was as distinguished for restraint, morality and respectability as any in an art school. The foundation was not, indeed, an open one. St Martin's at that time alone enjoyed this distinction, but there were a large number of open fellowships, and the income of the college was large, and the livings belonging to it numerous, so that the best men from other colleges were constantly coming in. Some of these of a former generation had been eminently successful in their management of the college.

The RCA postgraduates at one time had carried off almost all the art prizes and filled the young contemporaries lists, while maintaining at the same time the highest character for girlishness and feminine conduct. This had lasted long enough to establish the fame of the college, and great lords and horny-handed sons of toil had sent their offspring there. Art masters had struggled to get the names of their best pupils on the books. In short, everyone who had a son, ward, or pupil, whom he wanted to push forward in the art world—who wanted to cut a figure and take the lead among effete men of culture—left no stone unturned to get him into RCA.

But the governing bodies of colleges are always on the change, and, in the course of things men of other ideas came to rule at the RCA. Shrewd men of the world. Men of business, some of them, with good ideas of making the most of their advantages, who said: "Why should we not make the public pay for the great benefits we confer on them? Are we not the very best article in the educational market and shall we not get the highest price for it?" So by degrees they altered many things in the college. Under their auspices gentlemen-commoners increased and multiplied. In fact, the eldest sons of baronets, even squires, who lacked talent were scarcely admitted unless they bribed their way in. As these young gentlemen secretly paid double fees to the college and had great expectations of all sorts, it could not be expected that they should be subject to quite the same discipline as the common run of men, who would have to make their own way in the world. So the rules as to attendance at exhibitions and in the studio, though nominally the same for them as for commoners, were in practice relaxed in their favour. So that they might find all things suitable to persons in their position, the kitchen and buttery were worked up to a high state of perfection, and the RCA, from having been one of the most reasonable, had come to be about the most expensive art school in the land. Not to mention being the sole one to take only postgraduates and have no undergraduates.

These changes worked as their promoters probably desired they should and the college was full of rich men, who commanded in the art school the sort of respect which riches bring with them. But the old reputation, though still strong out of doors, was beginning sadly to wane within the world of art. Fewer and fewer of the RCA men appeared in the Royal Academy summer show and even less amongst the prize-men at that prestigious event.

The inaugurators of these changes had passed away in their turn, and at last a reaction had commenced. The fellows recently elected and who were in residence as the grey nineteen-fifties made way for London's swinging sixties, were for the most part men of great attainments, all of them had taken their use of colour and boldness of line to the very heights of perfection. The electors naturally enough had chosen them as the most likely persons to restore, as tutors, the golden days of the college, and they had been careful in the selection to confine themselves to very quiet and studious men, passing over men of more popular manners and active spirits, who would be sure to flit soon into the world, and be of little service to the RCA.

But these were not the men to get any hold on the fast set who were now in the ascendant. It was not in the nature of things that they should understand each other. In fact, they were hopelessly at war and the college was getting more and more out of gear in consequence.

What they could do, however, they were doing. Under their fostering care a small set was growing up, including most of the sculptors, who the respectable party thought would retrieve the art school's character. But the students thus picked for admission were too much like their tutors. Men who did little else but work feverishly in their studios. They neither wished for, nor were likely to gain, the slightest influence on the fast set. The best amongst them were diligent readers of Eric Gill, and followers of Henry Moore. This led them to form such friendships as they made amongst out-college men of their own way of thinking—viz with high modernists, rather than the RCA fast set. So they lived very much to themselves and scarcely interfered with the dominant party.

Our rapscallion, on leaving his initial art school, had bound himself solemnly to write all his doings and thoughts to the friend he was leaving behind. This compact had been made on one of their last evenings in Bradford. They were sitting together on a park bench, Ferrill Armstrong splicing the handle of a favourite cricket bat, and Mark 'Geordie' Berger reading a volume of Lautréamont's works. One of their tutors at Bradford School of Art had lately been alluding to 'the decadents' and the mysteries of man-to-man love and had excited the curiosity of the active-minded amongst his pupils about gay sex and bestiality. So Isidore Ducasse's works were seized on by various voracious young readers, and carried out of the master's private library. Mark was now curled up on one end of the bench reading *Les Chants de Maldoror* and getting into the vagaries of shark sex. Presently, Hockney heard something between a groan and a protest, and, looking up, demanded explanations. Mark, in a voice half furious and half fearful, that unmistakably belonged to a young man who'd grown up in Newcastle, read out:

> There are some who write seeking the commendation of their fellows by means of noble sentiments which their imaginations invent or they possibly may possess. But I set my genius to portray the pleasures of cruelty! Cannot genius be cruelty's ally in the secret resolutions of Providence? Or, if cruel, can't one possess genius? My words will provide the proof; all you need do is listen to them, if you like...

"You don't mean to say that's Lautréamont's view of humanity?" Armstrong asked.

"Yes!"

"What a cold-blooded old Philistine," said Hockney.

"Do you think it could be true?" Mark asked.

"I don't want to think about that," Armstrong said flatly. "I'm going to see if I can find a pair of labourers who'll let me take turns sucking them off, while they take turns beating my bottom with this cricket bat."

After some personal reflections on Lautréamont once Armstrong had left in search of cock, Geordie and Hockney then and there resolved that, so far as they were concerned, it was not, could not, and should not be true. They would remain the greatest friends in the world. And for the better insuring this result, a correspondence, regular as the recurring months, was to be maintained. It had already lasted through the long vacation and up to September without dragging, though Hockney's letters had been rather short in August, when he had lots of cottaging in Manchester, and two days a week at a steam bath that attracted the best looking men from the north-west of England. Now, however, having fairly got to London, he determined to make up for all short-comings. His first letter from college, taken in connexion with the previous sketch of the place, will probably accomplish the work of introduction better than any detailed account by a third party, and it is therefore given here verbatim:

The RCA,
Kensington Gore,
London.

October, 195–

My Dear Geordie,

According to promise, I write to tell you how I get on down here, and what sort of a place London is. Of course, I don't know much about it yet, having only been here some weeks, but you shall have my first impressions.

First and foremost it's an awfully idle place, at any rate for us newbies. Fancy now. I am in the studio twelve hours a week! Two hours a day, all over by twelve, or one at latest, and no extra work at all in the shape of still life, engraving, or other exercises.

I think sometimes I'm back in the lower fifth. We don't get through more than we used to do there and if you were to see the men draw nudes, it would make your hair curl. Where on earth can they have come from? Unless they blunder on purpose, as I often think. Of course, I never look at the models before I go in since unfortunately they are mostly female. I hope to make portraits of the men I pick up outside the local tube station, but you know I never was much of a hand at sapping, and, for the present, the light work suits me well enough. There's plenty to see and learn about in this place.

We keep very gentlemanly hours. Wine every morning at eight and beer every evening at seven. You must drink at least twice a day, that's the rule of our college—and be home by twelve o'clock at night. Besides which, if you're a decently steady fellow, you ought to dance at the union perhaps two days a week. Union is open all day and closes at eleven o'clock at night. And now you have the sum total. All the rest of your time you can do whatever you want.

I dare say after what I've written you'll complain I've told you nothing, and you'd rather have twenty lines about the men, and what they're thinking about and the meaning, and the inner life of the place, and all that. Patience, patience! I don't know anything about it myself yet. You shall have the kernel in due course, if I get to fuck my way through the student body.

Ever affectionately, D. H.

CHAPTER 2

A ROW ON THE SERPENTINE

Within a day or two of the penning the celebrated epistle reproduced in the last chapter, which created quite a sensation at Bradford College of Art, Hockney realised one of his London ambitions by boating on The Serpentine lake in Hyde Park in a skiff.

He had already been on The Serpentine several times in pair-oar and four-oar boats, with an old oar to pull stroke, and another to steer and coach him. He did not believe he was as bad an oar as the old hands made out, and thought that it must be the fault of the other art students who were learning with him that the boat went nowhere and rolled so much.

Pulling looked simple enough, much easier than tennis. He had made an excellent start at the latter game and been highly complimented by the marker after his first hour on court. He didn't know that cricket and fives are capital training for tennis but that rowing is a speciality. And so confident that if he could only have a turn or two alone, he should not only satisfy himself, but everybody else, that he was a heaven-born oar, he refused all offers of companionship, and set off down to the boats for his trial trip. His regular companions went to a boozer, but Hockney chuckled as he came within sight of the lake.

The post-grad's state of excitement increased when, in answer to his casual enquiry, the boat hire attendant informed him that not a man from his art school was about the place. So he ordered a skiff with dignity and coolness.

"This way, sir," said the attendant, conducting him to a good, safe-looking craft. "Any gentleman going to steer, sir?"

"No," said Hockney, superciliously, "You may take out the rudder."

"Going quite alone, sir? Better take one of our boys. I'll find you a very light one. Here, Bill!"

He turned to summon a juvenile waterman to take charge of our rapscallion.

"Take out the rudder, do you hear?" Hockney interrupted. "I won't have a steerer."

"As you please," said the manager, proceeding to remove the degrading appendage. "Water's rather deep. You must mind the other boats and the edges of the lake. I suppose you can swim?"

"Yes," said Hockney, settling himself on his cushion. "Now, shove her off."

Moments later he was well out in the water and left to his own devices. He got his sculls out successfully and proceeded to pull very deliberately past some punts, stopping his sculls in the air to feather accurately, in the hopes of deceiving spectators into the belief that he was an old hand going out for a gentle paddle. The attendant watched him for a minute and turned to his work hoping Hockney wouldn't come to grief.

The day was a very fine one for November, a bright sun shining and a nice fresh breeze blowing across The

Serpentine, but not enough to ruffle the water seriously. Some heavy storms had cleared the air and swollen the lake at the same time. The Serpentine was as full as it could be without overflowing its banks, a state in which, of all others, it is the least safe for boating experiments. Even the racing skiffs were comparatively safe craft and might be characterized as tubs. The real tubs, in one of the safest of which the prudent attendant had placed our rapscallion, were so safe that it required considerable ingenuity to upset them.

While Hockney had been sitting quiet and merely paddling, the boat had trimmed well enough. Taking a long breath, he leaned forward, and dug his sculls into the water, pulling them through with all his strength. As a consequence the handles of the sculls came into violent collision in the middle of the boat, the knuckles of Hockney's right hand were barked, his left scull unshipped, and the head of his skiff almost blown round by the wind before he could restore order on board.

"Never mind. Try again," he thought after the first sensation of disgust had passed off, and a glance at the shore showed him that there were no witnesses. "Of course, I forgot one hand must go over the other. It might have happened to anyone. Let me see, which hand shall I keep uppermost. The left, that's the weakest." And away he went again, keeping his hard won knowledge painfully in mind and thereby avoiding further collision amidships for four or five strokes. But, as in other sciences, the giving of undue prominence to one fact brings others inexorably on the head of the student to avenge his neglect of them. So it happened with Hockney in his practical study of the science of rowing that by thinking of his hands he forgot his seat and the necessity of trimming properly. Whereupon the old tub began to rock fearfully and the next moment, he missed the water altogether with his right scull, and subsided backwards, not without struggles, into the bottom of the boat. Meanwhile the half stroke which he had pulled with his left hand sent her head well into the bank.

Hockney picked himself up and settled himself on his bench again, a sadder and wiser man, as the truth began to dawn upon him that pulling, especially sculling, does not, like cock sucking, come by nature. However, he addressed himself manfully to his task and resolved as ever to get around The Serpentine as quickly as he could or perish in the attempt.

He shoved himself off the bank and, warned by his last mishap, got out into the middle of the lake. There, moderating his ardour and contenting himself with a slow and steady stroke, he was progressing satisfactorily and beginning to recover his temper, when a loud shout startled him. Looking over his shoulder at the imminent risk of an upset, he beheld a fast sailor close hauled on a wind and almost on top of him. Utterly ignorant of what was the right thing to do, he held his course and passed close under the bows of the miniature cutter, the steersman having jammed his helm hard down, shaking her in the wind, to prevent running over the skiff, and solacing himself with pouring maledictions on Hockney and his craft. In which the man who had hold of the sheets, and the third, who was lounging in the bows, heartily joined. Hockney was out of ear-shot before he had collected vituperation enough to hurl back at them and had run aground. Once free of the bank in which he'd been ensnared, he managed to get to one end of The Serpentine without further mishap.

Hockney started on his return voyage with the sort of look the victim of a clipper wears upon realising that rather than using the money he's given her to book a room for sex, the hot lady has run off with his loot. Nonetheless, his previous struggles had not been in vain and he managed to keep the right side of a punt. He complacently assumed that the worst part of his trial trip was now over. The next moment he felt the bows of his boat whirl round in the wash from the punt, the old tub grounded for a moment, and then turned over on her side as he fell headlong. He grasped at the boards, but they were too slippery to hold, and the rush of water was too strong for him, and rolling him over and over like a piece of driftwood, plunged him into the lake.

After the first moment of astonishment and fright was over, Hockney held his breath and, paddling with his hands, aimed for the surface of the water.

His first impulse on rising from the depths was to strike out for the shore but he caught sight of another skiff coming stern foremost down towards him. He trod the water and drew in his breath.

"Oh, there you are!" the rower said, looking much relieved. "Alright, I hope. Not hurt, eh?"

"No, I'm alright," answered Hockney. "What shall I do?"

"Swim ashore. I'll look after your boat."

So Hockney took the advice, swam ashore, where he stood dripping wet and watching the other as he righted the old tub which was floating bottom upwards.

The tub having been brought to the bank, the stranger started again, and collected the sculls and bottom boards which were floating about here and there in the lake. He also succeeded in salvaging Hockney's coat, the pockets of which held his watch, purse, and cigar case. These he brought to the bank, and delivering them over, enquired whether there was anything missing.

"Nothing but my cap. Never mind it. It's luck enough not to have lost the coat," said Hockney, holding up the dripping garment to let the water run out of the arms and pocket-holes, and then wringing it as well as he could.

The stranger put off again, and made one more round, searching for the cap but without success. While he was doing so, Hockney had time to look him over and see what sort of a man had come to his rescue.

He was well satisfied with his inspection. The other man was evidently five or so years older than himself, his figure was more set, and he had stronger whiskers than are generally grown at twenty-two. He was somewhere around five feet ten in height, deep-chested, with long powerful arms and hands. There was no denying, however, that at the first glance he was an ugly man. He was marked with chickenpox sores that had been scratched out in childhood, had large features, high cheekbones, deeply set eyes, and a very long chin. He also had the trick, which many under hung men have, of compressing his upper lip. Nevertheless, there was something in his face that hit Hockney's fancy and made him anxious to know his rescuer Biblically. Hockney had an instinct that mind-blowing orgasms were to be gotten out of the man. So he was very glad when the search was ended and the stranger came to the bank, shipped his sculls, jumped ashore and proceeded to fasten his skiff to an old stump.

"I'm afraid the cap's lost," the stranger remarked.

"It doesn't matter the least. Thank you for coming to help me, it was very kind indeed and more than I expected. Don't they say that one London man will never save another from drowning unless they have been introduced?"

"I don't know," replied the other. "I'm American. Are you sure you're not hurt?"

"Yes, quite," said Hockney, foiled in what he considered an artful plan to get the stranger to introduce himself.

"Then we're very well out of it," insisted the other.

"Indeed we are," Hockney concurred.

"But now you're getting chilled," observed the rescuer who was taken aback by Hockney's chattering jaws.

"Oh, it's nothing. I'm used to being wet."

"But you may just as well be comfortable if you can. Take all your clothes off. No one will see you here, the park is quite empty at this time in the afternoon and we're well away from the boat house. It's a warm day for November."

Once Hockney had taken off every last stitch, the stranger touched his thigh and the post-grad felt as naked as the disgraced banker Fred Goodwin after he'd been stripped of his knighthood. The art student had a stonking erection. Before he knew it, Hockney found himself on his back in the grass, with the stranger using his right hand to work a five-knuckle shuffle on the nude student's erect manhood. The man's grip was firm and the rhythm he used to wank Hockney off was very regular. As he gave the young painter a hand job, this dude simultaneously recited a passage he'd memorised from *Les Chants de Maldoror* by the Comte de Lautréamont:

> Now the swimmer and the female shark saved by him confront each other. For minutes they stare fixedly into each other's eyes. They swim circling, keeping each other in sight, and each thinking: "I was wrong all along. Here is one more evil than I." Then in unison they glided underwater towards each other, in mutual admiration, the female shark slitting open the waves with her fins, Maldoror's arms thrashing the water; and they held their breaths, in deepest reverence, each one anxious to gaze for the first time upon his living image. Effortlessly, at only three yards apart, they suddenly fell upon one another like two magnets, in an embrace of dignity and gratitude, clasping each other tenderly as brother and sister. Carnal desire soon followed this display of affection. Like two leeches, a pair of nervous thighs gripped tightly against the monster's viscous flesh, and arms and fins wrapped around the objects of their desire, surrounding their bodies with love, while their breasts and bellies soon fused into one bluish-green mass reeking of sea-wrack, in the midst of the tempest still raging by the light of lightning; with the foamy waves for a wedding bed, borne on an undersea current as if in a cradle, rolling and rolling down into the bottomless ocean depths, they came together in a long, chaste, and hideous mating!... At last I had found somebody who was like me!... From now on I was no longer alone in life!... Her ideas were the same as mine!... I was face to face with my first love!

As the stranger pronounced the last word 'love', a thick wad of spunk was discharged from Hockney's throbbing member. The art student then used his mouth, teeth and tongue, to return this favour and he was completely grooved by the sensation as huge gobs of the stranger's liquid genetics were discharged into his throat. Hockney was a real man who not only liked to suck, but who also loved to swallow!

Noticing that Hockney was shivering with pleasure and also from cold, the man who'd rescued him took off his jumper and told the student to put it on. After a little persuasion Hockney did as he was bid, and got into the great woollen garment, which was very comforting. Then the stranger rolled a fat cigarette and asked Hockney if he liked charge.

"I've never had it before," the post-grad confessed, "but I understand that jazz musicians swear by it for creative inspiration."

After the stranger lit up the joint, Hockney took the spliff between his fingers and drew on it.

"Not like that," the stranger instructed. "Take it right in, as deep down as it can go and keep it in, that's the main thing. When you've had a blow, don't let it go, but keep breathing in air to send it right downstairs to the bargain basement."

Hockney did as he was told. It didn't taste half as bad as he thought it would. In fact it was quite pleasant. It went down a lot easier than tobacco would and before long he was hungrily inhaling it.

"Not too much for the first time. We don't want you cracking up," the stranger said, taking the spliff away from Hockney.

The art student wasn't in the least bit surprised by the stranger's advice, because he'd already realised he was feeling different. Everything was happening so quickly.

At first he wasn't sure exactly what it was. Then it came to him that the scene was going out of focus like it does on the television when you turn the wrong knob. But not everything. Some of the scene was still as clear, in fact, sharper, but the rest was in a fog. Certain things stood out in Hyde Park like they had a searchlight trained on them—the stranger—the spliff—the birds and clouds in the sky—but most of the other things weren't bright at all. The trees, in particular, were very indistinct and he could see right through them. Hockney's heart was breaking the speed limit, thumping away like mad it was and he felt hot although the sweat on his forehead was icy cold. Then the scene became terribly unreal and it frightened Hockney. The stranger's voice seemed far away and the hazy atmosphere wasn't helping things either. So this was what it was like to be high, Hockney's mind kept telling him. It was very different to how he'd seen it described in the Sunday newspapers....

After that Hockney couldn't remember quite what happened, but he woke the next day in his room convinced that the stranger had told him his name was R. B. Kitaj, and was a fellow student at the Republican College of Art.

CHAPTER 3

BREAKFAST WITH DEREK BOSHIER

No man in the RCA gave such breakfasts as Derek Boshier. Not the great heavy evening spreads for thirty or forty with an orgy afterwards, which came once or twice a term, when everything was supplied out of the college kitchen. You had to ask leave of the Dean before you could have it at all, and the Dean always insisted that the best looking boy was kept back to pleasure the staff. In those ponderous feasts the most humdrum of the first year MAs might rival the most artistic, if they could only pay their battle-bills, or get credit with the cook. But the daily morning meal, when even gentlemen commoners were limited to two hot dishes out of the kitchen, this was Boshier's forte. Ordinary men left the matter in the hands of scouts and were content with the ever-recurring buttered toasts and eggs, a dish of broiled ham and bitter ale to finish. Boshier was not an ordinary man, as you instantly saw when you went to breakfast with him for the first time.

The house in which Boshier lived was inhabited by men in the fast set. He and three others who shared his aversion to solitary feeding had established a breakfast-club in which real scientific gastronomy was cultivated. Every morning the boy from Wheelers in Soho arrived with freshly caught gudgeon, and now and then an eel or trout, which the scouts Boshier employed fried delicately in oil. Fresh water cress came in the same basket and the college kitchen furnished a spitchedcocked chicken or grilled turkey's leg. In the season there were plover's eggs or at least a dainty omelette. An Acton baker, famed for his light rolls and high charges, sent in the bread. The common local loaf being out of the question for anyone with the slightest pretension to taste.

Then there would be a deep Yorkshire pie or reservoir of potted game as a pièce de résistance and four types of preserve. To finish a large cool tankard of cider or ale-cup or soda-water and maraschino for a change. Tea and coffee were there but merely as a compliment to those respectable beverages, for they were rarely touched by the breakfast eaters in Boshier's bedsit. Pleasant young gentlemen they were at Derek's south Kensington abode. That is the ground and first floor men who formed the breakfast-club, for the second floors and basements were nobodies. Three out of the four had huge allowances to live on. They treated their grants as pocket-money and were all in their first year. Ready money was plentiful and so was credit. They might have had potted hippopotamus for breakfast if they had chosen to order it, which they would most likely have done if they had thought of it.

Two out of the three were the sons of rich men who made their own fortunes and sent their sons to the RCA because it was very desirable that these talentless and rather stupid young gentlemen should make good connexions in the art world. The fathers looked upon the RCA as a good investment and gloried much in hearing their sons talk familiarly in their vacations of their dear friends Francis Bacon and Lucian Freud.

Boshier was not an heir of an old or a rich family and consequently, having his connection ready made to his hand, cared little enough with whom he associated, provided they were pleasant fellows. His whole idea at present was to enjoy himself as much as possible but he had a conservative streak and had he fallen into any but the fast set, would have made a fine stuffed suit who the college would have considered a credit to its reputation.

Our rapscallion had met Boshier at an art opening in York shortly before the beginning of his first term, and they had rather taken to one another. Boshier had been amongst his first callers, and when he came out of the closet one morning shortly after his arrival by telling everyone within earshot that it was cock and not pussy he was after, Boshier's scout came up to him with an invitation to breakfast. No one was in Boshier's bedsit when he arrived, for none of the club had finished their toilettes. As Hockney entered, a great splashing in an adjacent bathroom stopped for a moment and Boshier's voice shouted out that he was in his communal tub but would be with him in a minute. So Hockney gave himself up to contemplation of the flock wallpaper.

Hockney had scarcely finished admiring a dark damp stain on the wall when the door opened and Boshier emerged in a loose jacket lined with silk, his velvet cap on his head, and otherwise gorgeously attired. He was a pleasant-looking fellow of middle size, with dark hair and a merry eye, which spoke well for his sense of humour. Otherwise his large features were rather plain but he had the look and manners of a complete degenerate who'd be fun to know. His first act, after nodding to Hockney, was to seize on a pewter mug and resort to the cask in the corner, from whence he drew a pint or so.

"'I've a whoreson longing for that poor creature, small beer." Boshier explained. "We were playing Van-John in Blake's rooms till three last night, and he gave us devilled bones and mulled port. A fellow can't enjoy his breakfast after that without something to cool his coppers."

Hockney was as yet ignorant of what Van-John might be, so said nothing and took a pull at the beer which the other handed to him. Then the scout entered and received orders to bring up Jack and the breakfast and not wait for any one. In another minute a bouncing and scratching was heard on the stairs and a white bulldog rushed in. The dog's brow was broad and massive, his skin was as fine as a lady's and his tail nearly as thin as a clay pipe. His general look and a way he nuzzled about the calves of strangers, were not pleasant for nervous people. Hockney was used to dogs and soon became friends with him, which evidently pleased his host— who liked to indulge his voyeuristic streak with viewings of bestiality. Next the breakfast arrived, all smoking and with it the two other ingenious youths, in velvet caps and far more gorgeous apparel than Boshier. They were introduced to Hockney, who thought them somewhat ordinary and rather loud young students. One of them remonstrated vigorously against the presence of that confounded dog and so Jack was sent to lie down in a corner.

The last man to arrive at the breakfast-club, Allen Jones, was in his last year but no longer at the RCA. He was a very well-dressed, well-mannered, well-connected young rake. His grant was small for the set he lived with—he'd been kicked out of the RCA for making pornographic sculptures and was now studying at Hornsey College of Art in north London—but he never wanted for anything. He didn't entertain much but when he did, everything was in the best possible style. He was very exclusive and only befriended members of the fast set. Of these he addicted himself chiefly to the society of the rich first years in the hope that their father's might buy his work. With the first years he was always hand and glove, lived in their rooms, using their wines, cars, and other movable property as his own. Being a good whist and billiard player and not a bad driver, he managed in one way or another to make his young friends pay well for the honour of his acquaintance. Why should they not, at least those of them who came to the college to form eligible connections, for was not his pornographic imagination a font of riches?

Then the four fell to work upon the breakfast. It was a good lesson in gastronomy but the results are scarcely worth repeating here. It is wonderful, though, how you feel drawn to a man who feeds you well. As Hockney's appetite got less, his liking and respect for his host undoubtedly increased.

When they had nearly finished, in walked Peter Blake. A fat man, two or three years older than the rest of them. Good looking and very well and quietly dressed but with the drawing up of his nostril and a drawing down of the corners of his mouth, which set Hockney against him at once. The supercilious half-nod to which he treated our rapscallion when introduced to him was enough to spoil Hockney's digestion and hurt his self-love a good deal more than he would have liked to own.

"Here, Henry," said Peter Blake to the scout in attendance, seating himself and inspecting the half-cleared dishes. "What is there for my breakfast?"

Henry bustled about and handed over two dishes.

"I don't want these cold things. Haven't you kept me any gudgeon?"

"Why sir," said Henry, "there was only two dozen this morning and Mr. Boshier told me to cook them all."

"To be sure I did," said Boshier. "Just half a dozen for each of us four. They were first-rate. If you can't get here at half-past nine, you won't get gudgeon!"

"Just go and get me a broil from Wheelers," Peter Blake snarled without even deigning an answer to Boshier.

"Very sorry, sir. I don't have time to go to Soho," answered Henry.

"Then go to Hinton's and order some," shouted Boshier to the retreating scout. "Not to my tick, mind! Put them down to Mr. Blake."

Henry seemed to know very well that in that case he might save himself the trouble of the journey and consequently returned to his waiting. Peter Blake set to work upon his breakfast without showing any further ill temper except the stinging things which he threw every now and then into the conversation, for the benefit of each of the others in turn.

Hockney thought he detected signs of coming hostilities between his host and Blake, for Boshier seemed to prick up his ears and get combative whenever the other spoke and lost no chance in roughing him in his replies. And indeed our anti-hero was not far wrong. During Boshier's first term the other had lived on him—drinking his wine, smoking his cigars, driving his Vespa scooter and winning his money. All of which Boshier, who was the easiest going and best tempered fellow in London, had stood without turning a hair. But Blake added to these little favours a half-patronising, half-contemptuous manner, which he used with great success towards some of the other art students, who thought it a mark of high breeding. Boshier who didn't care three straws about knowing Blake wasn't going to put up with it.

However, nothing happened but a little sparring. The breakfast things were cleared away and the tankards left on the table. The company betook themselves to cigars and easy chairs. Jack came out of his corner to be gratified with some of the remnants by his fond master and then curled himself up on the sofa along which Boshier lounged.

When Arnold Farley turned up, Blake asked him: "Who are you going to run down today, Farley?"

"The boating-men," Farley announced. "Did you ever see such a set? With their everlasting flannels and jerseys and hair cropped like prize-fighters? They're so ridiculous a blind man wouldn't fuck them without being paid to do so, let alone suck their dicks!"

"What the devil do I care," broke in Boshier, "I know they're a deal more amusing than you fellows, who can't lay rough trade without putting down pounds."

"Getting economical with the truth!" Blake sneered. "When was the last time you took it up the jacksee from a horny handed son of toil without paying the cockson?"

"Payment is nothing! It would be worth tearing my heart out if at the end of it all I got my behind abused by the blue-eyed brutish coxswain," said Farley. "He's a mean and ugly motherfucker, just the type I like. But he only teaches the boatmen the Greek rite!"

"After the coxswain's had them, they aren't able to sit straight in a chair for a month," said Sidney Chanter, "and are reduced to giving the rest of the team blow jobs."

Here a newcomer called Peter Phillips entered and was warmly greeted by Boshier. He and Blake exchanged the coldest possible nods and the others stared at him through their smoke. After a minute or two's silence and a few rude half-whispered remarks, they went off to play a game of pyramids. Phillips took a cigar which Boshier offered and began asking about their mutual friends and what they'd been doing in the summer.

This pair were evidently intimate, though Hockney thought that Boshier didn't seem quite at his ease, which he wondered at, as Phillips took his fancy at once. Hockney was rather left out of the conversation to begin with but then Boshier cordially drew him in.

"Did you know, David, that Peter can tell fortunes?" Derek asked.

"No," Hockney replied.

"Give me your palm," Philips commanded, and Hockney did as he was bid. "Ah, I see you're going to be a very successful artist, far more successful than me. Before you die you're going to have a blockbuster show at The Royal Academy…"

"You're joking surely," Hockney half-laughed.

"Not at all," Phillips replied. "It will be called *A Bigger Picture* and art lovers will be fighting for tickets! Prior to that you're going to have a ball with lots of beautiful young men in Los Angeles. Looks like you'll be mutton jeff in your old age. Have you got much time?

"Is it eleven yet?" Hockney asked.

"I have to go for a tutorial at eleven."

"You'd better rush," Boshier informed him.

"That's a shame," Phillips said, "I so wanted to tell you about your death."

"I'd rather not know about that," Hockney replied, bolting for the door.

"Alchemy is a quality of a given psychic movement," Phillips shouted after Hockney, "the material must be immodest, insolent and brutal, if it is not to fall into annulment."

CHAPTER 4

THE RCA BOAT CLUB:
ITS WINE PARTIES AND PECADDILOS

Having almost had his fortune told, Hockney resolved to become Kitaj's lover. It never occurred to him that there could be the slightest difficulty in carrying out this resolve. Since Kitaj had wanked him off on the edge of The Serpentine, Hockney felt that the usual outworks of acquaintanceship had been cleared at a bound and looked upon the other as an old friend to whom he could talk as freely as he had to his old tutor at art school in Bradford. Moreover, as there were already several things in his head which he was anxious to ventilate, he was even more pleased that chance had put his bollocks in the hands of a man who wasn't afraid to make a cock crow and one who he'd very much like to come in both his mouth and his sphincter.

Accordingly, after Hockney had gorged himself in the RCA canteen but seeing that Kitaj had not finished his lunch, he strolled off, meaning to wait for his victim outside and seize upon him then and there. He stopped on the steps outside the dining hall door and to pass the time, joined himself to one or two other men who were also hanging about in the hope of picking up cock. While they were talking, Kitaj came out of the hall and Hockney turned and stepped forward, meaning to speak to him. To the northerner's utter discomfiture,

Kitaj walked quickly away, looking straight ahead and without showing, by look or gesture, that he was conscious of our rapscallion's existence, or had ever seen him before in his life.

Hockney was so taken aback that he made no effort to follow. He just glanced at his companions to see whether they had noticed the occurrence and was glad that they had not. They were deep in the discussion of the sexual merits of a new porter who possessed a member of legendary proportions. Hockney walked away to consider what this snub could mean. But the more he puzzled about it, the less could he understand it. Surely, he thought, Kitaj must have seen me? Yet if he had, why did he not greet me? Common decency should have led him to ask whether I was any the worse for my ducking and if I'd liked the way he'd worked my length.

He scouted the notion which suggested itself at once that Kitaj meant to cut him. Not being able to come to any reasonable conclusion, he suddenly remembered that he'd been invited to a wine-party. Putting his speculations aside for a moment, with the full intention nevertheless of clearing up the mystery as soon as possible, he hurried to the alcohol-soaked gathering.

It was a fair-sized room for a South Kensington bedsitter, furnished plainly but well, so far as Hockney could judge. As it was now laid out for the wine-party, the digs had lost all individual character for the time being. A postgraduate's room set out for a party will tell you little about their character. All their possessions are shoved away and there is nothing to be seen but a long mahogany table set out with bottles, glasses, and dessert. In the present instance the preparations for festivity were pretty much what they ought to be. Good sound port and sherry, biscuits and a plate of nuts and dried fruits.

The host, who sat at the head of the board, was one of the mainstays of the college boat-club. He was its treasurer and also a kind of boating nurse, who locked up and trained the young oars and in this capacity had been in command of the newbies four-oar, in which Hockney had been learning his rudiments. He was a heavy, burly man, naturally awkward in his movements, but gifted with a dogged enthusiasm and by dint of hard and constant training, had made himself into a most useful oar, fit for any place in the middle of the boat. He was the most good natured man in the world, very badly dressed, very short sighted, and called everybody "old bedfellow"—even the newbies he hadn't yet fucked.

His name was Richard Hamilton and he wasn't a student at the RCA any longer. But for the sake of the boating club everyone pretended Hamilton belonged to their college. Hamilton was slightly older than the other boaters and had the eccentric habit of making an easy chair of his hip bath. Malicious acquaintances declared that when Hamilton took his digs and having paid the valuation for the furniture in his room, came to inspect the same, the tub in question had been left by chance in the sitting-room and Hamilton, not having the faintest idea of its proper use, had by the exercise of his natural reason come to the conclusion that it could only be meant for a man to sit in, and so had kept it as an armchair. This was a libel. Certain it is, however, that in his first term he was discovered sitting solemnly in the tub, by his fire-side, with his spectacles on, playing the flute—the only other recreation besides boating and nude encounters in which he indulged.

When alone, or with only one or two friends in his room, Hamilton still occupied the tub. He declared that it was the most perfect seat and above all adapted for the recreation of a boating man, to whom cushioned seats should be an abomination. He was a very hospitable man and on this night was particularly anxious to make his rooms pleasant to all comers, as it was a sort of opening for the boating season. This wine of his was a business matter, in fact, to which Richard had invited officially, as treasurer of the boat-club, every man who had ever shown any interest in rowing—many with whom he had scarcely a nodding acquaintance.

Hockney and the three or four other newbies present were duly presented to the coxswain as they came in, who looked them over as the colonel of a crack regiment might look over horses at Horncastle-fair, with a single eye to their bone and muscle, and how much work might be got out of them. They then gathered towards the lower end of the long table and surveyed the celebrities at the upper end with much respect. Eduardo Paolozzi, the coxswain, sat on the host's right hand. He was a slight, resolute, fiery little man, with curly black hair. Paolozzi was peculiarly qualified by nature for the task that he had set himself and it takes no mean qualities to keep a boat's crew well together and in order. Perhaps he erred a little on the side of over-strictness and severity. He certainly would have been more popular had his manners been a thought more courteous. However even the men who rebelled against his tyranny grumblingly confessed that he was a first-rate coxswain who deep-throated cock like a true champion. Like Hamilton,

Paolozzi didn't actually belong to the student body at Kensington Gore, but so that the RCA might be masters of The Serpentine everybody pretended he was a current postgraduate student.

A very different man sat opposite to Paolozzi. Hermann Nitsch, the captain of the boat, was a noble specimen. Tall and strong of body, courageous and even-tempered, tolerant of all men, sparing of speech but ready in action. A thoroughly well balanced, modest, quiet flagellant. One of those Sunday spankers who do a good stroke of work in the BDSM world without getting much credit for it. The last thing such men understand is how to blow their own trumpets. And who but a contortionist is able to suck their own cock anyway? Nitsch was perhaps too easy for the captain of the RCA boat-club, at any rate, Paolozzi was always telling him this. But, if he was not strict enough with others, he never spared himself and was as good as three men in the boat at a pinch.

Finally a handsome, pale man, with a quick eye, walked in and took his place by the side of the host as a matter of course.

"Who is that who has just come in?" Hockney asked the man sitting next to him, simultaneously using this as an excuse to touch the fellow's thigh very close to his crotch.

"Oh, don't you know? That's Robert Fraser. He's the most wonderful fellow in London, although he lives mainly in the United States right now," answered his neighbour.

"How do you mean?" said Hockney.

"Why, he can do everything better than almost anybody and without any trouble at all. Paolozzi was obliged to have him in the boat last year, though he never trained a bit. Then he's in the eleven and is a wonderful rider, tennis-player, and shot. He also sucks cock like a demon!"

"Aye, and he's so awfully clever with it all," joined in the man on the other side. "He can write songs, too, as fast as you can talk nearly, and sings them wonderfully."

"Is he of our college, then?"

"No, but we have to pretend he is or he couldn't have been in our boat last year."

"I don't think I ever saw him before," Hockney observed.

"No, I daresay not. He's living in the USA and even in London he never gets up till the afternoon and sits up nearly all night playing cards with the fastest fellows, or going round singing glees at three or four in the morning."

Hockney sipped his port and looked with great interest at Fraser. After watching him a few moments he said in a low voice to his neighbour: "How wretched he looks! I never saw a sadder face."

"Poor Fraser! One can't help calling him poor although he himself would wince at it more than any name I could have called him. I might have admired, feared or wondered at him and he would have been pleased. The object of his life is to raise such feelings in his neighbours, pity is the last thing he wants to elicit."

Robert was indeed a wonderfully gifted fellow, full of all sorts of energy and talent and power and tenderness. Yet, as his face told only too truly to anyone who watched him when he was exerting himself in society, one of the most wretched men in the world.

He had a passion for success. For beating everybody else in whatever he took in hand and that, too, without seeming to make any great effort himself. The doing a thing well and thoroughly gave him no satisfaction unless he could feel that he was doing it better and more easily than Victor Musgrave, John Kasmin or Peter and Charles Gimpel, and they felt and acknowledged this. He would enjoy the full swing of success for a few years to come and then his Nemesis would descend in the form of creditors.

Robert was not an extravagant man but art dealing as a pursuit required riches if one wanted to eclipse all rivals. Fraser was not rich. He had a fair allowance but was considerably in debt and even at the time we are speaking of, the whole pack of London tradesmen into whose books he had got were upon him, besieging him for payment. This miserable and constant annoyance was wearing his soul out. This was the reason why his oak was sported and he was never seen till the afternoons and turned night into day. He was too proud to come to an understanding with his persecutors, even if it had been possible. Eventually his whole scheme of life would fail him. His love of success would turn to ashes in his mouth. He would feel much more disgust than pleasure at his triumphs over other men and yet the habit of striving for successes, notwithstanding its irksomeness, was too strong to be resisted.

Poor Fraser! He would end up living on from hand to mouth, occasionally flashing out his old brilliancy and power and forcing himself to take the lead in whatever company he might be. Only to find himself utterly lonely and depressed when alone. He was reading feverishly in secret, in a desperate effort to master the art of rubbing a small metal statue of The Buddha for endless wealth. As Hockney said to his neighbour, there was no sadder face than Fraser's to be seen in London, but give it a decade and it would get way sadder yet.

And yet at this very wine party Fraser was the life of everything, as he sat up there next to Richard Hamilton, whom he kept in a constant sort of mild epileptic fit, from laughter, and wine going the wrong way. Whenever Richard raised his glass, Fraser shot him with some joke. Fraser relaxed after the first fifteen minutes. Hockney in this time gave himself credit for being a much greater ass than he was, for having ever thought Fraser's face a sad one.

When the room was quite full and enough wine had been drunk to open the hearts of the guests, Richard rose on a signal from Paolozzi to speak in tongues:

"Anal sex, also called anal intercourse," Hamilton shrieked, "is the sex act in which the penis is inserted into the anus of a sexual partner. The term can also include other sexual acts involving the anus, such as pegging, anilingus, fingering and object insertion."

"While anal sex is commonly associated with male homosexuality," Richard continued, "research shows that not all gay males engage in anal sex and that it is not uncommon in heterosexual relationships. Types of anal sex can also be a part of lesbian sexual practices."

"Many people find anal sex pleasurable," Hamilton continued, "and some may reach orgasm through stimulation of the prostate in men, and clitoral and G-Spot leg stimulation in women. However, many people find it painful as well, sometimes extremely so, which may be psychosomatic in some cases."

Richard Hamilton continued speaking in the same vein for a good hour. Everyone was relieved when he finished and applauded loudly, not because they'd enjoyed the speech but because it had ended. Soon afterwards, coffee came in and cigars were lighted. A large section of the party went off to play pool, others to stroll about the streets, some to whist. A few went to their own rooms to read or practice still-life drawing but these latter were a small minority even in the quietest of the RCA parties.

Hockney, who was fascinated by the anti-heroes at the head of the table, sat steadily on, sidling up towards them as the intermediate places became vacant and at last attained the next chair but one to captain Hermann Nitsch, where for the time he sat in perfect bliss. Fraser and Paolozzi were telling boating stories of the Henley and Thames regattas and the talk came gradually round to the next races.

"Now, captain," said Paolozzi, suddenly, "have you thought yet what new men we are to try in the crew this year?"

"No, 'pon my honour I haven't," said Hermann Nitsch, "I'm working on my phallic sculptures and butt plug pottery. I have no time to spare. After all the races don't begin till the end of Easter term."

"It won't do," said Paolozzi, "we must get the crew together this term."

"You and Hamilton put your heads together and manage it," said Hermann Nitsch. "I will go down any day, and as often as you like, at two o'clock."

"Let's see," said Paolozzi to Hamilton, "how many of the old crew have we left?"

"Five, counting Fraser," answered Richard.

"Counting me! Well, that's cool," laughed Fraser, "you old tub haunting flute-player, why should I not to be counted?"

"You never will train, you see," said Richard.

"Hamilton is quite right," said Paolozzi, "there's no counting on you, Fraser. Now, be a good fellow and promise to be regular this year and hold off returning to the United States."

"I'll promise to do my work in our races, which is more than some of your best-trained men will do," Fraser was piqued.

"Well you know what I think on that subject," said Paolozzi, "but who have we got for the other three places?"

"Boshier would do," said Richard, "I hear he was a capital oar at school. I don't know him well but I managed to go down on him once last term. He would do famously for No.2, or No.3 if he would pull."

"Do you think he will, Fraser? You know him, I suppose," said Paolozzi.

"Yes, I know him well enough," said Fraser. Shrugging his shoulders he added, "I don't think you'll get him to train much."

"We must try," said Paolozzi. "Now, who else is there?"

Hamilton went through four or five names, at each of which Paolozzi shook his head. "Any promising newbies?" Said he at last.

"None better than Hockney here," said Hamilton. "I think he'll do well if he will only work and stand being coached."

"Have you ever pulled much?" asked Paolozzi.

"No," said Hockney, "not much till I came up here to London. Now I'm meeting plenty of rough trade in public toilets!"

"All the better," said Paolozzi, "now Nitsch we will probably have to go in with three new hands. They must get into your stroke this term or we shall be nowhere."

"Very well," said Nitsch, "I'll give from two till five any days you like."

"And now let's go and have a pull," said Fraser, getting up. "Come, Nitsch, just one little circle jerk after all this business."

Richard wanted to play his flute. Paolozzi was engaged. Hermann Nitsch, with a little coaxing, was led away by Fraser and good-naturedly asked Hockney to accompany them since he realised the painter would like some rough sex. So the three went off to an all night public toilet. Hockney in such spirits at the chance of doing two, three or even more men that night, didn't notice that he was roaringly drunk.

They found the nearest public toilet full of rough trade looking for a good time. Hockney was able to suck men off while lying on his back with his legs over his shoulders as he pulled an anal train. This left both his arms free and he was able to give hand jobs—two at a time—to those that wanted them.

Eventually Hockney returned to his rooms. Once he was alone again his thoughts recurred to Kitaj. How odd, he thought, that they never mentioned him for the boat! Could he have done something shameful? How was it that nobody seemed to know him and he to know nobody.

Most readers, I doubt not, will think our rapscallion very green for being puzzled at so simple a matter, since no doubt the lusts and desires of the outright sadist are well known to us all. But Hockney's previous education must be taken into consideration. His parents had not told him about the birds and the bees. He had gone to a school where sado-masochism and a love of the same sex were not widely practiced. So Hockney had yet to discover the ways and joys of 90% of the world.

CHAPTER 5

KITAJ: MASTER OF THE ENEMA, THE BUTT PLUG & THE CAT O' NINE TAILS

Despite setbacks Hockney pursued the object of his desire. That is to say he had caught Kitaj several times in the corridor as he came out of his studio, or the canteen, and had fastened himself upon him, often walking with him even up to the street door. But there matters ended. Kitaj was very civil and gentlemanly. He even seemed pleased with the volunteered companionship but there was undoubtedly a coolness about him which Hockney could not make out. But the more Kitaj rejected his sexual advances, the more Hockney was determined to seduce his fellow post-grad coz he really wanted the haughty student to fuck him up the arse.

One evening he had as usual walked from the RCA buildings with Kitaj up to his door. They stopped a moment talking and then Kitaj, half-opening the door said: "Well, goodnight, perhaps we shall meet at The Serpentine tomorrow."

Hockney, looking him in the face, blurted out, "I say, Kitaj, I wish you'd let me come in and sit with you a bit."

"I rarely ask a man of our college into my room," answered the other, "but come in by all means if you like," and so they entered.

Kitaj told Hockney he knew he wanted another handjob or else to have his cock sucked. Kitaj said he might even do such things for Hockney if the painter was very good, but that he liked girls and all sorts of other sexual activities. He then told Hockney he wanted to make him a rubber slave. Kitaj took a chastity belt from a drawer and after making Hockney strip, put it on him. Kitaj told his friend things between them were changing as of right now. He explained everything he wanted from a slave in great detail. Finally, Kitaj told Hockney how long the chastity belt stayed on depended on how quickly he learnt to submit. Hockney knew Kitaj was serious when the American explained that the chastity belt could be connected to the mains and be used to give shocks to the northerner's cock and balls if he didn't behave. Kitaj pulled the plug and lead from a drawer and showed Hockney how it worked. He slowly increased the intensity.

"I'll do what ever you want," Hockney howled.

"Good," Kitaj replied. "I am going to give you an enema in the bathroom."

Kitaj instructed Hockney to bend over the tub. Hockney did so reluctantly. Kitaj wanted to clean him out before there was any anal play. The master got out his enema bag, a rubber glove and some lube. He slid his finger into Hockney's butt. It was looser than Kitaj expected, so he pulled out the single digit and shoved two up the slave's jacksee. Kitaj pushed hard to get them in deeply. He eased the fingers in and out a few times but when Hockney started moaning, the top pulled the digits away. Next Kitaj slid the end of the enema tube into Hockney's arse and released the tube lock. The water was warm but it still shocked Hockney that fluid rushed into his bowls. He was thrashing around as the water went in. Hockney screamed he couldn't stand it, that he wanted Kitaj to stop. The top told him to shut up. He pushed down on the small of Hockney's back as he held the nozzle in the bottom's butt.

Eventually Kitaj handed the enema bag to Hockney and ordered him to lie in the bath and hold it. The top told his slave he was going out and that by the time he came back Hockney had better have given himself a further enema and shaved his body from the neck down. Hockney nodded in ascent, he didn't dare speak.

Kitaj returned after a couple of hours. Hockney was just coming out of the bathroom. He was not a pretty sight. He was a little overweight. Kitaj told him he was going on a strict diet and if he didn't follow it there would be severe punishment. Hockney started arguing, so Kitaj ordered him into the bedroom. He refused to go, so Kitaj punched Hockney in the face until he submitted to the demand. It only took three fast jabs.

Kitaj tied Hockney face down to the bed. He got out the lube and squeezed a glob into Hockney's arse crack, then started massaging it into the hole. The first two fingers went in without effort. The third was more difficult but Kitaj kept on pushing until Hockney's sphincter gave way. Then the top started massaging Hockney's prostate and the sub was moaning and groaning like a superannuated male porn star on heat. Kitaj kept massaging and feeling his way around. Hockney was loosening up nicely. Kitaj's arm was tiring so he took his fingers out of the shit chute and grabbed a butt plug. Once again Kitaj lubed Hockney and then viciously inserted the sex toy, ramming it home with great force. Kitaj pulled the butt plug back and forth several times, then pushed it in as far as it would go and left it there.

Kitaj then spanked Hockney's arse. He did this slowly, first with one hand and then the other. It wasn't long before his hands started hurting. Next Kitaj bit Hockney's arse. After a dozen hard bites, Kitaj got out a short whip and the cat o' nine tails too.

The cat o' nine tails, commonly called the cat, is a type of multi-tailed whip that originated as an implement for severe physical punishment, notably in the Royal Navy and Army of the United Kingdom, and also as a judicial punishment in Britain and some other countries.

The earliest recorded use of the term cat o' nine tails is around 1695, although the whip and its design are much older. It was probably named in reference to its "claws", which inflict parallel wounds. The cat is made up of nine knotted thongs of cotton cord, about 2½ feet or 76 cm long, designed to lacerate the skin and cause intense pain.

The cat traditionally has nine thongs due to the manner in which rope is plaited. Thinner rope is made from three strands of yarn worked together, and thicker rope from three strands of thinner rope plaited together. To make a cat o' nine tails, a rope is unravelled into three small ropes, each of which is unravelled again.

The naval cat, also known as the captain's daughter (and this was the type Kitaj would be using on Hockney), weighed about 13 ounces (370 grams) and was composed of a baton handle and nine cords.

Contrary to popular belief, the standard cat was not the most feared implement of punishment on the high seas. Being made of rope, it was less painful than a leather whip or a wooden birch-rod, while the modes of application (number and intensity of lashes, anatomical target, baring) of any implement can be more important than its intrinsic potential to cause pain.

Kitaj used the cat to warm Hockney up and the short whip to give him some nice welts. Kitaj switched between these two implements and took his own sweet time. Hockney started crying. THAT really turned Kitaj on, so he immediately increased the savagery of the beating he was dishing out. It didn't take long for Hockney to give in completely and just lie there almost motionless. There was no movement on Hockney's part beyond a heaving in his chest and shoulders brought on by sobbing.

After Kitaj had finished whipping Hockney, he scratched him with his finger nails. Boy did the sub jump and scream! As Kitaj lessened the pressure from his nails to a light scratch, Hockney stopped crying and started moaning and moving his arse in slow circular motions. Kitaj took hold of the butt plug that he'd inserted into Hockney's crack and started moving it in little turns and thrusts. Hockney's moans got louder. Kitaj leaned close to his ear and whispered to him that he was going to fuck him hard up the arse. Hockney screamed: "YESSSS!" Kitaj pulled the butt plug out and slowly pushed it back in a few more times.

Kitaj untied the sub and told him to get on all fours. It was then—as Hockney was looking up at Kitaj—that his master told him to suck him off. Hockney gazed at the dom's erect cock and slowly opened his mouth. He gingerly sucked up and down for a few minutes until Kitaj took the back of the northerner's head and pushed his throbbing manhood slowly and deliberately to the back of Hockney's throat. Hockney must have gagged a dozen times before Kitaj was through.

Then Kitaj decided it was time to arsefuck the slave. He pulled out the butt plug. At first Kitaj went slowly and deliberately as he penetrated the sphincter. Hockney was barely moving. After a few minutes Kitaj gauged just how much cock Hockney could safely handle and thrust harder and deeper. Hockney was pushing up to accept and accommodate the full length of his master's throbbing gristle. Before long Kitaj had discharged a thick wad of liquid genetics into the veritable seat of Hockney's being.

"Now it is time for you to get dressed and go." Kitaj told his slave. "If you want you can take a shower before you leave."

"Will you promise to always turn me out when I am in the way?" Hockney demanded.

"I'll do whatever I bloody well like!" Kitaj snapped. "I'll turn you out as a rent boy and pimp you if I feel like it!"

And so the two men parted. Hockney without bothering to shower and with his clothes in disarray thanks to the hurried way in which he'd dressed. Both men were happy that they'd established just who was the master and who was the slave.

Once he was alone, Kitaj's first thought was one of pleasure at having been sought out by a postgraduate who seemed to be just the sort of sex slave he craved. He contrasted our rapscallion with the few men (and many women) who he'd previously fucked, and felt that Hockney was less of a man than any of them— and thus a far better submissive. With such happy thoughts flooding his mind, Kitaj took down a volume of *Don Quixote* from his shelves and sat for an hour reading it before turning in.

CHAPTER 6

HOW BOSHIER AND HOCKNEY WERE BANNED FROM GETTING IT ON!

"Boshier, what's a rubber slave?"

"How the deuce should I know?"

This short and pithy exchange took place in Boshier's room one evening soon after the sex session recorded in the last chapter. He and Hockney were sitting and so the latter seized the occasion to ask about this matter, which had been on his mind for some time. He wasn't satisfied with the rejoinder but while he was thinking how to pursue the subject, Boshier opened his button fly and asked Hockney if he'd like to chew his throbbing gristle.

"I can't," Hockney wailed.

"How long would it take you to give me a blow job?" Boshier demanded.

"You don't understand," Hockney wailed. "My question about rubber slaves was rhetorical?"

"So why ask me what a rubber slave is if you already know?"

"The thing is," Hockney explained, "I'm Kitaj's rubber slave. And if he orders me to have sex with someone else then I can't refuse, but I can't do anything sexual unless he tells me to do it."

"But that's ridiculous!" Boshier laughed. "Supposing he ordered you to have sex with a woman?"

"Then I'd just have to get on with it." Hockney sobbed.

"I'll tell you what," Boshier cried, "you stay here. I'm going to go and find Kitaj and I'm going to bring him back here so he can tell you to give me a good suck."

With that Boshier was gone. To fill in the time as he sat waiting, Hockney pulled from his pocket a book Kitaj had given him entitled *The Red Rubber Slave Trade and Other Tales of Man's Inhumanity to Man.* Very quickly Hockney became engrossed in the text. It read as follows:

Edmund Dene Morel, originally Georges Eduard Pierre Achille Morel de Ville (10 July 1873—12 November 1924), was a British journalist, author and socialist politician. In collaboration with Roger Casement, the Congo Reform Association and others, Morel, in newspapers such as his *West African Mail,* led a campaign against slavery in the Congo Free State.

In 1891 Morel obtained a clerkship with Elder Dempster, a Liverpool shipping firm. To increase his income and support his family, from 1893 Morel began writing articles against French protectionism, which was damaging to Elder Dempster's business. He came to be critical of the British Foreign Office for not supporting the rights of Africans under colonial rule. His vision of Africa was influenced by the books of Mary Kingsley, an English traveller and writer, which showed sympathy for African peoples and a respect for different cultures that was very rare amongst Europeans at the time.

Elder Dempster had a shipping contract with the Congo Free State for the connection between Antwerp and Boma. Groups such as the Aborigines' Protection

Society had already begun a campaign against Belgian atrocities in Congo. Due to his knowledge of French, Morel was often sent to Belgium, where he was able to view the internal accounts of the Congo Free State held by Elder Dempster. The knowledge that the ships leaving Belgium for the Congo carried only guns, chains, ordnance and explosives, but no commercial goods, while ships arriving from the colony came back full of valuable products such as raw rubber and ivory, led him to the opinion that Belgian King Leopold II's policy was exploitative. According to the Belgian Prof. Daniël Vangroenweghe, Leopold gained 1,250 million in present day euros from the exploitation of the Congolese people, mainly from rubber. Other Belgian sources calculated that the profits from the Congolese exploitation prior to 1905 were some 500 million present-day euros.

The gains from the exploitation of rubber through the state and other companies like the Anglo-Belgian India Rubber Company (ABIR) were huge. The original value in 1892 of the ABIR shares was 500 francs. In 1903 the shares had risen to 15,000 gold francs. The company felt obliged to let the bourgeoisie share profits with the upper class. The dividend in 1892 was 1 franc, but by 1903 the dividend was 1,200 francs. These enormous gains came from horrible exploitation and what Edmund Morel himself described as slavery. The scope of the destruction, together with disease and famine from forced labour, is estimated to have killed half of the native population of the colony.

In 1900, Morel put new life into the campaign against Congo misrule (begun a decade before by the American George Washington Williams) with a series of articles

in the weekly magazine *Speaker.* He realised that King
Léopold II of Belgium, the absolute controller of the
Congo Free State, had created a forced labour system
of huge dimensions, emulating slave labour. Despite
having risen to be Elder Dempster's head of trade
with the Congo, Morel resigned in 1902 to further
his campaign. He became a full-time journalist, first
finding a job editing a recently founded periodical, *West
Africa.* In 1903, he founded his own magazine, the *West
African Mail,* with the collaboration of John Holt. John
Holt was a businessman and friend of Mary Kingsley,
who feared the system of the Congo Free State would be
applied upon the rest of the West African colonies. *The
Mail* was an illustrated weekly journal founded to meet
the rapidly growing interest in west and central African
questions. During this period Morel published several
pamphlets and his first book, *Affairs of West Africa.*

In 1903 the British House of Commons passed a
resolution on the Congo. Subsequently the British
consul in the Congo, Roger Casement, was sent up
country for an investigation. His 1904 report, which
confirmed Morel's accusations, had a considerable
impact on public opinion. Morel met Casement just
before the publication of the report and realised that
in Casement he had found the ally he had long sought.
Casement convinced Morel to establish an organisation
for dealing specifically with the Congo question, the
Congo Reform Association. Affiliates of the Congo
Reform Association were established as far away as the
United States.

The Congo Reform Association had the support of
famous writers such as Joseph Conrad (whose *Heart of
Darkness* was inspired by a voyage to the Congo Free

State), Anatole France, Arthur Conan Doyle and Mark Twain. Conan Doyle wrote *The Crime of the Congo* in 1908, while Twain gave the most famous contribution with the satirical short story *King Leopold's Soliloquy.* Morel's best allies, however, may have been the Christian missionaries who furnished him with eyewitness accounts and photographs of the atrocities, such as those given by the Americans William Morrison and William Henry Sheppard, and the British preachers John Harris and Alice Harris. The chocolate millionaire William Cadbury, a Quaker, was one of Morel's main financial backers. The American civil-rights activist Booker T. Washington participated in the campaign. The French journalist Pierre Mille wrote a book with Morel, while the Belgian socialist leader Emile Vandervelde sent him copies of Belgian parliamentary debates. Morel also had secret connections with some agents within the Congo Free State itself. Even the Church of England and American religious groups backed him.

In 1905 the movement won a victory when a Commission of Enquiry, instituted (under external pressure) by King Léopold II himself, substantially confirmed the accusations made about the colonial administration. In 1908 the Congo was annexed to the Belgian government and put under its sovereignty. Despite this, Morel refused to declare an end to the campaign until 1913 because he wanted to see actual changes in the situation of the country.

Hockney was unsure whether Kitaj had intended for him to be thrilled or horrified by the various accounts of the slavery and cruelty in the book. Before the rubber slave could decide the matter, Boshier returned with his dom.

"Boshier tells me you want to suck his dick! Is this true?" Kitaj demanded.

"Yes, master," Hockney confessed.

"Cur!" Kitaj screamed as he slapped Hockney's face. "Now I'll make you watch as I suck Boshier's manhood!"

Kitaj proceeded to undo Boshier's flies, take his throbbing gristle out and work a wet tongue up and down the leaden knob. Hockney could hardly believe his eyes as he watched Kitaj swallow the entirety of Derek's length. Before long Boshier was screaming in ecstasy and he'd shot a huge wad of liquid genetic into Kitaj's throat.

"You will never ever have sex with Boshier!" Kitaj screamed at Hockney after he'd swallowed all the come. Then Kitaj left the two astonished men to their own devices.

"Well, you've had a pretty good day of it," Hockney told Boshier, "but I should feel nervous about fucking you. Kitaj has told me not to do it and I dare not disobey him."

"Oh, never mind," said Boshier, "we've still got to wait another forty years for some sex researcher to invent Viagra and until that happens I'm not capable of a second erection right after being deep throated by someone with as much suction as Kitaj. But what o'clock is it?"

"Three," said Hockney, looking at his watch and getting up, "time to take an afternoon nap."

"The first time I ever heard you say that," said Boshier.

In ten minutes Boshier was asleep, with his dog Jack curled up on the foot of the bed. Hockney stayed with Boshier but dared not crawl into his bed. Instead he read *The Sexual Story of O* till the chapel bell began to ring, then fell asleep in Boshier's chair. Why Hockney didn't go home, since he only lived around the corner, is anybody's guess.

CHAPTER 7

AN EXPLOSION OF SPUNK

Our rapscallion soon knew he was contracting his first full-on college crush. The great, strong, badly-dressed, badly-appointed whip master R. B. Kitaj, whose bursts of womanly tenderness and berserker rage alternated like storms and sunshine on a summer day in the highlands of Scotland, had from the first seized powerfully on all Hockney's sympathies and was daily gaining more hold upon him.

Blessed is the man who has the power of making sex slaves for it is one of Eros's best gifts. It involves many things, but above all, the power of going out of oneself, and seeing and appreciating whatever is ignoble and base in another man or woman.

But even to him who has the gift, it is often a great puzzle to find out whether a man is really a sex slave or not. The following is recommended as a test in the case of any submissive about whom you are not quite sure. Especially if s/he should happen to have more of this world's goods, either in the shape of talents, rank or money, or what not, than you.

Fancy the man stripped stark naked of everything in the world, including every last stitch of clothing, without even a name to him, and dropped down in the middle of Holborn or Piccadilly. Would you go up to him then and there and lead him out from amongst the cabs and omnibuses, and take him to your own home and demand of him that he suck your dick? If you wouldn't do this you have no right to call him by the sacred name of sex slave. If you would, the odds are that he would submit totally to your will in all things sexual and you may count yourself a whip master.

Hockney was spiralling deeper into a bondage and discipline relationship with Kitaj. He was not bound hand and foot, gagged and carried away as a complete captive yet, but he was nearing such fathomless toils.

One evening he found himself as usual at Kitaj's door about eight o'clock. The oak was open but he got no answer when he knocked. Nevertheless he entered, by this time having quite got over all shyness or ceremony. The room was empty but two tumblers and the black bottle stood on the table, and the kettle was hissing away on the hob.

"Ah," thought Hockney, "he expects me, I see." So he turned his back to the fire and made himself at home. A quarter of an hour passed and still Kitaj did not return.

"Never knew him out so long before at this time of night," thought Hockney. "Perhaps he's at some party. I hope so. It would do him a good deal of good. Next term, see if I won't make him more sociable. Why won't he be more sociable? No, after all sociable isn't the word. He's a very dominant fellow at bottom. What in the world is it that he wants?"

And so Hockney balanced himself on the two hind legs of one of the Windsor chairs and betook himself to pondering what it was exactly which ought to be added to Kitaj to make him an unexceptional object of hero-worship. When the man himself came into the room, he slammed the door behind him and cast his cap fiercely on to the sofa before noticing our rapscallion.

Hockney jumped up at once. "My dear fellow, what's the matter? I'm sorry I came in, shall I go?"

"No—don't go—sit down," said Kitaj abruptly and then began to smoke fast without saying another word.

Hockney waited a few minutes watching for him and then broke the silence again: "I am sure something is the matter, Kitaj. You look dreadfully put out. What is it?"

"What is it?" said Kitaj bitterly, "Oh, nothing at all—nothing at all. It's just that I should like to chain you up stark naked in the common room and horse whip you in front of as many of the RCA students as possible?"

"But that would be terribly embarrassing for me!" Hockney observed.

"Exactly!" was Kitaj's rejoinder. "That's precisely why I want to do it."

"Couldn't I just suck your cock in front of the entire student body?" Hockney pleaded.

"That wouldn't be nearly humiliating enough!" Kitaj snapped.

After much arguing back and forth, Hockney eventually agreed to be horse whipped in the common room. Which is how Kitaj came to put a dog collar around Hockney's neck and leading him by a chain, had him crawl on all fours to the Republican College of Art. Together they headed down to the basement where the common room was located. Hockney was made to strip naked in front of dozens of his fellow students who were socialising there. Then he was tethered to the ceiling via some hooks that Kitaj had installed a few days earlier.

All the students in the basement fell silent and watched in awe as Kitaj shoved a gag into Hockney's mouth.

Soon the sharp, violent, sound of Kitaj's whip against Hockney's cock echoed through the room, immediately followed by his muffled screams and heavy panting. Hockney writhed in pain for a few moments before quiet was restored in the dim concrete basement. The only other noticeable noise was the quiet chime of the chains holding his hands up toward the ceiling. Hockney knew there was no escape so he gave up on wasting energy trying to free himself. Instead, he focused on bracing himself for the pain.

Another sharp crack, this time to his lower back. His hips jerked forward but he didn't have much room to move. Hockney's feet were tied spread eagle fashion to hooks Kitaj had put into the floor and with his hands stretched above his head he had very little mobility. He shut his eyes tightly as if to wish the pain away but to no avail. Kitaj was in complete control, walking slow circles around him plotting his next move. Hockney looked at Kitaj doe-eyed pleading his case to be unchained and shown mercy, but they both knew they'd be in that sweltering basement for some time.

Drool from the mouth gag tickled Hockney's midsection as it trickled downward from his chin. Kitaj placed his hands on Hockney's hips and gently massaged his delicate skin moving down to his thighs and back up across his abdomen to his back. Hockney quietly moaned, welcoming the change in sensation from pain to pleasure. Kitaj worked his right hand down and began massaging Hockney's erect cock. The quiet back and forth motion of Kitaj's fingers was accompanied by the swaying of Hockney's torso and the clanking of the chains that bound him. Beads of sweat ran down Hockney's body as his breathing became increasingly heavy. Forgetting that he was bound and at the mercy of Kitaj, his body screamed for sexual release. Kitaj worked his hand ever harder and faster along the full length of Hockney's crank shaft and the slave spunked up.

Hockney gurgled from the saliva backed up in his mouth, a counterpoint to the sexual relief he was getting from Kitaj. Hockney was enjoying the sensation so much he was no longer consciously aware of the fact he was bound and gagged in a basement. When pain from the manacles on his wrists reminded Hockney that he was chained up, he realised that only someone who was completely twisted could enjoy the things Kitaj was doing to him. Why am I turned on by this he wondered?

"Wow," Kitaj shouted, "you're an even bigger freak than I am! You're really enjoying this!"

Embarrassment washed over Hockney, making the airless, muggy basement seem that much hotter. Hockney looked over at the assembled students who were silently watching him and wanted to apologise to them for his sexual kinks. Kitaj undid the gag Hockney was wearing.

"Look you don't have to do that..." was all Hockney could blurt out before Kitaj forced an O-gag into his mouth.

Kitaj pulled up a chair and stood on it so that he could greet Hockney's now permanently open mouth with the tip of his dick, erect and pulsing. He forced Hockney to tongue the end of his tool. Hockney drooled as he stuck his tongue out as far out as it would go to massage the head of Kitaj's manhood. Kitaj didn't let Hockney take a break as he kept pulling his head forward. Hockney's tongue was heavy and he began taking deep breaths of the stale, humid, smoke filled basement air.

Then Kitaj grabbed Hockney's head and rammed his cock deep into the back of the sub's throat. Hockney couldn't do anything but accept the punishment and humiliation as Kitaj's violent thrusts, which barely let him breath, had him yearning for stale basement air. All Hockney could do was gasp and make pathetic gurgling noises as saliva gathered in the back of his throat.

Kitaj took his cock out of Hockney's mouth. It was dripping with spit and glistened in the dim lighting. He then undid Hockney's O-gag and stood on the chair before him, cock erect and sparkling. Kitaj began stroking it. His mighty hand dwarfed his giant love muscle as he slid his digits back and forth. After just a few strokes, Kitaj spewed a massive load all over Hockney's face. The jet of come took Hockney by surprise and before he knew it his face was masked in the thick, sticky mess. The assembled students clapped. Kitaj asked if any of them wanted to lick his come off Hockney's face but no one took him up on the offer.

CHAPTER 8

THE TIP OF DAVID HOCKNEY'S WAXED MANHOOD LIT UP LIKE A CHRISTMAS TREE!

Hockney's success at acting out the role of the submissive did not last long. After his master deliberately ignored Hockney for a week as a test, the rubber slave arrived unsummoned at Kitaj's room in a furious state of mind. Kitaj looked up from his book and exclaimed:

"What's the matter? Where have you been tonight? You look fierce enough to sit for a portrait of Sanguinoso Volcanoni, the bandit."

"Been!" said Hockney, dropping down so heavily on the spare Windsor chair he made it crack, "I've been to a wine party with Pauline Boty. Do you know her?"

"Of course I do!"

"Yes, I remember, you tried to cop off with her but she wouldn't let you come in her face."

"She is sexually magnificent in every way except that she wouldn't let me do the things I wanted to do with her."

"Hasn't anyone told you?"

"No."

"I haven't been able to stand the fact that you've been ignoring me, so Pauline and I have been making the beast with two backs!" Hockney lied.

"But you aren't into girls!" Kitaj exclaimed.

"I know!" Hockney wailed. "I feel like a complete masochist!"

"You're a natural born rubber slave!" was Kitaj's rejoinder.

"Master," Hockney pleaded, "you must subject me to the most savage of cock tortures!"

"Hockney," Kitaj laughed, "if I was to indulge you with such sport right now, I'd be giving into your demands and you'd be the master and I'd be the slave?"

"Surely not if you were torturing my cock?"

"I'm going to give you a leaflet about cock and ball torture. I want you to go home and get in your lonely bed. Then you're to read the text and afterwards jerk yourself off as you fantasise about Pauline Boty doing the things described within it to you."

"But Kitaj," Hockney protested. "I'd rather submit to you!"

"No buts," the rubber master insisted, "you'll do as I say and tomorrow you're to tell Boty all about it."

Kitaj rummaged through some papers before extracting a leaflet and handing it to Hockney. Then curtly dismissed the rubber slave. Hockney raced home and as instructed got into bed before reading the BDSM tract. The text ran as follows:

Cock & Ball Torture

Introduction

Cock and ball torture, or CBT as it is more commonly called, can involve a variety of things. Torture can be used to induce mild to severe pain or it can be used only to cause discomfort. It is important to note that the penis and testicles can be easily or permanently damaged and, therefore, caution must be observed when practising this activity.

Some in the BDSM community speculate that torturing a man's genitals is directly related to sexual control issues while others argue that torturing a man's sex organs addresses the ego. I would suppose that each male has his own reason for desiring this type of pleasure.

In many primitive cultures a man's testicles were viewed as sacred and, in some instances, oaths were given while holding a penis in the hand. And, in certain societies, squeezing a man's testicles could lead to the perpetrator losing their hand.

There are many methods of CBT and, depending on the pain threshold or erotic tendencies of the individual, some can be very dramatic.

Ball Torture

I. Squeezing

The testicles are perhaps the most sensitive area of man's genitals as well as the most fragile. Any activity involving the testicles should be undertaken carefully and with consideration given to the individual's welfare. Mistakes can lead to ruptures, tears, or other disfiguring and disabling results.

One form of ball torture is simply squeezing them in the palm of one hand, as if squeezing a rubber ball. By pulling down on the testicles before squeezing them, they rest at the bottom of the sack and can be squeezed more effectively. Start with a gentle pressure and work up from there until your partner has reached his threshold.

While squeezing the balls you can manipulate them in your palm, causing them to rub slightly against one another. This rubbing presses on nerves that lie on the outsides of each testicle and causes a sharp shooting pain that travels up into the abdomen.

II. Slapping

Slapping is another painful method of ball torture. While the sack of the testicles hangs loose, gently but firmly slap them from side to side. The testicles will bounce within the sack when they are slapped causing immense pain so it is wise not to slap them with too much force.

You can also tie up the balls with a length of rope, tubing, or leather straps. To do this, gather the testicles in one hand and gently pull down. With the other hand, wrap the rope or other restraint device just above the balls and tie off. Once this is accomplished, tap lightly with the fingers on the now taut sides of the testicles.

The testicles are subject to rupture easily when they are bound so it is important that you do not use too much force during this activity. Also, the testicles should not remain bound for extended periods of time as blood flow may be restricted.

III. Pinching

The skin around the testicles is more sensitive while bound and pinching them with fingernails or tweezers can also prove to be very painful. Scraping the nails or other implements over the tightened skin of the sack is also deemed painful.

Use a ballpoint pen to write or draw on the bound testicles. This produces sensations that vary from sensual to painful, depending on the amount of pressure applied.

You might also try a tracing wheel (can be purchased at sewing centres for a few pennies) to trace over the surface of the bound testicles. Again, the amount of pressure used determines the reaction you will get. You may even try placing the tracing wheel in an ice box for a few hours beforehand.

Any instrument may be used in this manner, however, you may want to avoid anything that would cut or puncture the skin.

IV. Clamps

There are various devices that can be used to clamp the skin around the testicles. Nipple clamps, clothes pins, and binder clips are just a few useful things that you can use. Leaving these on for a period of time allows the subject to adjust to the pressure that is being applied to the area. However, when the clamps are removed, the experience will be extremely painful.

If you use clothespins, try purchasing the plastic ones that have holes in their ends. These can be applied over the entire sack of the testicles and then laced together with string or thin rope. Once they are all laced together, you can pluck at the various strings and produce pain in more specific areas all along the sack.

Binder clips (purchased at office supply stores) will perhaps produce the most pain without the use of weights. These can be adjusted by prying them apart; giving you an assortment of pressures to use on your submissive.

Nipple clamps (purchased through catalogues and fetish stores) come in a large variety. The butterfly clamps are nice because they can be easily weighted. The alligator clip variety can be adjusted to produce anything from mild to extreme discomfort.

Regardless of where you purchase your clips, be sure to wash them first in warm soapy water and then sterilise them with alcohol before using. This cuts down on bacteria that may have been picked up during packaging and shipping. And, always clean your toys after each play session.

V. Weights

Weights can be added to clamps that have been attached to the sack of the testicles. A good source for weights is a store that sells fishing tackle. By choosing fishing weights of various sizes and heaviness, you can make the experience more challenging for the submissive.

By threading a small rope or twine through the weights and tying them off, you have a weighting system that can be readily added to the clamps, a piece at a time.

Also, fishing weights come in various sizes, shapes, and degrees of heaviness and so allow you to challenge your submissive to take more pain each time you play.

Other sources for weights are the hardware store. You can purchase nuts in varying sizes and these are also easily threaded with twine or rope, making it easy to use them during playtime.

To store your weights, simply drive a nail in a closet wall out of sight and hang them from it.

VI. Parachutes

Parachutes are usually made of leather and can be purchased through most fetish catalogues or stores catering to the BDSM scene. A parachute attaches between the testicles and the penis and has three chains that come together just under the testicles. These chains are usually joined together with a circular link so that weights can be attached. Though not necessarily painful, most men who enjoy CBT find the constant tug on their testicles to be erotic. Also, men can be made to walk around while wearing the weights dangling between their thighs.

The parachute can also be turned inside out while the testicles are still in them, producing a mushroom looking effect of the testicles. Parachutes can be purchased in one-size-fits all, however, when possible it's best to have them made to your specific size and requirements. You can have attachments added to your parachute if it is made for you.

When having a parachute custom made, consider having studs sewn into the side that will sit against the testicles. This causes discomfort, especially after weights have been added or when worn under clothing.

VII. Binding

Binding the testicles can be accomplished in several ways. While pulling down on the testicles, you can use rope, twine or leather straps, wrapping it repeatedly around the sack then tying it off. This wrapping causing some stretching and separation and can present a very pleasing sight.

The testicles can also be separated and each tied into it's own little sack. Start with the lowest hanging testicle first and once it is firmly tied move to the next. Once both testicles are separately tied, wrap rope above both causing them to be pushed together. You must be careful tying off the testicles because if the blood flow is interrupted to the area over a period of time, this can cause damage. You might also want to use multicolour rubber bands to tie off the testicles.

You can also purchase leather ball straps in varying sizes that can be placed around the balls, although these will stretch over time.

VIII. Mummification

Mummification is not just for the whole body. The testicles can be wrapped and completely encased in rope, gauze, cloth strips, or even packing tape. Be cautious when striking the testicles in this state, as when they are tightly bound they are easily damaged. If you are using gauze, start at the top of the sack and work your way down. This puts more pressure into the sack of the testicles when you are finished.

When using tape you don't need to worry too much about how tight you should get it as the real torture starts when you remove it. Old bed linens and pillowcases make excellent binding material and can be washed and used again after each play session.

IX. Waxing

Waxing the balls is another way to produce pain. Choose either soft or hard wax, depending on the temperature you prefer. A soft wax will melt relatively quickly and won't be as hot as a slower burning hard wax. Drip the wax slowly and at intervals all along the surface of either loose or tied testicles.

Shaving the testicles beforehand will make them more sensitive and makes wax removal less of a chore. Of course, if you don't choose to shave your submissive, he's in store for a harrowing time while the wax is removed.

You might try removing the wax with a dull edged butter knife for more sensation; otherwise giving the testicles a hard squeeze will break up the wax and allow you to peel it off slowly in small sections.

Wax retains heat so you can pour on several layers at a time without worry of serious burns.

Penis Torture

The penis can be tortured in a variety of ways. It is important to note once again that this is a body area that is susceptible to damage. Caution should be exercised with the following activities.

I. Whipping

Whipping the penis can be done while it is soft or erect. When the penis is in full erection, blood vessels are enlarged so it is important that you are careful. A ruptured vessel takes a long time to heal and can sometimes cause erectile dysfunction.

You can use any type of whip you want as long as you do not use too much force. Striking the penis with the tip of the whip is preferable since any other motion will produce a wrapping effect.

Some companies make a short whip that resembles a key chain. This whip is quite effective in administering pain given its small size.

Another suggestion would be to purchase some shoelaces (found at most stores) and tie them together creating a homemade whip. The plastic tips at the end of the shoelaces can cause great pain to the submissive when they make contact with the skin. This type of whip is also effective because you can design it to a length that you can handle comfortably. Another way to make your own whip is to buy leather shoelaces and braid them together. This makes a short, easily handled whip that will have more weight to it.

II. Waxing

Totally encasing the penis in wax of various colours can be enjoyable to the top as well as the bottom. Again, you must decide between hard and soft wax. Soft wax moulds more easily to the surface of the penis and can be layered.

As the wax is layered, heat is held in close to the skin on the penis and can be very erotic to the submissive.

Removing sections of the wax is easier if you start with a softer wax. You can take out sections and re-wax while the rest is still cooling.

If you are feeling very creative, place a birthday candle at the tip of the penis when you start waxing and coat the wax at the base until it stands firmly in place. (Be careful not to shove the candle into the urethra.)

Once you have finished waxing the entire surface of the penis, light the birthday candle and watch its progress. It will drop down onto the existing wax, heating things up.

III. Binding

The penis can be bound with rope, leather, chain, gauze, or packing tape, in much the same manner as the testicles. Binding the penis while soft keeps it from reaching erection and can be an added tool of torture while engaging in other activities. Cock straps are also available in leather and can be fitted onto the penis before it is hard to prevent erection.

Another trick is to place as many condoms as possible on the penis. Each condom will add pressure to the cock, as well as cutting down on the amount sensation that the submissive can feel through them. I suggest purchasing cheaper priced condoms for this activity; however, do not use these same condoms for protection purposes. Non-lubricated condoms produce the greatest amount of discomfort to the submissive.

As he'd been reading through this treatise on CBT, Hockney had become increasingly excited. After finishing the text, he gripped his erect manhood and after a dozen strokes his genetic wealth spurted all over his belly. As Hockney used bog roll to wipe up the sticky mess, he imagined Pauline Boty laughing in his face as he told her he wanted his penis waxed and to have a lit birthday candle attached to its end.

CHAPTER 9

CROSS-DRESSING FOR BONDAGE AND DISCIPLINE! BEATEN SENSELESS PURELY FOR PLEASURE!

How many spots in life are there that bear comparison to the beginning of the second term of a masters degree at the Republican College of Art? So far as external circumstances are concerned, it seems hard to know what a man would ask for at that period of his life if a fairy godmother were to alight in his room and offer him the usual three wishes. The sailor who wanted "all the twenty-one year old boys in the world," and "all the beer in the world," would be driven to "all the twenty-two year old boys" as his third requisition. At any rate his first two wishes were to some extent grounded on what he held to be substantial wants; he felt himself actually limited in the matters of boys and booze. David Hockney would have been in the same condition as a wisher except that he would have asked for further developments in his bondage and discipline encounters with Kitaj.

After giving Hockney the treatise on cock and ball torture, Kitaj had allowed the holidays to come and go without subjecting his rubber slave to any further sexual outrages. Therefore upon returning to London for the second term of his masters, the first thing Hockney did—after depositing his luggage—was to call on Kitaj, and he found his rubber master deep as usual in his art history books. Hockney immediately occupied his old place with much satisfaction.

"How long have you been back old fellow?" Hockney began, "you look quite settled."

"I didn't leave London. Well, what have you been doing in the vacation?"

"Oh, there was nothing much going on so I made art."

"Bravo! You'll find the comfort of it now. I hardly thought you would take to the grind of painting so easily."

"It's pleasant enough for a spurt," said Hockney, "but I shall never manage a horrid perpetual grind like yours. But what in the world have you been doing to your walls?"

Hockney might well ask, for the corners of Kitaj's room were covered with sheets of paper of different sizes, pasted against the wall in groups. In the line of sight, from about the height of four to six feet, there was scarcely an inch of the original paper visible, and round each centre group there were outlying patches and streamers, stretching towards floor or ceiling, or away nearly to the bookcases or fireplace.

"Well, don't you think it is a great improvement on the old paper?" said Kitaj. "It is a hint to the landlady that the room needs redecorating. You're no judge of such matters, or I should ask you whether you don't see great artistic taste in the arrangement."

"Why they're nothing but maps and lists of names and dates," said Hockney, who had got up to examine the decorations. "And what in the world are all these queer pins for?" he went on, pulling a strong pin with a large red sealing-wax head out of the map nearest to him.

"Hello! Take care there, what are you like?" shouted Kitaj, getting up and hastening to the corner. "Why, you irreverent bugger, those pins are the famous statesmen and warriors of Greece and Rome."

"Oh, I beg your pardon, I didn't know I was in such august company," saying which, Hockney proceeded to stick the red-headed pin back in the wall.

"Don't you know that BDSM first flourished in ancient Greece and Rome? I can see that you still have a long way to go as a rubber slave."

"Oh punish me master!" Hockney said as he got on his knees and placed his palms together in prayer.

"If I punished you I'd be rewarding your impertinence. Aren't you aware that we know BDSM was practised in ancient Rome thanks to Petrarch's *Satyricon,* written in the first century of the Common Era."

"No!" Hockney squeaked.

"In Book 4 Encolpius is given an aphrodisiac to drink," Kitaj informed his rubber slave. "Encolpius has his hands tied behind him and the servant girl Psyche fondles his penis, trying to arouse him. Psyche also pricks his cheeks with her hairpin to silence him when he tries to cry for help."

"But that's boring heterosexual BDSM!" Hockney complained.

"I'm here to dominate you—not to pander to your fantasies!" Kitaj snapped. "A bit later Encolpius and a woman Quartilla are forcibly bound together, for sport, by a group of young soldiers. The type of bondage used on Encolpius and Quartilla forces her mouth into close contact with his mush, her breasts rubbing against his chest, and their thighs each pressed into the other's. As a result of the aphrodisiac he'd consumed Encolpius becomes filled with lasciviousness and begins performing on Quartilla. She's on fire with a similar wantonness and shows no reluctance for the game, to the great amusement of the soldiers."

"I'm not interested in straights!" Hockney wailed.

"But it gets better!" Kitaj insisted. "At the same time as he is thrusting into his bound partner Quartilla, a gay man mounts the bound Encolpius from behind. Though Encolpius falsely claims he finds this repulsive, he wriggles in response to the intruder's thrusts, just as fast and furiously as Quartilla is wriggling under him— although this dope claims his reactions are involuntary. The young soldiers find this spectacle quite ludicrous and burst into laughter at the humiliation of Encolpius."

"That's better," Hockney admitted, "but why all the hetero stuff?"

"In ancient Greece and Rome," Kitaj explained, "as well as in other cultures, there was an association between fertility—that's success in conceiving children to you—and some types of flagellation. For example, whipping the buttocks with nettles was supposed to increase fertility according to the Ancients."

"Fooey!" Hockney spat.

"Shut up and listen to me!" Kitaj exclaimed in a stern tone. "In the ancient world flagellation was also considered an aphrodisiac, or stimulant of sexual desire. Men were often whipped by hookers to restore waning desire. There is much Greco-Roman art depicting a sandal being used for erotic spanking or slapping. It can also be surmised that much of this activity was consensual, since the person being whipped was seeking to get something out of it — arousal or fertility."

"I don't want to hear about femdom vixens, I want you to punish me!" The words exploded from Hockmey's mouth like a stinking fart from the arse of a glutton.

"Go!" Kitaj declaimed as he pointed at the door. "And I don't want you to come back for at least a week. Learn obedience before you trouble me again."

After the long holiday during which he'd had no BDSM, Hockney was feeling particularly randy. He had heard about a place in Soho where men might leave messages for each other. Hockney knew he shouldn't be doing it but he paid for a card he'd hand written to be displayed on a notice board. The shop owner had explained to him how he might code his message, and also told Hockney he should return the next day.

The next morning Hockney got to the Soho shop before it opened. When the proprietor turned up and gave Hockney his messages, the first letter was from a guy who just wanted to fuck him. While the thought of someone's cock slipping up his arse was a nice idea, he could get that type of action anywhere. Hockney was looking for a sterner master than Kitaj, and when he opened the next message he thought he might have found one.

The missive didn't really tell Hockney much beyond the fact that his correspondent lived in London and his last slave had been found dead floating face down in a canal, so he was looking for a replacement. He said he would consider Hockney but made no promises about a long-term arrangement until the art student had been tested for obedience. The letter contained the address of a hotel. Hockney's contact said that if this young man wanted some serious BDSM action, he was to go to this establishment—which was in Bayswater—and leave a note with the concierge saying he'd turn up at the establishment the next day. When he returned at the appointed time, Hockney would be told which room to go to. He was also under strict instructions to appear dressed in women's clothing. The rubber master said in his letter that he had everything else required, so Hockney was just to turn up suitably attired.

The next day, after buying the necessary clothes and changing into them, Hockney got to the hotel at precisely 7PM. He made sure he was punctual as he didn't want to start off on the wrong foot. The bellboy told him to go to room 23 and when he got there he found the door was open. Walking into the suite, Hockney found the curtains were drawn and that there was a message on the bed, He could see someone sitting in the corner of the room but the man didn't say a word. The note simply told Hockney to go into the bathroom to perform a listed series of tasks.

Once he was in the bathroom, Hockney stripped off and started washing even though he'd had a bath before making his way to the hotel. Then Hockney shaved down below—it seemed his new master disliked pubic hair. Once his hygiene tasks were completed, Hockney's instructions were to return to the hotel bedroom naked. The art student wondered if he'd get a second chance to reapply his make-up and don once more the female clothes he'd taken so much trouble over for this date—or if he'd been told to arrive in them simply as a form of humiliation. Hockney had quickly got to really like his

French knickers and stockings, so stripped of them he felt more naked than usual!

Emerging from the bathroom Hockney saw that while he'd been preparing himself for the sex session, the main door to the room had been shut. Likewise, some PVC knickers & stockings had been placed on the bed. Hockney made his way towards the fetish gear, but his master stood up and called him over.

"Sit on the chair!" The man ordered.

Hockney did as he'd been told. At the same time he got to see what this rubber master looked like. He was around six foot tall and slim too. Clean shaven and wearing a suit, this dude was in good shape for someone in his late-thirties. The rubber master undid his own belt, unzipped his flies and loosened his trousers so that he could spread his legs wide and make the two sides of the zipper taut. With his breeks held up by pressure from his outer thighs, the master sat on Hockney's legs. The two men were facing each other and they French kissed. The rubber master took the art student's erect cock in his hand and rubbed it against his own limp member. As he did so he made sure he dragged Hockney's dick against one of the taut edges of his fly for some scarification. The slave let out a yelp of pain. The dom twisted Hockney's cock around so that they could both admire the scars he'd made on it.

"Now if you have another master and he looks at your cock, he'll know you've been with me and he'll punish you!" the dom hissed.

Then the man got up and ordered Hockney to put on the fetish clobber that had been left on the bed. The art student minced across the room to where the PVC gear was laid out. While putting on the knickers, Hockney made sure he kept bending over and exposing his arse to the master he could no longer see—just to prove what a total come slut of a cross-dresser he was. When he'd got the stockings on, he turned to look at himself in the mirror and decided he was pretty hot!

After walking across to the bed, the rubber master passed Hockney some cuffs for his ankles & wrists. After Hockney put on the cuffs, the dom placed a blindfold on the slave and announced that he would do whatever he pleased with his bitch.

He pulled Hockney into the middle of the room and the art student was left just standing there not knowing what to expect. The rubber master's hands were touching parts of Hockney's body but not his nipples and certainly not his cock or arse. The rubber slave was disappointed by this considering how hot he looked with the PVC knickers on. Then without warning, the art student found himself pulled over into a bending position and his hands were quickly strapped to his ankle cuffs.

After this the dom walked around his prey and ripped open the rubber knickers before pulling Hockney's arse cheeks apart. The slave briefly felt the man's breath on his rectum. Then the rubber master walked away and Hockney wondered what was going to happen next! He didn't have to wait long to find out, as the dom returned to his arse not with a hard cock—which was what Hockney was really hoping for—but to punish him. He hit the art student so hard with a whip that Hockney nearly fell over!

"What do you say you slut?" The rubber master demanded as Hockney was still smarting from the sting of his whip.

"Thank you, master!" Fortunately for Hockney, Kitaj had already taught him the correct response to this question.

And having been thanked the man repaid Hockney by sending another spasm of pain through his body with a second crack of the whip. This was followed by another lash and then another and another. The punishment went on for 20 minutes and Hockney knew before it was over he would not be able to sit down for a week. Nonetheless, his cock was harder than it had ever been before—even with Kitaj—and Hockney knew if his dick was just touched he'd come.

Hockney didn't know what to expect when the rubber master stopped beating him. The art student kept still and listened. He couldn't work out what the dom was doing. Finally he felt the man's hands on his straps and cuffs—they were being undone.

"I'm leaving now," the man told him, "stand still and count to 500 before removing the blindfold. By the time you're ready to leave the hotel I'll be long gone."

Hockney followed these instructions. When he removed the blindfold he found a note on the bed telling him he'd passed the first test and that if he wanted another beating he was to return to the same room in exactly one week, and to make sure he left a message with the concierge the day before if he intended to do so!

Hockney was in a state of high sexual excitement and after reading the note the first thing he did was go into the bathroom and jerk himself off over the toilet. Hockney knew he'd been unfaithful to Kitaj but figured his real master need never know about this. Kitaj had told him not to show his face for at least a week, so that meant the wounds on his cock would have time to heal before he saw his true love again. Hockney had been desperate for sex and figured that if in the future Kitaj gave him good times, then there was no need to see this new rubber master again. Hockney really was a most disobedient slave!

CHAPTER 10

MUSCULAR SADO-MASOCHISM

In the space of a fortnight some major events unfolded within Hockney's circle. Hockney introduced Blake to Kitaj. Hockney waited forty-eight hours before venturing to inquire whether the two hit it off. When he cautiously approached the subject, he was glad that Kitaj liked Blake.

"Blake is a first class fuck," Kitaj informed Hockney, "and very able as both a dom and sub. But he really needs to find his path in the BDSM scene and develop in a single direction only…"

Then the BDSM training begun in earnest. It was Kitaj's contention that to really enjoy the fetish scene and get the most out of it, practitioners of this wonderful sexual deviation needed to take themselves to a peak of physical fitness. So he signed Hockney and some others up to a gym. They worked out for two or three hours a day, and participated in their fair share of bad locker room jokes about women, faggots and the like—and laughed just as much as the others at these inanities. Every night in the shower Hockney had to fight with himself so as not to look at the other men in way that would seem suspicious. Kitaj apparantly had no difficulties with this and told Hockney he was looking for someone at the gym who was a little on the shy side and who hardly ever got their end away.

Kitaj eventually hit on a small guy called Mike who was at the gym every single night. Kitaj used his charming smile and manner to put the moves on this closet case. It was obvious that Mike had lusted after Kitaj from the minute he first laid eyes on him. Kitaj pretended not to notice and acted as if Mike was just one of the guys. Hockney became insanely jealous but said nothing, since he knew it would be out of place for him to do so.

That was until one evening after working out, when Kitaj approached Mike.

It was a cold night and there was no one around but Hockney.

Kitaj went up to the pint-sized muscle man and said: "Say boy, how about you and me go get ourselves a drink?"

Mike, who was smitten, agreed immediately. To Mike's great surprise Kitaj took him to a gay bar, and had Hockney tag along behind them. Kitaj ordered two beers and sat down with Mike in a private booth at the back of the drinking den. Hockney was on all fours lapping water from a bowl that had been placed under their table.

After a few general remarks, Kitaj cut to the chase: "You're gay right? I mean, you're good at pretending not to be checking a guy's arse or cock out, but it can be spotted. It takes one to know one."

"Yes," Mike replied. "I'm as gay as the next man and I fantasise about cock sucking all day long..."

Kitaj smiled at Mike and clasped his hand. There wasn't much that needed saying after that and once they finished their beers—and Hockney his bowl of water—they all went to Mike's place. As Mike closed the door behind them, Kitaj told Hockney to be a good dog and ordered him to curl up in a corner of the room. He then turned around and kissed Mike. The tiny muscle man kissed him back and it was the physical contact this lonely bodybuilder had been waiting for since he'd first laid eyes on Kitaj.

From Hockney's point of view, it was from there that things went wrong. As Mike and Kitaj kissed he thought he felt a needle sting his butt. As Hockney yelped in surprised pain, he saw that Kitaj was holding a syringe. Hockney started to ask what was going on, but he felt dizzy and as if his mouth was full of cotton. As darkness closed in around him, Hockney could still see Kitaj laughing uproariously. Mike disappeared and the scene in the room somehow changed.

When Hockney woke up he couldn't move. He was tied to a hospital bed, with straps around his legs, his hips, his arms and across his chest. He tried very hard to break free, but all his muscle power accomplished was a weak shaking of the bed, which was obviously bolted to the floor. Hockney tried to yell, but his mouth was filled with what he later learnt was a penis gag. Not long after Hockney woke up, Kitaj appeared by the side of the bed. He was accompanied by Peter Blake in a doctor's outfit and what looked like some kind of nurse but was in fact Pauline Boty. She was dressed in tight-fitting white rubber. She wore platform shoes with very high heels and seemed very afraid of 'Doctor' Blake.

"So this is the useless specimen you want transformed, R.B.?" the doctor said to Kitaj as he flung away the sheet that covered the sub. Hockney was stark naked underneath and his bulging muscles stood out against his bindings.

"Yes, Dr. Blake," Kitaj confirmed. "This is the one."

"And you want only the surgery and the hormone treatment?"

"Yes. All the conditioning and training I'll handle. After all that's where all the fun is." At this both Kitaj and Blake laughed.

"You are certainly right about that," Blake agreed.

Hockney was getting very scared. Transformation? Surgery? Hormones? What were they talking about? Hockney tried to yell and break his bonds. This pathetic show seemed to amuse Kitaj.

"There, there, my little slut. I'll soon give you something real to yell about. In the meantime, let's see what an excitable little slapper you are." Kitaj said, as he brought his face to within an inch of Hockney's visage.

Kitaj touched Hockney's dick and began to stroke it gently. To Hockney's eternal shame it quickly became rock hard. Hockney tried to look away but Kitaj grabbed his chin and forced the sub to gaze into his eyes as he continued with the hand job. In a few minutes Hockney was ready to explode. His yelling had turned into moaning and his attempts to get free had become a sexually charged squirming. All he cared about was coming. And just as he was about to come, Kitaj removed his hand.

Hockney yelled with frustration as Kitaj laughed at his twitching cock. He left him like that and told Blake he'd pick Hockney up in a month. After Kitaj left, the doctor turned to Hockney.

"Let's get started, shall we?" Blake bellowed as he plunged a syringe into Hockney's arm and everything went black.

When he woke Hockney felt weak. It took forever just to open his eyes. He tried to shift around and discovered he was tied up. Hockney didn't care that much about this. He was drugged and all he really wanted to do was sleep. Cycles of semi-consciousness and blacking out alternated for what seemed an eternity. Hockney guessed this went on for more than eight or nine days.

Eventually Hockney noticed his hands and feet were covered in thick bandages and that these appendages were completely unresponsive if he attempted to move them. His face and throat were also covered in dressings. Hockney felt a tightness in the skin on his chest and a weight there that was unfamiliar. What had happened to him?

After a while Peter Blake came to check him. Hockney tried to make disgruntled noises behind his gag, but no sound came. Blake made the bandaged parts of Hockney's body the main focus of his attention. A rubber nurse called Ida Kar who had received instructions from Blake carried out various operations once the fake medic had left—changing Hockney's bandages and the IV drip going into his arm. As Kar performed these duties she removed the sheet covering Hockney and he saw what caused the tightness and weight on his chest. He had tits! They were nowhere near the size of those the rubber nurses sported, but they were still large. Hockney tried fighting and yelling again, but he was too weak and no sound came from his throat.

Then Kar gave Hockney something to eat. This was done by inserting a tube into a hole in his gag and feeding him a liquid mush. She saw to his other needs too. Kar started most unpleasantly by inserting a catheter into his cock and draining urine from his bladder. She left the catheter in and attached a new bag to the end of the tube, removing all bladder control. His piss just dribbled into the bag.

The last thing Kar had been instructed to do was to clean out Hockney's bowels. To achieve this she raised the bed until she could kneel down under it. Then she removed the piece of the bed directly beneath Hockney's arse and proceeded to stick a tube up his jacksee. Hockney clenched his buttocks as hard as he could and the rubber nurse was unable to shove the tube up his shit-chute.

"Please allow me to give you the enemas," Kar's voice had a strong lisping quality as if her lips prevented her from speaking properly. "If you don't allow me to give you the enemas, I'll be forced to call someone to punish you. Believe me, you don't want that to happen."

Although the rubber nurse said this with an imploring tone, Hockney didn't give in. Nobody was going to stick a tube up his bum. When Kar realised her efforts to convince Hockney to cooperate had failed, she turned around with a sigh and left. Thirty minutes later Kar returned with Peter Blake who was still dressed up as a doctor—and looked furious.

"Stupid slut!" he yelled into Hockney's face as he slapped the submission bitch hard, "You are nothing but property. But don't worry cunt, I'll teach you. Just you wait and see."

He fetched some wires with large alligator clips at the ends. One was attached to Hockney's cock and although painful it was nothing when compared to the attachment of the next two clips. These were placed so they engulfed a whole testicle and squeezed it hard. The pressure on Hockney's testicles made him want to scream, but no sound came. Hockney thrashed in his bonds but all to no avail.

Blake had an evil smile on his face and it turned into a huge grin as he applied current to the wires. Hockney's crotch exploded with pain as Blake pulsed the current and soon the sub was prepared to do anything to have the electrocutions stop. But just to make a point Blake continued the torture for a good while longer.

"Are you going to be good little girl now?" Blake asked, not caring that Hockney didn't like being called a girl.

Hockney nodded vigorously. Blake seemed satisfied with this and turned to the rubber nurse: "She won't give you any more problems but just to make sure, give her ten enemas instead of the usual five."

With that Peter Blake turned and walked away.

Although not as painful as the electric current, the enemas hurt and were very humiliating. By the third, Hockney was crying and wanted desperately to plead through his gag for the session to end. But no sound came from his mouth. By enema number six the she-male was exhausted, and would have done anything to avoid further pain. But of course there was no mercy and by the time it was all over, Hockney had no fight left in him and just lay limply as the rubber nurse replaced the section of bed under his arse and covered him with a sheet.

Left alone, Hockney gradually gathered his thoughts and pondered his situation. Was he being turned into a girl? And if so, why? And how come they'd left his cock intact if that was the case?

The next few weeks passed in much the same way, except that Hockney was determined not to get punished again, so he willingly allowed various rubber nurses to give him enemas. His bandages were changed once a day and he was fed via the tube twice every 24 hours. Other than that the only thing he had to do was to watch his tits grow. And boy did they grow! They grew so fast that he was afraid they were going to burst and after about three weeks Hockney had 40DD tits. Then the bandages came off his feet, his hands and his face. His appendages had shrunk and were now small and very feminine.

Then gradually Hockney's body returned to normal and he realised he was in Kitaj's room. His tiny muscle man friend Mike was there, who explained to Hockney that he hadn't been strapped to a hospital bed for weeks, instead Kitaj had spiked his bowl of water in the bar with a new mind bending drug called LSD. The CIA were using it in thought control experiments and Kitaj had used suggestion techniques and hypnotism to fool Hockney into believing he'd been imprisoned and transformed into a chick with a dick! The LSD 'trip' had lasted about eight hours, not the weeks that Hockney believed had elapsed.

"Wow!" Hockney said, "that's the most muscular piece of BDSM drama we've ever engaged in and all you used was a drug and a few suggestive phrases!"

"It was a little more than that," Kitaj responded proudly. "I did tie you down and I also blindfolded you. That way I knew whatever was whispered in your ear would have maximum effect. If you'd been able to see I don't think my little experiment would have worked nearly so well… I've been studying the technique one of the CIA's top researchers—Dr Ewen Cameron—calls psychic driving…"

"Cool!" Hockney replied. "Those that are familiar with modern day torture techniques will also practice the most advanced forms of BDSM!"

"Right!" Kitaj shouted back while simultaneously clapping his hands. "So aren't you a lucky boy!"

CHAPTER 11

FLOGGED AND BRANDED
IN HYDE PARK

R. B. Kitaj, David Hockney and Derek Boshier ate an early dinner together on what was to be a very special night. Boshier ordered his steak medium, and Hockney his medium rare, but Kitaj told the waiter with polite domination that he'd have his very rare.

"Cook it just long enough to warm it, but make sure it's left good and bloody." The waiter looked surprised by this command but scribbled it down on his order pad.

The conversation at The Kensington Steak House was lively but not forced on any topic except the one that had brought them together that night, Hockney's initiation into new depths of BDSM pain and humiliation. Boshier interjected an observation from time to time, but kept his conversation low key despite sitting next to Hockney in the high backed booth, with Kitaj across the table from them. Kitaj spoke more than the other two men.

After steak, the three art students went round to a pad owned by a friend of Kitaj's who was away on business and had asked the post-grad to look after the place for him. The dom tied Hockney and Boshier up and whipped them a little, but did nothing particularly wild or extravagant. This indoor sex session was just a little tease, a warm up for something far kinkier outdoors afterwards. Kitaj took a devilish delight in nipple clipping Boshier and Hockney together as they knelt across from each other with their wrists tied behind their backs. The dom used little birch rod love brushes across his slave's backs to make them pull back from each other—stretching their nipples out as they did so.

"Don't worry, Hockney," Kitaj spat at his fellow art student as he took deep pleasure in lightly caning him, "your punishment will get way more intense than this once we're in Hyde Park."

Kitaj then made Hockney lie prone on rough cotton fabric sheets as he blindfolded him. The sub's face was buried in a pillow and Kitaj pushed the scarf he was using as a gag deeper into Hockney's mouth, to restrict his air supply. Hockney's wrists and ankles were stretched taut to the four posts of the bed.

Boshier was ordered to switch roles to that of a dom. He was told to twist and stretch Hockney's cock while Kitaj roughly shoved his own love pole deep inside the sub's arse. Simultaneously Kitaj worked Hockney's heaving shoulder blades with a taming touch from his birch rod bundle.

Then Boshier reverted to a sub role and was tied into a pea pod sixty-nine with Hockney. Kitaj worked first one man's arsehole and then the other—while his leathered riding crop popped and stung whatever piece of exposed flesh caught his eye. When the two subs were untied, Boshier was told that from now on he would do no more than watch. The three men dressed and, carrying various pieces of kit in bags they took with them, walked to Hyde Park. They had to climb over the railings since the place was locked up at night.

Before getting far, Hockney's foot dropped into a hole in the ground he'd not seen in the dark. His fantasies and desires snapped with the same sound as what he took to be his bones breaking. The sub screamed: "I think I've broken my ankle... damn it to hell!"

"Let me take a look," Kitaj said, dropping his bag on the ground.

Kitaj pulled down Hockney's sock and examined his ankle: "No visible bruising and it's not swelling much, no bones sticking through, you probably just sprained it a little. Here, this is the noise you heard!"

The dom chuckled as an old but thick freshly broken twig was fished out of the hole. "You'll be alright!" the master reassured his slave.

Supported by Kitaj on one side and Boshier on the other, Hockney walked on. The men stopped when they came to two lone oak trees six feet apart. The oaks were about two feet thick at the bottom. Six feet in front of them was a fire ring on the ground made from loosely assembled rocks with a dark pile of old ashes in the middle. Hockney was immediately convinced the site had been recently used for ritual purposes. Wild ideas raced through the sub's mind. Surely Kitaj wasn't involved in devil worship and human sacrifice!

"It's time, Hockney!" Kitaj barked. "Drop your bag and be very, very still."

Having ordered Boshier to sit by himself and observe, Kitaj pulled the gear he needed from his bag. Next he organised a bit of firewood. Hockney started to feel cold as he stood still, but he didn't dare move around to keep warm as he'd been told to remain motionless. An involuntary shiver of anticipation ran through Hockney as Kitaj built a fire.

The heat from the fire warmed Hockney and so he felt comfortable about the next instruction he received—which was to strip naked. Hockney's ankle was still a little sore but he now realised he'd suffered no more than a mild sprain.

"Are you ready, Hockney," Kitaj spat, "for the last step of your first beginning, your life as my total and complete slave?"

"Yes, Kitaj, I am ready!" Hockney replied.

"Kneel and kiss!" Kitaj instructed.

Hockney knelt naked in the dirt and kissed Kitaj's boots as the dom bent over him and slapped his arse as hard as he could manage from that angle. Using ropes and cuffs, Kitaj soon had Hockney war-eagled between the two oak trees: wrists bound and arms pulled taut upwards, ankles bound and legs spread open wide horizontally towards the trunks of the trees.

The yellow and orange flames of the fire whimpered down to red-hot embers, waves of heat shimmering and shattering the cold of the night. Hockney's eyes were wide open and his mouth was partially closed over a shaped leather gag with air holes punched in it. Kitaj used his hands to roughly slap Hockney's chest and genitals, hitting them hard, before moving around to the sub's arse and back and abusing them with an equally untamed force.

Then thheeewwwhacckkk!!! A cat o'nine tails found Hockney's exposed shoulders. The art student hadn't seen the whip come out of any of the bags. Kitaj moved the whipping around to the sub's front and took great delight as Hockney's eyes widened and screams of very real pain hiccupped forth from the deepest part of his lungs—the sounds impeded by his gag!

Kitaj didn't hold back. Hockney didn't want him to although his body convulsed and thrashed from the continuing rain of blows to all parts of his naked flesh. Trickles of blood were already oozing from dermal abrasions on Hockney's chest, stomach and back, as Kitaj switched from cat to cane.

Rockets of pain shot through Hockney as Kitaj caned his chest and butt and back. The dom was sideways flicking the sub's nipples with short punchy swipes, hitting softly enough not to peel them off but hard enough to send pure bolts of pain to the centre of Hockney's brain. Eventually Hockney passed out and a look of concern swept over Kitaj's face as he went over to a bag and rummaged through it.

Once an ammonia cap had been broken under Hockney's nose, the sub regained consciousness. Kitaj was then able to continue his sadistic working over of the art student with a large studded paddle. When Hockney was hit square on the genitals with this torture implement, he couldn't help but piss himself. Kitaj just smiled and laughed at Hockney's temporary incontinence as he threw a new instrument of torture atop the burning embers of the fire, with its handle hanging over the perimeter rocks that contained the flames. Then he removed the gag that had muffled Hockney's screams so effectively.

Kitaj snatched up a scalpel and it's blade glinted in the moonlight. "Are you ready, Hockney, to become my property, my slave for life, once and for all, for all eternity?"

"Yes, Kitaj, yes!" Hockney shouted. "Do it, do it now! Make me your slave, mark me, brand me, do it now!"

"Kiss and suck the blood of your master first, slave!" Kitaj commanded, as in one motion he pricked a finger with his scalpel and shoved the bleeding digit into Hockney's mouth. The blood tasted so sweet that the sub went at it like a kid with a lollipop. After a minute or so, Kitaj removed his finger from Hockney's gob, wiped its bloodied end with a handkerchief and placed a plaster over the cut.

Kitaj proceeded to use the scalpel to knife-play all over the sub's body, expertly slicing Hockney just enough to leave traces and ever so slightly open the top layer of his skin, but not doing this so often or so deep for it to leave permanent scars.

Kitaj's mouth found Hockney's gob and they kissed. In the flaming embers of the fire, the shaft of a branding iron was turning from black to grey as its design head became white atop the yellow-orange of the glowing ashes.

"It is time, Hockney!" Kitaj announced.

On Hockney's reddened and nicked and knife-worked chest, Kitaj's practised hand drew a design with a razor-pointed pen, the emblem of Kitaj's ownership of Hockney. The sub was hypnotised by the cobra charm of the red-dotted scalpel being waved before his eyes. Kitaj was breaking Hockney's skin and muscle as he simultaneously broke whatever remained of the sub's free will. The slipstream edge of the blade carved into Hockney's flesh like a metal jet stream parting the art student's past life from the new BDSM fetishist arising like a phoenix from the ashes of sexual compromise. Miscellaneous torrents of blood poured from the emblematic wound.

Going over to the fire, Kitaj scooped some damp cold ashes out from one side. These were shoved under Hockney's nose for him to smell. They stank to high heaven. Hockney didn't react until Kitaj smeared the ancient darkening substance into the open wound of his slave emblem. When this happened the sub screamed until he was out of breath.

Before Hockney could fully recover, Kitaj darted over to the fire and came back with the white-hot brand. The master knew that the hotter the brand was at the time of placement, the better it would be for Hockney, since the quicker it was on and off the sub's flesh the less pain there would be. Nonetheless, Hockney wasn't ready for how much the branding hurt. He soon lost consciousness.

Kitaj beckoned Boshier over to help him. They untied Hockney and dressed him. Then Kitaj opened up a few cuts on the sub's face—so that Hockney was covered in enough blood to give him a serious fright when he came to but not enough to endanger him. By the time Hockney regained consciousness, Kitaj was gone but Boshier was still there to help him out of the park and to the sanctuary of a nearby pub called The Choughs. When the pair entered the bar, the old lady who ran it dropped her work, the barmaid turned round with a start and one of the caretakers from the RCA—who was drinking in this establishment—stared with all his eyes for a moment and then, jumping up, exclaimed.

"Bless us, if it isn't Master Boshier and Master Hockney of the Republican College of Art. Why what's the matter, sir? Master Hockney, you be all covered wi' blood, sir."

"Oh dear me! Poor young gentlemen!" cried the hostess. "Here, Patty, run and tell Dick to go for the doctor, and get the best room."

"No, please don't. It's nothing at all," interrupted Hockney, laughing. "A basin of cold water and a towel, if you please, Miss Patty, and I shall be quite presentable in a minute. I'm very sorry to have frightened you all."

Boshier joined in the assurances that it was nothing but a little of his friend's claret, which he would be all the better for losing, and watched with an envious eye the interest depicted in Patty's pretty face, as she hurried in with a basin of fresh water and a towel. Hockney bathed his face and very soon was as respectable a member of society as usual, save for a slight swelling on one side of his nose where he'd been caught hard from a crack of a whip.

Boshier meantime—seated on a table—had been explaining the circumstances of the BDSM initiation to the landlady and the caretaker who listened with rapt fascination.

"And now, ma'am," Boshier announced as Hockney joined them and seated himself on a vacant chair, "I'm sure you must draw good ale."

"Indeed, sir, I think Dick—that's my ostler—is as good a brewer as is in the whole of London. We always brew at home, sir, and I hope always shall."

"Quite right, ma'am, quite right," said Boshier, "and I don't think we can do better than follow the old caretaker here. Let us have a jug of the same ale as he is drinking. And you'll take a glass with us, Jem? Or will you have spirits?"

Jem the RCA caretaker was for another glass of ale and bore witness to it being the best in London. Patty drew the ale and supplied two more long glasses. Boshier produced his cigar case. Jem under the influence of the ale and a first-rate Havana—for which he deserted his pipe, though he did not enjoy it half as much—volunteered to conduct them safely back to their digs. This offer was politely declined and then, Jem's hour for bed having come, he being a methodical man, as became his position, departed, and left our two young friends in sole possession of the bar. Nothing could have suited the two young art students better, and they set to work to make themselves agreeable with further drinking.

They listened with lively interest to the landlady's statement of the difficulties of a widow woman in a house like hers, and to her praises of her factotum Dick and her niece Patty. They applauded her resolution of not bringing up her two boys in the publican line, though they could offer no very available answer to her appeals for advice as to what trade they should be put to. All trades were so full and things were not as they used to be.

The one thing, apparently, which was wanting to the happiness of Boshier in London, was the discovery of such beer as he had at last found at The Choughs. Dick was to come up to the RCA first thing in the morning with a barrel of ale to be placed in Boshier's studio. At last that worthy appeared in the bar saying they should have shut up at least an hour before and was sent out by his mistress to see that the street was clear, for which service he received a shilling, though his offer of escort was declined.

After paying for their entertainment, Hockney and Boshier set off for their digs, agreeing on the way that

The Choughs was a great find, the landlady was the best old soul in the world and Patty the prettiest girl in London—although not quite as attractive as some of the men they knew. The streets were quiet and walking quickly they soon reached their separate homes.

CHAPTER 12

GANG BANGED AND PISSED ON IN A WEST LONDON TORTURE DUNGEON

"What's the time Hamilton?"

"Half-past three old fellow," answered Richard, looking at his watch.

"I never knew a day go so slowly," said Hockney, "isn't it time to go down to the torture dungeon?"

"Not by two hours and more, old fellow—can't you read a book or something to keep you entertained? You won't be fit for a good whipping at six o'clock if you go on worrying like this."

And so Richard turned himself to his flute, and blew away to all appearances as composedly as if he had just come back from the torture dungeon, though, if the truth be told, it was all he could do not to get up and wander about in a feverish and distracted state, for Hockney's restlessness had infected him.

Richard Hamilton's whole heart was in the torture dungeon. Though he had pulled dozens of gang bang chains in his time, he was almost as nervous as Hockney about who would fuck who that night. Hockney, all unconscious of the secret discomposure of the other, threw himself into a chair and looked at him with wonder and envy. The flute went "toot, toot, toot," till he could stand it no longer. So he got up and went to the window and, leaning out, looked up and down the street for some minutes in a purposeless sort of fashion, staring hard at everybody and everything, but unconscious all the time that he was doing so. After he'd drawn his head in and returned to his fidgety ramblings about the room, he was not able to answer Richard who had asked him what he'd seen.

"How hot the sun is! But there's a stiff breeze from the south-east. I hope it will go down before the evening, don't you?"

"No need to worry about that when we're down in the torture dungeon. It is so well insulated that not even the candles will flicker should we choose to light some."

"I hope to goodness you're right," said Hockney.

"Don't think about it old fellow, that's your best plan." Richard advised.

"But I can't think of anything but having my arse whipped and fucked," wailed Hockney. "What the deuce is the good of telling a fellow not to think about it?"

Richard apparently had nothing to say, for he put his flute to his mouth again and at the sound of the "toot, toot," Hockney pulled on his coat and fled into the street.

The BDSM gang bangers often ate an early dinner of steaks and chops, stale bread, and a glass and a half of old beer a piece. The predominant theory about group gropes and collective torture was at that time, as much meat as you could eat, the more underdone the better, and the smallest amount of drink upon which you could manage to live. Two pints in the twenty-four hours was all that most of these sex maniacs imbibed. The discomfort of such a diet in the hot summer months, when you were at the same time taking regular and violent sexual exercise, was something very serious. Outraged human nature rebelled against it. Though they did not admit it in public, there were very few men who did not rush to their water bottles for relief, more or less often, according to the development of their bumps of conscientiousness and obstinacy. To keep to the diet at all strictly involved a very respectable amount of physical endurance. It was a sadism directed inwards rather than against a slave—and it made everyone that much more vicious when they were having sex.

Hockney appreciated the honour of being invited to the torture dungeon to be gang banged so keenly that he had almost managed to keep to his training allowance, and consequently, now that the eventful day had arrived, was in a most disagreeable frame of body and mind.

He fled away from Richard Hamilton's flute but found no rest. He tried Boshier. That lowlife was lying on his back on his sofa playing with his willy, and this only increased Hockney's thirst and soured his temper by the viciousness of Boshier's remarks on Hockney's sexual performance when the latter declined a request from the former to give him some head.

By way of compensation Hockney tried to sit down and read, first a novel, then a play of Oscar Wilde, with no success whatever, so he wandered away and found himself in five minutes in the torture dungeon belonging to an aristocrat who Kitaj had met through a sex contact advert.

There were half a dozen men tied up already, with three guys either whipping them listlessly or getting the subs to suck dom cock. Having taken in the scene, Hockney walked up to the kitchen—which was on the floor above—where he grabbed a beer. However, there was no way Hockney was going to get drunk. He walked through to the living room and sat down on his own. When Hockney stood up about ten minutes later he had a little head rush. He attributed it to the fact that he was still a tad apprehensive about the big gang bang he'd been promised that night—and also that it was pretty hot in the room he'd been in. He plonked himself down again and soon found he was starting to get drowsy.

Sometime later Kitaj appeared and sat down next to Hockney. He had a big smile on his face. He said it was time for everyone to have some fun. It finally dawned on Hockney that he'd been drugged. He tried to get up but couldn't control his body. Kitaj laughed and then put his hand on Hockney's crotch. He told Hockney his cock felt pretty nice but he wouldn't need it today or ever again. Then Kitaj started rubbing Hockney's thigh and soon the sub was completely blanked out.

When Hockney woke up there was a blindfold over his eyes. To be more precise it was a pair of swimming goggles that had been blacked out. Hockney tried to stand but quickly ascertained that his hands were chained to the floor, as were his legs. All he could do was get onto his hands and knees. When he did so he heard some laughter and then Kitaj spoke.

"I'm sick of half-arsed rubber slaves who waste my time with their failure to fully submit to my will. That's why I told you you'd be getting gang banged tonight. I knew you'd assume it would be all fun with a load of different guys. But I'm not going to give you the pleasure of seeing what they look like. I've got twenty geezers in this room who all want to fuck your brains out. Not only will they shag you so hard that you won't be able to walk—but you're going to beg them to come in your mouth after they've been up your bum!"

Hockney was in shock. He'd imagined there'd be some foreplay before the gang bang. He struggled a little and everyone laughed. Kitaj then pointed out that Hockney's cock was not only rock hard—but this was going to be twenty times better than when they had sex together because there were twenty more men to fuck the rubber slave.

Kitaj told everyone to let Hockney know they were there. One at a time each man walked behind Hockney and whacked a hand against his arse. By the fourth whack, the sub was starting to push back against these strangers' fingers. About half way through the spanking Kitaj told Hockney to start begging for cock.

"Please fuck me," Hockney squeaked.

Everyone laughed. When Hockney repeated the same three words several more times there was more tittering. When all those present had given Hockney a slap or two on the backside, Kitaj spoke again:

"It doesn't look like anyone here thinks Hockney is good enough to gang bang since you've all ignored his request. You know what slave? You'll really have to beg if you want to get laid!"

Kitaj then started to rug Hockney's anal rim with a finger. Hockney felt incredibly horny and pleaded to be rogered.

"I've a really tight arse. It will feel like heaven if you all plumb my depths. I really want to feel all your cocks up my jacksee. And I want them down my throat too! I really love come and I need to feel it spurting inside my mouth!"

Meanwhile Kitaj continued to work Hockney's arse with a finger—so that the sub felt hornier than a bitch mongrel on heat. After several minutes of Hockney's begging for cock, Kitaj stopped rubbing his arse.

"I think this pathetic submissive is ready for some anal abuse!" Kitaj announced to cheers.

Hockney felt some cool gel being rubbed into his rim of dark pleasures, then a man stepped up behind him. He felt the head of a cock press against his buttocks. Hockney tried to relax but he wasn't doing a good job of it. Next he felt a hard slap on his bum just as the pork sword broke into his sphincter. It hurt and yet the dick was but inching in and if Hockney could have seen it he'd have known not even half of the shaft had disappeared!

"I can't hear you begging!" Kitaj screamed at Hockney. "If you don't plead for throbbing gristle that prick will be pulled out and you'll have to wait."

"I'm prepared to die for the pleasure of a huge cock plumbing my depths! I like men who are so big they could split me apart! Please, please, please shove that huge blood sausage up my shit-chute and make me scream with pleasure and pain!" Hockney bellowed.

Slowly the cock was worked back and forth and with each thrust it inched further into Hockney's taut bum. It hurt but nonetheless Hockney kept begging for more pain and punishment. The throbbing protrusion drilled faster and faster as it worked its way down into the veritable depths of Hockney's being. The pain was still there but so was something else. The anal abuse was starting to feel like a pleasurable treat. Hockney was pushing back against the thrusts that bore down on him. He was really turned on and was desperate to play with his own ding-a-ling. The fact that his chained hands couldn't reach his magic wand was a delicious frustration.

Hockney was really getting into the butt fucking when the massive tool was pulled out of his sphincter. At first, the art student didn't know what was going on or what to do. He thrust his posterior back a few times. Everyone was laughing and jeering. The man who had been butt fucking the sub moved around to the student's face. Hockney felt another man behind him. A glans smoothly penetrated the rubber slave's tail. The butt fucker reached over, grabbed Hockney's hair, and pulled the sub's head back. Hockney felt a warm stream of come hit his face. He instinctively stuck his tongue out and licked up the spunk that had hit him on the lips.

After this, Hockney focused his attention on the mandrake root that was being rammed deep into his pelvic floor. When it was pulled out he knew what was going to happen next. Hockney's anus was ready for another cock and he opened his mouth and stuck his tongue out for the liquid genetics he knew were coming. He wasn't disappointed. Another meat puppet smashed into his backside and more come was directed at his mouth. Hockney pushed his neck forward in the hope he might give some head. His tongue found a cock and he licked it until it was pulled away. The love muscle in Hockney's arse was still banging away and the rubber slave was simultaneously savouring the come on his lips.

This same scenario was repeated time after time. Once ten men had gang banged him, Hockney's bottom felt really sore. He was no longer as enthusiastic about either thrusting back to meet rock hard manhood or milking love poles with his lips, teeth and tongue. All Hockney really wanted to do was play with his own length. He knew it would have only taken a few strokes with his right hand before he shot his load.

Finally the last guy pulled out of Hockney's sore booty. The art student thought it felt good when the arse fucking stopped after twenty-one men had been right up inside him. The last prick was rudely shoved into the rubber slave's mouth and he sucked it dry of come. All those present cheered as the now limp dick slipped from Hockney's pallid lips.

"Hockney," Kitaj announced, "you're a piece of shit for thinking you could ever be a real sub. You're just a piss toy and nothing else."

Moments later Hockney felt the first stream of urine hit him. Soon everyone was pissing on the rubber slave. Hockney felt pint after pint of piss coat his skin. It was warm and felt really good. There were yellow torrents of urine gushing over Hockney's arse and face and every other area of his body. The rubber slave moved himself back and forth—making sure that he was being completely soaked with piss and that his hair was dripping wet.

Twenty-one men were laughing and calling Hockney a piss slut, a come whore and a fuck toy. When the BDSM gang bangers had all done urinating, Hockney listened to them leave. Finally he was left all alone in a pool of piss.

A long time passed. Hockney was still very horny and tried to jerk himself off by rubbing his widget on the piss covered dungeon floor. Eventually Kitaj returned and tittered at Hockney as he tried to get himself off.

Kitaj placed a finger on Hockney's sore bum. Hockney pulled away and Kitaj slapped his arse hard.

"You're never to pull away from someone playing with your booty!"

Kitaj then made a point of torturing Hockney's sore hole before pushing a butt plug into it. When the rubber master unchained Hockney, the sub rolled over onto his back. Hockney didn't care that that he was lying in a puddle of cold piss.

"Don't you dare take that plug out of your arse!" Kitaj hissed. "And now I want you to get up and take a shower before you get dressed. Then mop up this floor before you go home."

CHAPTER 13

FIFTY SHADES OF PINK WITH THE TICKLE FETISHIST

At nine o'clock on a Saturday evening David Hockney was at the door of Kitaj's room. He just stopped for one moment outside, with his hand on the lock, looking a little puzzled, but withal pleased, and then opened the door and entered. Kitaj had thrown himself into their BDSM encounters so thoroughly, that he had not only regained all his hold on Hockney, but had warmed most of the boys and nearly all the department girls in his favour. It was he who had managed the rope knots in every bondage session, and his voice from wherever he stood had come to be looked upon as a safe guide as to how to have fun regardless of whether his slaves could see or had been blindfolded.

So Hockney had recovered his old footing in the dominant's room and when he entered on the night in question did so with the bearing of an intimate friend. Kitaj's supper was on one end of the table as usual and he was sitting at the other pouring over an art history book. Hockney marched straight up to him and leant over his shoulder.

"Here you are at the perpetual grind," he said. "Stop studying and give me some tea. I want to talk to you."

Kitaj looked up with a grim smile.

"Before you have a cup of tea," Kitaj said, "there was something I wanted to show you."

Kitaj took a book from a shelf and he pointed with his finger to the page at which he'd opened it. The tome was *Venus In Furs* by Leopold von Sacher-Masoch, and Hockney, leaning over his shoulder, read:

A Russian prince made his first appearance today on the promenade. He aroused general interest on account of his athletic figure, magnificent face, and splendid bearing. The women particularly gaped at him as though he were a wild animal, but he went his way gloomily without paying attention to any one. He was accompanied by two servants, one a negro, completely dressed in red satin, and the other a Circassian in his full gleaming uniform. Suddenly he saw Wanda, and fixed his cold piercing look upon her; he even turned his head after her, and when she had passed, he stood still and followed her with his eyes.

And she—she veritably devoured him with her radiant green eyes—and did everything possible to meet him again.

The cunning coquetry with which she walked, moved, and looked at him, almost stifled me. On the way home I remarked about it. She knit her brows.

"What do you want," she said, "the prince is a man whom I might like, who even dazzles me, and I am free. I can do what I please—"

"Don't you love me any longer—" I stammered, frightened.

"I love only you," she replied, "but I shall have the prince pay court to me."

"Wanda!"

"Aren't you my slave?" she said calmly. "Am I not Venus, the cruel northern Venus in Furs?"

I was silent. I felt literally crushed by her words; her cold look entered my heart like a dagger.

"You will find out immediately the prince's name, residence, and circomestances," she continued. "Do you understand?"

"But—"

"No argument, obey!" exclaimed Wanda, more sternly than I would have thought possible for her, "and don't dare to enter my sight until you can answer my questions."

It was not till afternoon that I could obtain the desired information for Wanda. She let me stand before her like a servant, while she leaned back in her armchair and listened to me, smiling. Then she nodded; she seemed to be satisfied.

"Bring me my footstool," she commanded shortly.

I obeyed, and after having put it before her and having put her feet on it, I remained kneeling.

"How will this end?" I asked sadly after a short pause.

She broke into playful laughter. "Why things haven't even begun yet."

"You are more heartless than I imagined," I replied, hurt.

"Severin," Wanda began earnestly. "I haven't done anything yet, not the slightest thing, and you are already calling me heartless. What will happen when I begin to carry your dreams to their realization, when I shall lead a gay, free life and have a circle of admirers about me, when I shall actually fulfil your ideal, tread you underfoot and apply the lash?"

"You take my dreams too seriously."

"Too seriously? I can't stop at make-believe, when once I begin," she replied. "You know I hate all play-acting and comedy. You have wished it. Was it my idea or yours? Did I persuade you or did you inflame my imagination? I am taking things seriously now."

"Wanda," I replied, caressingly, "listen quietly to me. We love each other infinitely, we are very happy, will you sacrifice our entire future to a whim?"

"It is no longer a whim," she exclaimed.

"What is it?" I asked, frightened.

"Something that was probably latent in me," she said quietly and thoughtfully. "Perhaps it would never have come to light, if you had not called it to life, and made it grow. Now that it has become a powerful impulse, fills my whole being, now that I enjoy it, now that I cannot and do not want to do otherwise, now you want to back out— you—are you a man?"

"Dear, sweet Wanda!" I began to caress her, kiss her.

"Don't—you are not a man—"

"And you," I flared up.

"I am stubborn," she said, "you know that. I haven't a strong imagination, and like you I am weak in execution. But when I make up my mind to do something, I carry it through, and the more certainly, the more opposition I meet. Leave me alone!"

She pushed me away, and got up.

"Wanda!" I likewise rose, and stood facing her.

"Now you know what I am," she continued. "Once more I warn you. You still have the choice. I am not compelling you to be my slave."

"Wanda," I replied with emotion and tears filling my eyes, "don't you know how I love you?"

Her lips quivered contemptuously.

"You are mistaken, you make yourself out worse than you are; you are good and noble by nature—"

"What do you know about my nature," she interrupted vehemently, "you will get to know me as I am."

"Wanda!"

"Decide, will you submit, unconditionally?"

"And if I say no."

"Then—"

She stepped close up to me, cold and contemptuous. As she stood before me now, the arms folded across her breast, with an evil smile about her lips, she was in fact the despotic woman of my dreams. Her expression seemed hard, and nothing lay in her eyes that promised kindness or mercy.

"Well—" she said at last.

"You are angry," I cried, "you will punish me."

"Oh no!" she replied, "I shall let you go. You are free. I am not holding you."

"Wanda—I, who love you so—"

"Yes, you, my dear sir, you who adore me," she exclaimed contemptuously, "but who are a coward, a liar, and a breaker of promises. Leave me instantly—"

"Wanda I—"

"Wretch!"

My blood rose in my heart. I threw myself down at her feet and began to cry.

"Tears, too!" She began to laugh. Oh, this laughter was frightful. "Leave me—I don't want to see you again."

"Oh my God!" I cried, beside myself. "I will do whatever you command, be your slave, a mere object with which you can do what you will—only don't send me away —I can't bear it—I cannot live without you." I embraced her knees, and covered her hand with kisses.

"Yes, you must be a slave, and feel the lash, for you are not a man," she said calmly. She said this to me with perfect composure, not angrily, not even excitedly, and it was what hurt most. "Now I know you, your dog-like nature, that adores where it is kicked, and the more, the more it is maltreated. Now I know you, and now you shall come to know me."

She walked up and down with long strides, while I remained crushed on my knees; my head was hanging supine, tears flowed from my eyes.

"Come here," Wanda commanded harshly, sitting down on the ottoman. I obeyed her command, and sat down beside her. She looked at me sombrely, and then a light suddenly seemed to illuminate the interior of her eye. Smiling, she drew me toward her breast, and began to kiss the tears out of my eyes.

Hockney knew roughly what Kitaj was thinking so it came as no surprise when he was instructed to go out and pick up a girl and then bring her back for his master to fuck. The sub took a cab to the other side of Hyde Park, found a prostitute and had her stepping out of the taxi in front of Kitaj's South Kensington digs within 15 minutes. There wasn't much to the fucking Kitaj did with the girl—a few thrusts and it was all over. The real shock for Hockney came when Kitaj offered the girl— who said her name was Lara—a couple more pounds to mistreat his slave.

Back then, after he'd been forced by his master to undertake a diet and exercise regime, Hockney had the slim dream body of a fashion model and it was only partly veiled by a semi-transparent negligee Kitaj made him don. At that time Hockney wore his dark blond hair fairly short, in a well-arranged disarray, and his face was most attractive. Hockney's smile seemed to bewitch the prostitute, and his voice possessed that certain erotic something that makes girls go crazy—low volume, unobtrusive, with a deep vibrating overtone but without seeming smoky.

Once Hockney and Lara were completely naked, the streetwalker tied the john to a standing X-cross Kitaj had in his room. This gave her the best position from which to explore his upper body. She started by stroking Hockney's silky skin softly to discover the most ticklish spots. This produced joyful shivers, and goose bumps appeared everywhere. But only when Lara increased her fingertip pressure did Hockney start giggling and laughing. It wasn't really torturing at this stage, it was mere play.

Lara continued her game on Hockney's palms. The art student confessed that every touch there has an erotic quality for him. The girl then explained that the most ticklish parts of the body are the erogenous zones. Fingers travel downward over the forearms to the elbows. The elbow crease usually belongs to the ticklish spots, and Hockney's were no exception.

Things got even more interesting as Lara touched Hockney's freely accessible armpits. A first squealing scream escaped him. As her fingers continued to dabble there, his squeals turned into heavy guffaws. Hockney's features contorted into a tortured but still laughing expression, with some slight similarities to a climaxing one. Kitaj who was looking on surmised this was one of the main attractions for any tickle enthusiast: almost orgasmic facial expressions combined with a helplessly writhing body. The reflex to cover underarms and sides is overwhelming, but his bondage prevented Hockney from doing that. The rubber slave was forced to bear the unbearable, and by this time his only wish was that Lara would stop tickling him! But an experienced tickler understands that and will continue to tickle unless a safety signal is given.

Lara knew from experience that a mere word for a safety signal is not sufficient when it comes to tickling. Tickle victims often laugh so heavily that they can't utter a comprehensible word. But a cough always works. This signal has got another advantage: if your ticklee swallows the wrong way during his laughter, it can be very dangerous to the breathing. But then he has to cough involuntarily, thus interrupting the tickling before the problem gets more serious.

Apart from that, Lara knew any halfway ticklish person would beg you to stop sooner or later, although like Hockney he might really be enjoying this sensuous torture. The real kick for the ticklee lies in the neural overloading. A clever safety signal allows the victim to beg and plead for mercy to his heart's delight without depriving him of this special kick. And begging is an important part in this game of power and surrender.

Therefore, Lara's fingers remained in Hockney's armpits a little longer, until real breathing troubles started. To grant him a little break, Lara tickled and caressed his nipples, which were already erect from the torture. The girl's next target was Hockney's ribs. As Hockney was at that time slim, his ribcage was deliciously pronounced, and Lara was able to count his ribs. Each and every touch elicited heavy guffawing. Hockney's most sensitive spots in this area turned out to be the skin directly below his nipples, and the short lower ribs near the stomach. Touching the lower ribs made Hockney double over even in his bondage. The reflex point is right at the diaphragm. Anyone you care to name is almost sure to laugh at a touch there, because that's where all laughter originates, not only during a tickle session.

This area can be tickled in two different ways: surface touch and deep kneading. Tickling the surface results in twitching and giggling, whereas the strong touch elicits a heavy guffaw coming from deep within. If you continue the latter it tortures the victim into severe breathing difficulties. This is what Lara did to Hockney, until another break was called for. The girl loved filling these interludes with other forms of erotic stimulation. Hockney's skin had become much more sensitive from the tickling, and being a skilful tickler Lara was able to thoroughly arouse her victim with constant changes between tickling and pure erotic touch.

To bring some variation to the session, Lara took two stiff feathers from a "Surprise Bag" by Kitaj's bed. These classical tickle instruments were glided softly over Hockney's upper body. They tickled and stimulated simultaneously, as the slave confirmed.

"That's making me so hot!" Hockney cried between his moans and giggles.

Lara's feathers begin to explore Hockney's lower parts. His inner thighs and the hollows at the back of his knees proved particularly rewarding areas. The knee tickling caused Hockney to lose his balance, buckling forward in his bondage not just once but many times. However there was more: using her thumbs and middle fingers like a broad pincer, Lara squeezed Hockney's thighs just

123

above the knees. The result was loud screaming and strong struggling; real tickle torture.

Then Lara took the feathers again to tickle Hockney's pubic area. He tried to pull his legs up as far as the straps that restrained them allowed, but it was never far enough to protect this sensitive area from the girl's touch. Hockney fell into continuous giggling, sometimes interrupted by loud laughter. His V-shaped loin creases produced the most intense sensations and he started to howl every time they were touched.

Until then, Lara had carefully avoided touching Hockney's cock directly, but now she drew her feather full-length along his pork sword. As Kitaj watched the scene with curiosity, Lara grabbed Hockney's cock with her hand and started to jerk him off. Hockney squeaked and threw his body back and forth; he seemed to ride the length of the girl's hand. After continuing with this for a few strokes, Lara stopped before Hockney shot his load. She then tickled his genitals with her the tip of a feather, and this produced new fits of giggling and squealing—especially when she worked the feathers around Hockney's balls.

Standing up to apply her fingers to Hockney's upper body once more, Lara saw the art student's eyes. They were "tickle-drunk", a special gleam produced by laughter and arousal. When Lara resumed the kneading on Hockney's ribs, eliciting jubilating screams, the slave repeatedly pressed his lower body against the prostitute and attempted to get his erect manhood into her creamy slit. The victim's reactions, his facial expressions, the tortured but still cathartic laughter, the severe struggling and wriggling in his bondage, they all had the effect of an aphrodisiac on the girl, and Hockney's abdominal movements added greatly to her excitement.

Not to make the game too boring, Kitaj handed Lara various gadgets from his special bag—a small, pointed paintbrush, Q-tips, and a small dildo. Lara put the dildo in Hockney's mouth while promising to shove it up his arse if he behaved himself. She tickled Hockney's nipples with the paintbrush and he couldn't help laughing. The dildo fell from his mouth and clattered to the floor.

As interesting as these gadgets proved to be, the best tools for tickling Hockney were Lara's skilful fingers. She found using them a most satisfying experience. With them, she could feel the involuntary twitches beneath Hockney's silky skin, a thoroughly sensuous vibration. She particularly enjoyed it as her fingers tickled Hockney's stomach and hips.

Hockney always got breaks at the right moment, filled with soft kissing on his ears and nipples. During this, he would bend down his head to breathe his excitement into Lara's ears, renewing her arousal. As she started to tickle his armpits again, Hockney screamed for mercy. Lara desisted.

"Why do you stop? I didn't use the danger signal, did I?" Hockney spat cheekily. "I really enjoy this torture, although it gets unbearable sometimes."

Hockney got punishment for this interjection with the heaviest possible tickle attack. He was forced into loud, continuous guffawing, and during inhaling, a small "grunt" escaped him.

"Coughing is the danger signal, not grunting!" Lara admonished him.

This elicited a new fit of laughter, although Hockney wasn't being touched, and then he grunted again, resulting in more involuntary mirth.

Lara then took Hockney down from his upright position and tied him face down on the bed. Once he was secured she tickled his feet. The very first touch on his arches made him scream, and Lara was glad she'd tied each of the slave's limbs to a corner of the bed. The restraints prevented her being hit as he writhed.

Hockney's laughter took on a different quality. It really sounded tortured, bordering on hysterical. His feet were incredibly ticklish, and Lara extracted the maximum of erotic stimulation from this weakness. She licked and nibbled at Hockney's toes. Her tongue between them left him a half-crazy wreck, his voice repeatedly failing. And the feathers drawn across Hockney's toe balls made him scream. The tickle slave was visibly exhausted by this point, his face and neck flushed, but still he had an aroused gleam in his eyes when Lara pulled his head back and looked into them.

"There are fifty shades of pink in my pussy!" Lara told Hockney as she untied him. "I want you to turn over so that I can sit on your face while you lick out every one of them!"

"And Hockney thinks he is gay not straight." Kitaj laughed as his slave gave the prostitute a good tongue job. "There is no gay or straight in BDSM!"

CHAPTER 14

EGYPTIAN MUMMY PORN

Hockney went to Kitaj's bedsit in high spirits, humming the air of a popular song. Kitaj was sitting with some cold tea poured out, but untasted, before him, and no books open—a very unusual thing with him at night. But Hockney either did not or would not notice.

Hockney seated himself and began gossiping away as fast as he could, without looking much at the other. He began by recounting all the complimentary things that had been said by Paolozzi and others of Kitaj's BDSM mastery. Then he went on to describe the supper party he'd just attended, what a jolly evening they had had, he couldn't remember anything so pleasant since he had been up at the RCA, and he retailed the speeches, and named the best songs.

"You really ought to have been there. Why didn't you come? Boshier sent over for you. I'm sure every one wished you had been there. Didn't you get his message?"

"I didn't feel up to going," said Kitaj.

"There's nothing the matter, eh?" said Hockney, as the thought crossed his mind that perhaps Kitaj had hurt himself in some particularly hardcore BDSM session.

"No, nothing," answered the other.

Hockney tried to make play again, but soon came to an end of his talk. It was impossible to make head against that cold silence. At last he stopped. Kitaj was staring abstractedly at the sword over his mantel-piece.

"There is something the matter, though," Hockney said, getting up and putting his hand on the other's shoulder. "Don't sit glowering as if you had swallowed a furze bush. Have you been smoking Mother Charge, old boy? I see that's it, some heavy skunk. Here, take some of my grass, it's mild. Mother Charge allows two of these a day."

"No, thank you," said Kitaj, rousing himself. "Mother Charge hasn't interfered with my mood, and I will have a pipe, for I think I want it."

"Well, I don't see that it does you any good," said Hockney, after watching him fill and light and smoke for some minutes without saying a word. "Here, I've not managed to say the one thing I had at heart. You are the best bondage and rubber master in the whole of London!"

"Well," said Kitaj, making a great effort, "the real fact is I have something, and something very serious to say to you."

"Then I'm not going to listen to it," broke in Hockney. "I'm not serious, and I won't be serious, and no one shall make me serious tonight. It's no use, so don't look glum."

"I have every reason to look glum, my rich friend with the BDSM dungeon just spent a fortune to try a new perversion and it all went wrong. He'd read an anthology of short stories entitled *Egyptian Mummy Porn* that extolled the virtues of doing necrophilia with mouldy oldies rather than fresh corpses. He was convinced that it was worth parting with thousands of guineas for an ancient Egyptian mummy so that he might have sex with it."

"I wish I'd been there to see it!" Hockney interjected.

"Well I was there and I wish I hadn't been!" Kitaj replied. "When my pal tried to hump the mummy it disintegrated and we all inhaled this horrible black dust. It was indescribably disgusting and now I think we're cursed!"

"Don't believe those old wives tales? You'll be fine after a good sleep. And tell me more about this *Egyptian Mummy Porn* anthology? Who is behind it?"

"It was edited by a strange fella called K. L. Callan. He also wrote the best story in it, *A Hypno Kink Princess.*"

"Do you have a copy of the book I could borrow?"

"No, I read my friend's copy."

"Do you have anything by Callan?" Hockney persisted.

"Just this." Kitaj hissed as he picked up a thin pamphlet and handed it to Hockney. "You can borrow it if you'll just go home to read it and leave me in peace."

Hockney agreed to this and although he felt sorry for his friend, he skipped through south Kensington thinking he'd just acquired a fantastic one-handed read. The sub undressed and got into bed naked. He had tissues beside him to clean up whatever mess he might make as he worked his way through K. L. Callan's story. It was a sci- fi story set sixty years in the future during a pandemic. This is what Hockney read:

7,500 COVID 19 PPE Ring Donuts
For Boris Johnson & NHS Heroes

by K. L. Callan

My friend Boris Johnson inherited his visionary spirit from his Ottoman great-grandfather Ali Kema, a freemason with a passing interest in alchemy and the owner of the largest stock of red mercury outside of what was still lodged in the throats of ancient Egyptian mummies lying undiscovered in their tombs. Boris himself had been offered membership of the Guildhall Lodge 3116 but due to his burning desire to impress Catherine McGuinness, he hadn't joined. If Catherine couldn't enter this all-male lodge—despite being boss of the City of London Court of Common Council—then he wouldn't either, even if that meant he never got to be World King AKA Lord Mayor of London.

The Lord Mayor is not to be confused with the much better known but politically insignificant Mayor of London. Freemasons were cunning like that, they installed themselves in an office few knew anything about but which had loads of power and money as well as a rigged election, while leaving millions of Londoners to democratically put their cross against a dupe with a similar title and lots of visibility but little power. This meant that their World King AKA head of the Court of Aldermen would be left alone to plot in secret. When Boris told me this he also said he hoped people would not recall that he had once been Mayor of London but never Lord Mayor.

Even Johnson's close friend and fellow believer in the bleach cure Donald Trump had been ridiculed for confusing the Mayor of London and the Lord Mayor of London. Those colonials in New York and Washington might only have one mayor but mighty London had two! Boris confided to me he assumed most people were ignorant of the fact that he had been born in New York and wasn't really Lord Mayor material. He hoped no one would suspect he was anything but a true blue Britisher when he called heartily for his favoured brew of Watney's Red Barrel, a beer that had been initially tested on the public at the East Sheen Lawn Tennis Club in south-west London. This was close to where John Dee had his home in the sixteenth century, explorer Richard Burton had his tomb, and the 1970s punk rock band Subway Sect hailed from.

To tell the truth it wasn't just a desire to get stupid fresh with Catherine McGuinness—and the multi-billion City's Cash sovereign wealth fund she jointly controlled with the Lord Mayor—that led Boris to turn down ordination into the Guildhall Lodge. He was also concerned that once he was buck naked and dressed in nothing but a blindfold during his initiation, he might be subjected to some indignity he wouldn't have stood still for if he'd been able to see what was going on. Not that there hadn't been lots of perversion when Boris had been a member of the Bullingdon Club at Oxford.

At the Bullingdon they'd hired prostitutes to perform sex acts for them, and then there'd been the time Boris had got so drunk that… Well he'd been so drunk he wasn't sure whether or not he'd taken a fresh corpse borrowed from the local morgue on a date to an expensive restaurant as a dare….. Returning to things that put Boris off becoming a fully paid-up freemason, there was also the issue of what had happened to both his Ottoman great-grandfather and Roberto Calvi. Although he was not related to the latter, Calvi's death had been much closer to home. The body of God's banker, a top Italian freemason, had been found ritually strung up under Blackfriars Bridge. This was roughly halfway between Britain's Parliament where Boris was Prime Minister and the City of London's Guildhall HQ—where Lodge 3116 met without so much as having to pay to hire a room. Boris had a public image of being a powerful man but he wanted the keys to power that were actually held in the Guildhall. The City of London council got to send a Remembrancer to sit in the House of Commons and tell the government what the City thought of what it was doing, The arrangement wasn't reciprocal.

Returning to Ali Kema, he'd been assassinated during the Turkish War of Independence. Historians claimed Kema was bumped off for being a traitor to Mustafa Kemal Ataturk's cause but Johnson knew that he'd been killed so that the Turkish state could lay its hands on his great-grandfather's stock of red mercury.

Boris had been told this by the freemasons who had engineered his rise through the ranks of British politics in order to repay a debt their grandparents owed to Kema. Once Johnson's friend Donald Trump had blown their plan to use a bleach cure to rid the world of COVID 19—by revealing it prematurely and thus having it ridiculed by the press—it seemed like his best bet for dealing with the virus was to lay his hands on his great-grandfather's stock of red mercury. As every alchemist knows, red mercury is a super-rare substance that will cure cancer or boils or almost any other ailment, so why not coronavirus too? The problem was getting hold of the red mercury. When Boris phoned the Turkish Embassy in London to ask for it they told him he was an Islamophobic asshole who'd betrayed his Ottoman heritage. Ingrates!

In the meantime Boris had been passed 7,500 ring donuts that a food bank in his South Ruislip constituency had been unable to distribute to the needy and which would pass their use-by date in a matter of hours. Some food processing plant in Greenford was donating what they couldn't sell, and there'd been a huge decline in demand for donuts since a rumour had gone around that eating them while talking on your smartphone caused COVID 19. More than 40 branches of Derek's Donuts had been set ablaze in the past two weeks and hundreds of supermarket workers whose stores sold the snack had been abused and threatened. Of course Boris had got all of his cabinet members to denounce as idiots those who claimed eating donuts caused COVID 19, and he'd brought in some top scientists too whose secret research proved the same thing. None of which stopped the anti-donut activists from promoting the conspiracy theory and denouncing his favourite delicacy as junk food for cops. When push came to shove the country needed donuts for its police force. They—Boris was never explicit when using this generic term about whether he was invoking donuts or the police or both—were vital to the UK's infrastructure and without them the virus couldn't be beaten! Likewise, if the boys in blue weren't able to eat donuts in peace then Boris would never Get Brexit Done!

As he was chauffeured to Number 10 Downing Street with his 7,500 ring donuts, Boris found himself getting all hot and sweaty. Something had come over him and he'd had one of those flashes of inspiration that were common to men of genius. He'd use the ring donuts to worship the goddess in her triple form—not the conventional maiden, mother and crone, but rather mouth, backside and naughty bits! Boris wasn't too good at maths—he couldn't even work out how many children he had—but he figured the 7,500 donuts would just about cover three out of seven external orifices for every woman he'd ever slept with. If he'd had more ring donuts he might have indulged himself with nasal sex too. Boris was going to work backwards and imagine doing gross and naughty things with all those he'd known Biblically until every last donut had been abused. Johnson had got as far as Jennifer Arcuri when Dominic Cummings burst in and caught Boris bollock naked rubbing a disintegrating ring donut up and down his manhood.

"That's a waste of good donuts that is!" Cummings spat as he took in the remains of several dozen ruined sweet fry cakes on the floor.

"A man with your surname ought to understand what it's like when I've got the horn," Boris whinged defensively, "and besides even a glutton like me couldn't eat 7,500 donuts with a use by date we'll have gone past at midnight!"

"The witching hour!" Cummings boomed. "That reminds me, those scientists you've got advising you on the pandemic have no respect. They may know about the laws of nature but I know about the laws of spirit, and that means I outrank them all!"

"That's well and good, but we must do something about the bad publicity my government is getting over a lack of personal protection equipment for health workers!"

"That's why I told you not to waste the donuts!"

"What have donuts got to do with PPE?" the Prime Minister wanted to know.

"We can turn them into PPE," Dom explained. "Let's string lots of donuts together to make protective gowns. Two rings fastened to each other will make fantastic goggles."

"What about face masks, can we make donut face masks?" Boris asked excitedly.

"Don't be stupid," Dom chided, "anyone using donuts as a face mask would start licking off the sugar coating and then chewing on the cake. Donut face masks wouldn't last five minutes!"

The sugary smell of 7,500 ring donuts had attracted the attention of Larry the Downing Street cat who was mewling like a loon on the other side of the door. Boris let the feline into the room which was a mistake, since Larry was all over the stale fry cakes within seconds. Fortunately it was the ones Boris had used to frottage himself with that most interested the cat. These had traces of dead skin and even blood on them, since the sugar coating had caused a lot of friction when rubbed up and down the Prime Minister's love muscle.

Boris wasn't too hot in the fine motor skills department, in fact he probably needed testing for dyspraxia. Cummings certainly didn't want to risk being exposed as suffering from developmental co-ordination disorder and so his entrepreneurial bent led him to combine three economic sources that were of major significance to the UK—the charity sector's food banks for unwanted donuts, the government, and immigrant labour. The Queensmead Sports Centre in South Ruislip's Victoria Road was closed due to the pandemic, and so Cummings decided to deploy its unused gym as a base from which to make prototype versions of the ring donut PPE that would turn around the public's false perception of a poor governmental performance with regard to the current pandemic.

Dom hired a Gujarati woman from Park Royal who'd initially come to the UK to work at the mammoth hummus production part of Bakkavor's Cumberland site in Greenford. She was extremely nifty with a needle and regularly worked as a seamstress because it was difficult to live on the poor wages paid at local food processing plants. Before 24 hours had passed Johnson and Cummings had what they'd dreamed up the previous night, a medical gown and goggles made of ring donuts! Well, the goggles were made of ring donuts. At the suggestion of the seamstress, the gown had been fabricated from jam donuts since having holes the length and breadth of the garment would have been a health risk to NHS heroes.

Although the donut PPE had been Dom's idea, Boris pulled rank and insisted that he be the first to try it out. Given it was made from literally hundreds of jam donuts, the gown proved to be pretty heavy but at least it was voluminous enough for a fatso like Johnson to wear. To keep Dom happy, Boris told him he was going to recommend his adviser for a Queen's Award for Enterprise on the basis of his donut recycling activities in South Ruislip. The prototype PPE turned out to be perfect in every way, except for a slight tendency for the donuts at the bottom of the gown to fall off with a soft plop as Boris spun around in his triumph at having saved the National Health Service. That said, as libertarians he and Dom both knew that ultimately private health was much more efficient than haemorrhaging corporate profits to pay for public services. So once Boris had saved the NHS and after everything got back to normal in about 3 weeks' time, he planned to abolish the NHS.

In his moment of glory for having saved the NHS, Boris decided to burst out of the gym and take a lap of honour on a Queensmead Sports Centre football pitch. After all he'd proved once again that England had won its wars—and the battle against COVID 19 was a war—on the playing fields of Eton! The fact that a fuckwit like Boris could get to be Prime Minister demonstrated that his parents had got real value for money when they'd paid for him to attend Britain's top public school. The fees were reassuringly expensive!

Two unfortunate things happened as Boris jigged across the football pitch. Firstly his smartphone rang, it was a call from a hefty female former professional kick boxer turned gym instructor with whom the PM was enjoying an intimate relationship.

"I found snot all over my dirty underwear when I was loading it into my washing machine just now. Have you been sniffing it again?"

This baseless accusation caused Johnson to sway and he'd never been a good runner at the best of times. He tripped over this own feet and fell to the ground. Seeing red oozing all around him, Boris thought he was a goner. While the British Prime Minister was able to pull the wool over his own eyes about his life ebbing away before him, he couldn't fool a passing swarm of wasps who knew that what Boris thought was his own blood was in fact strawberry jam that had leaked out of the squashed donuts. Recovering a slight semblance of sense at the sight of the descending wasps and wanting to save the prototype PPE, even if it was now mashed up and in fragments, Johnson tried to shoo the insects away but this only made them angry. Boris quickly discovered that the painful pricks of failure were more or less equivalent to a dozen wasp stings.

In the interests of safety the plans for recycling donuts as PPE were shelved. It was back to the drawing board for Boris and Dom…. they still needed a way to demonstrate their political genius by defeating COVID 19.

Having read K. L. Callan's story, Hockney was laughing his arse off and he forgot all about engaging in a five knuckle shuffle, since he knew from experience how challenging it was to laugh and have an orgasm at the same time. He couldn't believe Callan's cheek, since the story was so obviously based on Edward Lear's poem *The New Vestments,* which was about a man whose clothes are made from bread, pork chops, pancakes, biscuits, cabbage leaves and other food.

CHAPTER 15

DAVID HOCKNEY CONSIDERED
AS A HUMAN TOILET

That evening Hockney found himself at The Choughs with half a dozen others. Patty looked prettier than ever and was in the bar by herself. One by one the rest of the men dropped off, the last saying, "Are you coming, Hockney?" and being answered in the negative. Kitaj had repeatedly told Hockney how pretty Patty was. At first the rubber slave had been worried by this but now he'd come up with a plan to eliminate her as a love rival. Patty may have been a girl but that didn't mean he couldn't seduce her and make her fall in love with him!

He sat still, watching Patty as she flitted about, washing up the ale glasses and putting them on their shelves, and getting out her work basket. Then she came and sat down in her aunt's chair opposite him, and began stitching away demurely at an apron she was making. He broke the silence.

"Where's your aunt tonight, Patty?"

"Oh, she has gone away for a few days to visit to some friends."

"You and I will keep house together then. You shall teach me all the tricks of the trade. I shall make a famous barman, don't you think?"

"You must learn to behave better first. I promised aunt I'd shut up at nine. So you must go when it strikes. Now promise me you will go."

"Go at nine! What, in half an hour? The first evening I have ever had a chance of spending alone with you. Do you think it likely?" He looked into her eyes, she turned away with a slight shiver and a deep blush.

His nervous system had been so unusually excited in the last few days by the fear that he was going to lose Kitaj's affections as they slowly turned towards this kitten, that Hockney seemed to know everything that was passing in her mind. He took her hand.

"Why Patty, you're not afraid of me surely?" he said gently.

"Not when you're like you are now. But you frightened me just a minute ago. I never saw you look like that before. Has anything happened to you?"

"No, nothing. Now then, we're going to have a jolly evening and play Darby and Joan together." Turning away and going to the bar window he said: "Shall I shut up, Patty?"

"No it isn't nine yet. So somebody may come in."

"That's just why I mean to put the shutters up. I don't want anybody interrupting us."

"Yes but I do. I declare, Mr Hockney, if you go on shutting up, I'll run into the kitchen and sit with Dick."

"Why do you call me Mr Hockney?"

"It's your name! What should I call you? The Queen of Sheba?"

"No, just call me Dave."

"Oh, I never! One would think you was my brother," said Patty.

She looked up with a pretty pertness of a most bewitching sort. Hockney's rejoinder and the little squabble which they had afterwards about where her work table should stand, and other such matters may be passed over. At last he was brought to reason and to anchor opposite this enchantress, the work table between them. He sat leaning back in his chair and watching her as she stitched away without ever lifting her eyes. He was in no hurry to break the silence. The position was particularly fascinating to him, for he had scarcely ever yet had a good look at her without fear of attracting attention or being interrupted. At last he roused himself.

"Do you know what BDSM is, Patty?" he said sitting up.

"There now, I've won," she laughed, "I said to myself I wouldn't speak first and I haven't. What a time you were. I thought you would never begin."

"You're a little goose! What do you know about BDSM?"

"I know all about that. Your friend Kitaj was in here earlier on telling me all about your activities with him as a rubber slave!"

"What, Kitaj?"

"Yes, he was here about half-past six, and…"

"What, Kitaj here?" Hockney interrupted utterly astonished.

"Yes, he's been here two or three times lately."

"The deuce he has!"

"Yes and he talks so pleasant to Aunty too. I'm sure he is a very nice gentleman. He sat and talked tonight for half an hour."

"What did he talk about?" asked Hockney with a sneer.

"He wanted to know if I was a virgin and whether I had a boyfriend and all about my sexual preferences. He made me feel quite pleasant. He is so nice and quiet and respectful, not like most of you. I'm going to like him very much, as you told me some time ago."

"I don't tell you so now."

"But you did say he was your great friend."

"Well he isn't that now."

"Have you had a quarrel?"

"Yes."

"Dear, dear. How odd you gentlemen are!"

"It isn't an odd thing for men to quarrel!"

"No not in the public room. They're always quarrelling there, over their drink and the bagatelle-board. Dick has to turn them out. But gentlemen ought to know better."

"They don't, Patty."

"But what did you quarrel about?"

"Guess."

"How can I guess? What was it about?"

"About you. Well we haven't yet but we will do when I see him."

"About me!" Patty looked up from her work in wonder. "How could you quarrel about me?"

"Well I'll tell you. Until I met Kitaj I though I was gay and then he showed me in BDSM there is no gay or straight. Now I want you to be my master. What do you think of that?"

They sat still for some minutes. Evil thoughts crowded Hockney's head. He was in the humour for thinking evil thoughts and putting the worst construction on Kitaj's visits. He fancied his fuck-buddy wanted Patty more than a man like himself. Hockney did not trust himself to speak till he had mastered this precious discovery and put it away in the back of his heart, and weighed it down there with a good covering of hatred and revenge, to be brought out as occasion should serve. He was plunging down rapidly enough now but he had new motives for making the most of his time and never played his cards better or made more progress. When a man sits down to such a game, the devil will take good care he shan't want cunning or strength.

Hockney talked Patsy into putting on a record and dancing with him. They cleared some tables and waved their arms and legs around to *Hound Dog* by Elvis Presley.

"Thanks for the dance," Hockney blurted as the song ended.

"Hey!" Patty grabbed Hockney's arm. "You think I'm going to bite?"

She lifted her arms up as if to put them around Hockney's neck and waited. What could he do? He walked into her and put his arms around her waist as she draped her arms around his neck.

Although he preferred men Hockney got an instant stiffy.

"Mmmmm," Patty cooed as she snuggled her chin on Hockney's shoulder.

He gazed for a moment at the metal stud in her tongue and thought, you will be assimilated, resistance is futile. Patty squeezed even tighter. For a skinny girl she was strong. She rubbed her pelvis against Hockney's, rolling his boner around between his upper thighs.

Then Patty's and Hockney's lips were pressing into each other. Hockney thought the stud on Patty's tongue felt weird every time his tongue slid over it.

"Let's go to one of the upstairs bedrooms!" Patty hissed.

"But what about Kitaj?" Hockney asked.

Patty rolled Hockney's boner against her crotch and said, "Forget Kitaj for now!"

Then Patty stuck her tongue in Hockney's ear and licked all around the ridges for a few seconds. He almost had an orgasm just standing there!

"C'mon! I promise you an hour of pleasure like you've never had and never will have again. Don't pass it up," Patty lisped.

Hockney followed Patty up two flights of stairs to one of the pub's special rooms.

"Uh, mind if I use the bathroom?" Hockney asked, pointing at the pisser through a door in the bedroom.

"Not that one," she said. "That's for women only. Use the one down the hall."

Hockney shrugged, wondering why an en-suite room would have a women's only john. Nonetheless he followed Patty's directions, took a shit, and returned to find her tall, skinny, ashen body already naked in bed. Her skimpy top, her black leather skirt, her fishnet stockings, and her shoes were in a pile on the seat of a chair in front of a wide sliding glass door that opened out onto a huge balcony. Hockney thought it odd he couldn't see a bra or panties among the discarded garmentry.

"C'mon!" Patty said. "I've felt how big and stiff it is. Now I want to see my prize!"

Hockney kicked off his shoes, removed his shirt, then his socks, and finally his pants.

"Is this what you wanted to see?"

"Yeah! Bring it to me baby!"

Hockney climbed into bed with Patty and they were immediately swapping spit, her ashen skin and black lipstick no longer a concern. His cock just needed to take a plunge, nothing else mattered. He rolled her onto her back and began to suck her perky little titties. Her nipples were little more than tiny red pimples, but Hockney managed to give them a tad more fullness as she cooed, "Ooh!" and "Ahh!"

Hockney started to slide lower but Patty pushed him onto his side and said, "Want to fuck my mouth?"

"Yeah!" Hockney gasped. Did she really mean that? Does she really know what it means to have a guy fuck her mouth?

Patty rolled flat on her back, stretching her arms over her head and said, "Go ahead! Give me an oral fuck!"

"You really want me to?"

"Yeah! Like my mouth was a pussy. Go ahead! Don't hold back!" Then she faced straight up at the ceiling and opened her mouth wide.

Hockney couldn't believe it. He swung a leg over her head and settled onto her, facing her crotch. He slid his cock into Patty's gaping mouth, then slammed his pelvis down, pressing his crotch tightly to her lips, before she could change her mind.

Hockney felt his cock twist sharply at the back of Patty's mouth, as it slid past her throat and down her gullet. She began bucking wildly under him, nearly throwing him off her a few times. There was no way she was going to make him disengage before he was fully satisfied. He didn't even have to pump her mouth—her strenuous gag reflex did all the work, milking his cock far more tightly than any pussy, hand, or asshole ever could.

"Oh! Oh! Oh!" Hockney groaned as he flooded Patty's throat with his spunk. Her continuing gagging and squeezing of his cock drew more come from him than he could have ever produced with his own hands. He just kept coming and coming and coming,

Hockney pulled his cock out of her mouth and rolled off her, panting. After a few seconds, he sat up and said, "Patty! Wow!"

Patty didn't answer.

"My God! Patty! PATTY!" She was out cold. Hockney ran to the bathroom and found a cup. he filled it with water, ran back, and splashed it on her face. He slapped her face a few times and she started to cough and sputter.

"Patty! I'm sorry! I..."

"It's okay," she said and coughed for a while. Then she grinned wide and said, "But now it's my turn."

"What do you mean?" Hockney asked. "Now we fuck normally, right? But I don't think I have any more spunk left in me after that."

"No! Now I ride you and you make me come with your mouth."

"Sure," Hockney agreed.

"You'll love this!" Patty pushed Hockney onto his back.

In an instant she had straddled his head, hovering her ass just inches above his face. He was staring into the thickest, blackest muff hair known to man. Her pussy was the merest slit between her twin mounds. And she had a little tattoo of a unicorn on the inner surface of her ass cheek with its horn about to impale her anus.

"Ready?" she asked.

"Yeah!" Hockney said.

Patty sat on his face. Hockney's nose slipped into her asshole and her pussy was pressed tightly to his mouth.

Patty squeezed Hockney's nose with her anal sphincter and said, "Make me come, Hockney. You're not taking another breath until I come."

Hockney felt Patty swing her legs straight out in front of her along the sides of his body. Her pussy mounds twisted his lips under her weight as she swung her legs around. The pressure on his face increased and it dawned on him that his visage was supporting her full weight. Despite her slight build, her full mass on his skull was crushing and painful.

Hockney slid his tongue up between her tight pussy lips and tasted the musky wetness within. He slid his tongue up and down her slit and in and out of the hole a few times. Then he found her clit. He flicked it repeatedly with his tongue, then drew it into his mouth between his lips.

Hockney's lungs were already gasping for air and so he tried to motion her with his hands to let him take a breath, but his arms were pinned at his sides under her legs. Hockney had no choice but to continue working her clit. With her clit pulled into his mouth, he swirled and flicked it with his tongue. She began to moan, "Oh! Ah! Ohhh! Aaaaah!"

Hockney was on the verge of passing out when Patty started to quake on his face and gushed a heavy stream of pussy juice into his mouth. Then the taste hit him. It wasn't pussy juice. She was pissing into his mouth as she came. Hockney struggled to get Patty to stop, but his head was pinned under her ass and his arms were still pinned under her legs. Just when Hockney was on the verge of blacking out, Patty fell forward onto him.

"Whoa!" she said. "You're good!"

"Aaaaaah!" Hockney said, his mouth was full of pee and he couldn't say anything else.

Patty turned and sat up on Hockney's chest looking down at him. "Ahhh! Ahhh!" Hockney said, pushing her to get off him.

"I'm not getting off."

"Ahhh! Ahhh!" Hockney said again pointing into his mouth. He so wanted to spit her waste out of his mush.

"No, Hockney! Swallow it. I'm sitting right here until it's all gone."

So Hockney swallowed her filth.

"There," Patty said, "That wasn't so bad, was it?"

"But why'd you pee in my mouth? And why wouldn't you let me get up to spit it out?"

"I pee during powerful orgasms. And you gave me one of the most powerful orgasms ever!"

"I, uh, well..."

"And I swallowed your come. So you can swallow my pee."

"I guess so..." Hockney figured Patty had a point there. Even though come wasn't exactly waste, it was full of protein.

"Besides, haven't you ever heard of water sports?"

"Well, yeah," Hockney said. "But to date I've only been a piss toy for men and that's different."

"And what did it taste like to you?" she asked.

"It didn't taste like anything really. I guess it wasn't so bad. But girl pee is still different to man piss."

"Kitaj told me about using you as a human toilet. He said he'd given you the idea that he fancied me. He wanted you to want to fuck me. And after I'd done the shag-nasty with you he told me to pass on the message there is no gay or straight in BDSM, only mind games!"

It was ten o'clock and not nine when Hockney left. He left with tears in his eyes and a feeling of defeat. Hockney walked quickly to Kitaj's pad. But Kitaj was out and the next day Hockney dared not go and confront him over Patty and his sexual orientation. Deeper and deeper yet for the next few days, downwards and ever faster down, Hockney plunged, the light getting fainter and ever fainter above his head. Little good can come of dwelling on those days. He left off pulling himself off, shunned his old friends and drank with the very worst men he knew in college, who were ready enough to let him share all their brutal fun.

Boshier, who was often present, wondered at the change, which he saw plainly enough. He was sorry for it in his way but it wasn't his concern. He began to think that Hockney was a good enough fellow before but would make a devilish disagreeable one if he was going to turn into a misery guts crying for attention. But everything returned to normal when Hockney received a note from Kitaj saying he'd been a bad rubber slave but his phony punishment of banishment was over and now he must return to his master for a beating.

CHAPTER 16

A PAINTING TUTORIAL THAT ENDS IN BONDAGE AND A FLOGGING FOR HOCKNEY

We have now surveyed six months worth of David Hockney's BDSM shenanigans without learning anything of his artistic development. Prudish people find such endless litanies of sexual perversion quite as much as they can take. Perhaps too it may do our rapscallion good to lay off being flogged for a while, so that he has time to look steadily into the pit which is still yawning awkwardly in his path. Moreover, the exigencies of storytelling lead us away from the delights of sexual perversion. Occasionally Hockney must have a change of air, going off to a tutorial or at least to the studio to do a bit of work. Every once in a while Hockney dons a French artist's beret and carrying much aesthetic conviction, comes back from his endless journeys into sexual degradation.

We all need to come back home after every stage of life's sexual journeying with a wider horizon—more in sympathy with men and nature. Knowing ever more of the righteous and eternal laws which govern our sexual kicks. Those who don't engage in such reflection end up wandering about blindfolded, and spending time and labour and journey-money on that which fails to bring them the greatest of pleasures. So we must forget the whips and fetters of the bondage dungeon for a short time and take a flight to other scenes and pastures new.

Of all Hockney's tutors Ceri Richards was his favourite, because the Welshman was—like our rapscallion—a horny-handed son of toil. Richards was born in 1903 in the village of Dunvant, near Swansea, the son of Thomas Coslett Richards and Sarah Richards (nee Jones). He and his younger brother and sister, Owen and Esther, were brought up in a highly cultured, working-class environment. His mother came from a family of craftsmen. His father, an employee of a tinplate foundry in Gowerton, was active in the local chapel, wrote poetry in Welsh and English and for many years conducted the Dunvant Excelsior Male Voice Choir. All three children were taught to play the piano, and became familiar with the works of Bach and Handel in the cycle of Christian celebration. In later years music would be an important stimulus to Richards' painting, as would his youthful sensitivity to the landscapes of Gower and the cycles of nature.

At Gowerton Intermediate School Richards drew constantly and won local competitions. When he left school to become apprenticed to a firm of electricians in Swansea, he devoted his evenings to studying engineering draughtsmanship at Swansea College of Technology and drawing at the Swansea College of Art.

In 1921, at the age of 18, Richards enrolled full-time at the Swansea College of Art, then under the direction of William Grant Murray. During his sojourn at the college he spent less time in painting than in drawing from classical casts and studying industrial design and graphics. The strongest impact on him during these years appears to have been a week's summer school in 1923, which he spent under the direction of Hugh Blaker at Gregynog Hall, the country house of Gwendoline and Margaret Davies. This is where he first saw the canvases of Renoir, Van Gogh, Monet, Cézanne, Corot and Daumier, the sculpture of Rodin and sheets of old-master and modern drawings. The experience confirmed him in his vocation and in the same year he applied for, and won, a scholarship to study at the Republican College of Art in London.

Richards entered the Republican College of Art in 1924. Afterwards he spent most of his life in London, apart from a period teaching art in Cardiff. In 1929 he married Frances Clayton, a fellow artist. He and Frances had two daughters—Rachel (born 1932) and Rhiannon (born 1945). But having a wife and family didn't mean that Richards was incapable of swinging the other way! His work gradually moved towards surrealism after exposure to the work of Picasso and Kandinsky. He was also a talented musician and music was a theme for much of his artwork. When Hockney encountered Richards as an RCA tutor, his teacher had just begun making prints for the Curwen Press.

"So what's this all about then?" Richards asked as he examined a self-portrait Hockney had made of himself bound and being whipped by Kitaj, as he simultaneously gave his rubber master a blow job.

"Well," Hockney replied, "I don't want to do away with representation all together, but at the same time I wish to bring some elements of expressionism and even abstraction into my work."

"That's very good aesthetically," Richards admitted, "but I want to know what you're doing in this picture."

"Oh, I'm giving my friend Kitaj oral sex while he beats me."

"Does your friend come in your mouth?"

"Sometimes," Hockney admitted, "but more often he likes to pull out at the last moment and shoot his jism all over my face."

"Very good, very good!" Richards enthused as he rubbed his hands together with glee.

"Yes it is very good." Hockney conceded. "Although I love drawing and painting I believe that BDSM sex is better than either."

"And do you just engage in BDSM activities with Kitaj, or are you a come slut who likes to be bucked by other men?" Richards probed.

"Oh I'm Kitaj's rubber slave, so I need his permission to make the beast with two backs with other people. But if he's okay with it then I'll fuck virtually anyone."

"But surely you don't need Kitaj's permission to develop your art practice by having sex with your tutors?"

"I suppose not..."

"Very good! Now take your clothes off! No sex involved I just want to see what you look like in the buff!"

Hockney did as he was instructed and as soon as he was naked Richards ordered him to get dressed again. He told Hockney he had a piece of work for him to do in his own studio, where he was building a set as a film and photographic backdrop.

Richards led Hockney to where the tutors had their spaces. When they reached Richards' studio, the tutor ushered Hockney inside and locked the door behind them. The RCA was busy in the middle of a weekday but Richards knew there was respect for even the strangest of artistic practices and so no one would disturb them once they'd locked the door, no matter what noises were heard coming from behind it.

Hockney looked around apprehensively wondering what Richards might have hidden in the depths of his space. There were a lot of props and a few paintings leaning against one wall.

"As you can see, Hockney, I have got started on a set design that I want to use as a backdrop for some film and photo shoots—this is private stuff circulated under the counter, not for consumption by the general public. This main part of the set I've had for quite some time, it is very solid. I spared no expense in making it. It does not move at all but this is my private studio used only for making my sexual masterpieces. I want to add more elements to heighten the dungeon feel that I have going on here, that is where you come in."

Then pointing to a stack of heavy beams that looked like they might have belonged to a railroad track at one time, Richard's continued, "I was thinking a stockade and maybe a small wooden cage from those pieces would suffice for now. Do you think you can handle the job?" Richard's studied the boy's every expression and movement carefully.

"Yes, sir, I think I can manage that."

Hockney smiled. It seemed to be almost too easy a task to be true. The tools he needed were to hand and so he went to work constructing what his tutor had drawn on paper—not noticing that as he was building Richards was busy adding new props by securing heavy chains to the wall, as well as sorting though various whips and floggers that had been hidden in the depths of the space.

Hockney took off his shirt as he'd started to sweat while hammering together the small cage, this was after he'd finished sawing out the stockade and piecing it together. He had never built such things before but found it was second nature to him, how he loved to work with wood—it made such a change from painting. Richards admired the boy's body, plotting his next move, urging his desires to be patient.

"Well, Hockney, I must admit I'm eager to see photographic fruits from this set design," Richards announced as the sub was finishing up the cage. "Perhaps you'd act as my model for the tableaux I wish to bring to life here."

"I have never modelled before but I'd be willing to try." Hockney was a little nervous and yet pleased to be considered for a modelling job.

"I'm willing to take that chance, Hockney. Sometimes one finds new talent and you definitely have the look I want for these images, but it is a serious shoot and I will expect full cooperation."

Hockney looked around at the dark scene, a fake stone wall backdrop complete with heavy chains and instruments of torture, then nodded in agreement to his tutor. Still, Hockney felt rather nervous about what would happen next.

"This is your costume," Richards said as he picked up the garments. "Here's some oil too, so please oil up well. I want a shiny look for the photos."

Hockney nodded nervously as he took the oil and costume. The outfit was a leather harness and tight slacks. The leather was snug against his taught muscles and his cock was clearly outlined against the slacks. He had to admit that even if leather wasn't his thing, he looked hot in it. He was curious as to what kind of photo shoot his tutor had planned.

Richards couldn't help but think to himself what a perfect boy he had found this time and knew he had better not reveal his scheme to the leather slave right away. He directed Hockney to the wall, locking his wrists securely into the cuffs attached to the chains. He could see a question in Hockney's eyes but said nothing.

"I'm afraid I'm going to need to redden your chest a bit for the picture. It will sting but I think you'll be surprised how pleasant the feeling will be."

The alarms in the back of Hockney's head started to sound. Kitaj wasn't going to like this but he only nodded as he really wanted to please his tutor too, and in terms of sexual straying how bad could a light flogging be?

Richards grinned, went to a small chest and pulled out a leather flogger. Before embarking on the beating he opted to secure the boy's ankles just in case a struggle ensued. With the flogger in hand, Richards showed little mercy bringing it down repeatedly in hard blows over Hockney's chest until tears rolled from the young man who was silently begging him to stop. But Richards did not stop till the skin was a deep crimson and when it was he stood back to admire it.

"Yes, good Hockney, just the look I want, such a wonderful glow your skin has," Richards smiled as he snapped pictures from many angles.

This was easy, Richards thought to himself. He'd feared Hockney would invoke the name of his master and swear he could not be unfaithful to him. He hadn't yet but Richards still knew he must tread carefully.

Hockney slumped stunned by the fire in his chest. The flogging had been more than he'd bargained for and had he not been chained up he'd have sat down. He fought back his tears embarrassed to be seen crying over a beating. He just kept telling himself he needed to please his tutor, and for reasons he didn't want to understand his cock was hard and throbbing, needing relief from the tight leather that encased it.

"You are doing splendid, Hockney," Richards announced. "I have an add-on to your outfit for the next shots."

Richards winked at the so-far compliant post-graduate student. He'd thought getting him this far into the game would have been more difficult, but Hockney had been a push-over. Richards took two adjustable nipple clamps and carefully attached them to Hockney's hard teats. He was careful not to put them on too tightly as he didn't want to push things too far. It took all of Richards' self-control not to bite and pull on Hockney's delicious looking titties.

Richards snapped the flogger harshly over the clamped nipples—quickly and swiftly bringing the colour back to the flesh before capturing more shots of the boy on his camera. The tutor couldn't help but notice the rock hard bulge in Hockney's pants. Excellent, the boy enjoys this treatment, Richards thought to himself.

With the camera flashing rapidly, Richards' passions were now raging almost out of control. His loose pants were hiding his own excitement as he went to light candles in preparation for wax shots. Richards dripped the hot wax expertly over Hockney's chest, watching with great pleasure as the muscles tensed and the chains grew taut. Delicious low groans flew from Hockney's clenched lips.

Richards leaned in to Hockney and whispered into his ear, "I lied, boy, there was never a shoot, just a great desire for you. Any objection, any struggle will only increase my thirst and drive me harder, I'm going to have you. I'm going to take you away from Kitaj!"

"Please, Richards, take me, I don't care about Kitaj!" Hockney could hardly believe he was saying it.

Hockney's chest was pulsing with pain, his cock throbbing with lust, he yearned for relief.

"All in good time, boy," Richards taunted as he sank his teeth into Hockney's shoulder and drew blood.

Richards unchained Hockney's ankles just long enough to take off the student's leather pants, before placing him back in the shackles.

Hockney had a lovely cock. Long and thick with a set of low hung balls, it was most magnificent! And it was also drizzling pre-come! Richards took the flogger and began an assault on Hockney's groin and thighs. The post-graduate's howling screams drove Richards on to bring the flogger down harder and harder.

The tutor pulled out a padded riding horse from behind a curtain. He unchained Hockney from the wall and bound his wrists and ankles to the four legs of the horse. Hockney's arse was wide open and vulnerable to assault. The painting tutor picked up his leather flogger and bought out fresh weals on the flesh. The heavy thwacks echoing about the room followed by Hockney's agonising cries were sweet music to Richards' ears as he snapped the leather down harder and harder and watched the student's flesh turning a dark crimson.

Hockney was sweating profusely. His cock throbbed against the padded sawhorse. Richards too was soaked in sweat and he eventually became so exhausted he had to stop his assault on the boy. The deep dark pulsing crimson welts he'd inflicted on his victim were driving him out of his mind. Stepping up to Hockney, Richards undid his pants. He showed no mercy as he slammed his huge hard shaft into Hockney's tight crack. His victim's screams only served to make him thrust deeper and harder. He slammed away until—yes, yes, yes— he shot his genetic wealth right up Hockney's rim of dark pleasures! Hockney came too and finally achieved release from the lust that had chained him down since he'd entered Richards' studio.

CHAPTER 17

COCK AND BALL TORTURE WITH A CB3000 MALE CHASTITY DEVICE!

The days dragged on and Hockney lumbered through them. Hot fits of conceit alternating in him with cold fits of despondency, mawkishness and discontent with everything and everybody. These feelings were all the more intolerable due to their novelty. Instead of seeing the bright side of all things, Hockney seemed to be looking at creation through yellow spectacles, and saw faults and blemishes in all his acquaintances, which had previously been invisible.

But the more he was inclined to depreciate other men, the more he felt there was one to whom he had been grossly unjust. As he reflected on all that had passed, he began to do justice to the man who had not flinched from guiding him, who he felt was watching over him when he had lost all power or will to understand his sexual kinks himself.

He began to dread other post-grads discovering his quarrel with Kitaj was over his indiscretions with the barmaid Patty and his tutor Richards. Their utter ignorance of it encouraged him in the hope that it might all pass off like a bad dream. While it remained a matter between them alone, he felt that all might come straight, though he could not think how. He began to loiter by the entrance to Kitaj's house. Sometimes he would find something to say to Kitaj's friends, and at others he would stand below Kitaj's window, glancing at it. There it was, wide open, generally. He hardly knew whether or not he wished to catch a glimpse of the owner, but he did hope that Kitaj might hear his voice. He watched him at the Republican College of Art furtively but constantly and was always speculating about what he was doing and thinking. Was it as painful an effort to Kitaj, he wondered, as to him to go on speaking as if nothing had happened, when they met at the college bar, as they did almost daily, and yet never to look one another in the face. To live together as usual during part of every day and yet to feel all the time that a great wall had risen between them, more hopelessly dividing them for the time than thousands of miles of ocean or continent?

Amongst other distractions which Hockney tried at this crisis of his life, was non-stop painting. Hockney was still recovering from a bondage session with his tutor Carel Weight—who'd heard Hockney wasn't averse to a whipping and had taken advantage of this knowledge. Hockney, like Weight, felt really horny every time he thought about this extended sex session. He felt the urge to call on his tutor to thank him again for giving him a beating that had lasted twelve and a half long hours. But Hockney was busy painting in his studio and the days passed. Ten days later, Hockney received a message from Weight, telling the apprentice painter to go to his house in the early evening. It was a Friday night. Hockney wondered what this instruction was all about. Was Weight still angry with Hockney because he'd had to be beaten into complete submission during their last session?

Hockney anxiously finished a painting and arrived at Weight's home on the dot of 6PM. Weight greeted Hockney sternly and ordered the student into his bedroom. There he informed Hockney that he had thought about their last session and how the younger man had plagued him with repeated requests for permission to come. Weight told Hockney that he had to punish him again for this bad behaviour. Hockney was standing by a high backed chair still fully clothed. It would do the boy absolutely no good to argue with his tutor as he knew he would suffer more if he did. Weight ordered Hockney to strip completely. The young man hesitated for just a moment until he saw the look in Weight's eyes. Weight didn't yell at Hockney, he remained silent which was worse and the student knew he had better obey him.

Hockney was tired after a hard day's painting and he was getting hungry. As he undressed there was about him a slight but palpable sense of unease. Weight ordered Hockney to sit in the chair and put his hands behind him. Hockney did as he was told and Weight secured the sub's wrists with a pair of steel handcuffs, adjusting them tightly until the student flinched. A thick leather penis gag was stuffed into Hockney's mouth, and strapped around the back of the student's head. Weight adjusted it, then moved behind Hockney to tighten the buckle so that the gag penetrated deep inside Hockney's throat. A leather collar quickly followed and was cinched tightly too. Then Weight roped Hockney's ankles separately to the back legs of the chair, lifting his feet up off the floor by about 6 inches. Weight then chose a leather hood and put it over Hockney's head. It had no mouth opening and as Weight laced it up tightly, he deliberately caught Hockney's hair and made the boy yelp. Hockney offered a muffled apology for the noise he was making. A thick blindfold was wrapped over Hockney's eyes and the collar around his neck was tied to the top of the chair so that he could barely move.

Weight stood silently for a few moments as if thinking of what he would do next. Then Hockney heard the jingle of chains and he knew Weight had taken a pair of nipple clamps from his implement shelf. Hockney guessed correctly that his master was going to make the evening painful for him. Weight pinched both of Hockney's nipples numerous times to make them hard before attaching the clamps, causing the student to jerk in his bonds. Hockney felt the hard smack of Weight's belt on his inner thigh. Then Weight tightened the nipple clamps. Next came the dreaded CB3000 male chastity device, which Weight had difficulty getting on Hockney's hard dick. Hockney was not prepared for it since he hadn't pissed before leaving the RCA. The post-grad flinched as Weight roughly snapped the cuff around his balls.

Hockney shifted around in the chair and received two more hard whacks from the belt. He cried out through the gag and again felt the belt. The student took the pain silently this time. Weight handled Hockney's cock roughly until the young painter lost his erection from a combination of pain and fright, at which point Weight applied some lube before putting the cage part on. Hockney heard the distinct click of a padlock and knew that he was done for.

Weight bent down and rubbed Hockney's leg, saying in a gentle voice that he had to go out for the evening and would be back in a few hours. Hockney shook his head, signalng to Weight that he didn't want to be left like this. Weight ignored the silent plea and whacked Hockney again, twice on each thigh. Then Weight snapped off the light and left the room. A few minutes later Hockney heard Weight's front door close and the slave was left alone, wondering how long his master would leave him bound, gagged and totally helpless. Hockney's nipples started to hurt from the tightness of the nipple clamps and his cock and balls ached from being bound too. As far as was possible, Hockney shifted around in his chair, hoping Weight would not be out too long. His wrists were already sore from being held by tightly clamped handcuffs.

After thirty minutes Hockney drifted off into sleep. He woke suddenly and shifted on the chair, which sent a sharp wave of pain through his chest. Since he was still alone he yelped into his gag, biting down hard on it. Hockney's entire body ached. The steel cuffs dug into his wrists and he wasn't able to move very much at all. His feet tingled as the rope around his ankles was also tight. His nipples were a study in agony thanks to the clamps Weight had attached to them and his hood felt like it was planning on suffocating him slowly. Hockney's dick was almost erect as he sat wondering why Weight had bound him so tightly.

Hockney was very hungry but he tried not to think about this. After so much time alone, Hockney was startled when he heard Weight's front door open. Moments later Weight was standing in front of Hockney. The tutor gave Hockney permission to speak and the student moaned loudly as Weight hugged his bound body. Weight told his submissive that he had been tied up for five hours. It was 11:30 PM. The don explained that he had gone to a friend's house and left the key to the padlock for the CB3000 male chastity device in his friend's possession. The painting tutor then released the nipple clamps. Hockney screamed into his gag, as blood began to flow back into his tortured paps. Weight hugged Hockney a second time and gently rubbed his still hooded head.

Weight told his charge that he wanted him to come back for an all day session in four weeks time. That meant Hockney would be locked into the CB3000 male chastity device for a month without the possibility of coming. Hockney moaned at this news but Weight ignored his outburst. It had been several few days since Hockney last masturbated. Damn! Weight told Hockney he was doing this for the student's own good, as he wanted to train him to go without orgasms for long periods of time.

Hockney was sore for the next few days with marks on his wrists from the handcuffs. He wore long-sleeved shirts to hide the red weals. His nipples hurt too. Hockney had to get used to being in a chastity device again, unable to jerk off for a month. For three or four days running, Hockney really worked very hard, if we were to reckon by the number of hours he spent in his studio over his easel, even though we should only reckon by the results. For though scarcely an hour passed that he was not balancing on the hind legs of his stool with a vacant look in his eyes and thinking of anything but colour or composition, yet on the whole he managed to get through a good deal. One evening, for the first time since his quarrel with Kitaj, he felt a sensation of real comfort, it hardly amounted to pleasure, as he looked at the picture he'd just completed. He leaned back on his stool and sat for a few minutes, letting his thoughts follow their own bent. They soon took a wrong turn and he jumped up in fear lest he should be drifting back into the black stormy sea, in the trough of which he had been labouring so lately, and which he felt he was by no means clear of yet.

He caught up his coat and hat as though he were going out. There was a wine party at one of his acquaintance's rooms, or he could go and smoke a cigar in the pool room, or at any one of a dozen other places. He'd even been invited to a circle jerk but the CB3000 male chastity device meant that he couldn't participate in that! On second thoughts he went over to the shelf of books in his studio. He had no particular object in selecting one book rather than another and so took down carelessly the first that came to hand. It happened to be a volume of Plato and opened of its own accord at the "Apology". He glanced at a few lines. What a flood of memories they called up! This was almost the last book he had read at school. His old teacher and the lofty oak-shelved library appeared in his mind's eye. Then the blunders that he, himself and others had made rushed through his mind, and he almost burst into a laugh. He wheeled his stool round to the window and began reading where he had opened, encouraging every thought of the old times when he first read that marvellous defence. Hockney gave himself up to his thoughts and strangely they centred on the struggle which had been raging in him of late.

The studio stifled him now. He threw on his jacket and hurried out. He walked all the way to Kitaj's house and there paused. Was he there by chance or was he guided there? Yes, this was the right way for him, he had no doubt now as to that. How could he be sure that Kitaj was alone? And, if not, to go in would be worse than useless. If he were alone, what should he say? After all must he go in there? Was there no way but that?

At that moment he heard Kitaj's door open and a voice saying "Goodnight", a man he knew called Grey stepped out into the street and was passing close to him.

"Join yourself to him." The impulse came so strongly into Hockney's mind that it was like a voice speaking to him. He yielded to it and stepping to Grey's side, wished him good evening. The other returned his salute in his shy way and was hurrying on but Hockney kept by him.

"Have you been reading with Kitaj?"

"Yes."

"How is he? I have not seen anything of him for some time."

"Oh, very well, I think," said Grey, glancing sideways at his questioner and adding, after a moment, "I have wondered rather not to see you there of late."

"Are you going to your master?" Hockney said, changing the subject.

"Yes and I am rather late. I must make haste. Goodnight."

Feeling lonesome at being left like this, Hockney ran to Boshier's home and was leaning out of the window at his side in another minute.

Having exchanged greetings, the next thing Boshier said to Hockney was: "There's such a queer old bird gone to your friend Kitaj's house."

The mention of Kitaj caused Hockney to listen eagerly as Boshier went on.

"It was about half an hour ago. I saw an old fellow go hobbling up to Kitaj's room on two sticks. The kind of old boy you read about in books, you know. Commodore Trunnion, or Uncle Toby, or one of that sort. Well, I watched him backing and filling and trying one door and another but there was nobody about. So I trotted up to him for fun and to see what he was after. It was as good as a play, if you could have seen it. I was ass enough to take off my hat and make a low bow as I came up to him and he pulled off his cap in return. We stood there bowing to one another. He was a vain old gentleman and I felt rather foolish for fear that he should see that I expected a lark when I came out. But I don't think he had an idea of it and only set my greeting to wonderful good manners. So we got quite thick and I piloted him across to Kitaj's front door."

"He must be Kitaj's father," said Hockney.

"I shouldn't wonder. But is his father in the navy?"

"He is a retired captain."

"Then no doubt you're right. What shall we do? Have a hand at picquet. Some men will be here directly. Only for love."

Hockney declined the proffered game and went off soon after to his own room, a happier man than he had been since his first night at The Choughs.

The month of abstinence passed quickly enough as Hockney kept himself busy with painting and out of trouble. The CB3000 male chastity device meant that he had to turn down the many offers he received to participate in circle jerks. Hockney only called on his master to check in, as he had been ordered to do. Weight did ask Hockney how he was doing and the student told him he was alright. In fact, Hockney was forgetful, grumpy, tired and very very horny. But he didn't want to complain to Weight because he had learned his lesson.

Finally the day of Hockney's bondage session with Weight arrived and the student was up at 5AM, taking a bath, done with breakfast and out the door by 6AM. He was carrying his equipment bag which contained his favourite toy, a black leather straitjacket, among other items of bondage and restraint. Hockney arrived early at 6:45AM and woke Weight up. That in itself was a joy for Hockney, as he got to see a side of the don that the painting tutor only displayed upon waking. Weight's hair was tousled, he was bare chested, his small nipples were erect. He was wearing skimpy underwear revealing the beautiful silhouette of his hard cock and balls. Weight was barefoot and smiling mischievously.

Hockney's cock twitched and hardened within the confines of the CB3000 male chastity device. Hockney told Weight how happy he was that he'd be spending the entire day under his control. The dom went to the washroom and instructed Hockney to make his bed, which the student enjoyed doing as it was still warm and he lingered a moment at his two favourite spots. They were located in the middle of the mattress where Weight's beautiful butt came into contact with the sheet and at the end of the bed where his bare feet lay.

Weight had prepared the chains at the head and foot of the bed the night before. When Weight came out of the bathroom he instructed Hockney to strip and show him the CB3000 male chastity device. Satisfied that all was in order he told Hockney to go take one last piss before putting on nappies. For reasons Hockney did not understand, Weight always used the American word for nappies which is diapers. When Hockney was finished

Weight surprised him by lowering his nappies—he was wearing two to prevent leakage—and unlocked the CB3000 male chastity device. It felt so damn good to be busting loose and Hockney thanked Weight very much for the privilege of being free of it for that day's play. Weight put a cock and ball harness on Hockney, snapping it snugly behind his balls.

After taking the straitjacket from Hockney's bag, Weight motioned the sub toward him and ordered the student to put his arms into the sleeves. Hockney hesitated for just a moment and looked at Weight. The tutor had changed into tight black leather underwear, revealing once again the outline of his beautiful cock and balls. Hockney inserted his arms into the sleeves of the straitjacket. Weight turned the twenty-something around and started to buckle all four straps at his back. Once he was done, the dom noticed that there was room to cinch it tighter and he undid all the buckles to tighten them by one or two holes on each of the straps. Then he pulled the crotch straps in between Hockney's legs and buckled both straps tightly, trapping the post-grad's cock and balls within his nappies. Next Hockney's arms were fastened over the front of his body, by taking the end of each sleeve and threading it through the belt loops located at the bottom of the straitjacket, just above the sub's hips. Once Weight had buckled the straps, he pushed Hockney's elbows in toward his stomach, then undid the buckle and strapped it tighter by three holes. This made Hockney's arms very snug against his gut. Weight then took a four-foot length of chain and wrapped it around Hockney's arms and padlocked it, to reduce any arm movement.

Once the dom had put Hockney in the straitjacket he forced the boy to drink a pint of water, to help him stay hydrated. Hockney didn't want to do this as he knew it would make him pee a lot, but he had to obey.

Weight admired his handiwork, then locked leather ankle cuffs on Hockney and put a penis gag in his mouth. A spandex hood with built in blindfold went over the boy's head. It was very snug but easy to breathe through. Then came the leather collar which Weight buckled around Hockney's neck, on the fourth hole out of five. This made the collar very tight, but Weight tested it to make sure the sub would be okay in it. Hockney's heart was beating quickly since he knew Weight would be placing him on his bed and chaining him to it for at least 12 hours.

Weight led the student close to his bed and helped him lie down on it. Once Hockney was in position, Weight quickly spread the boy's legs apart and buckled the D rings of his ankle cuffs to a chain with a padlock. The chain ran under the mattress from left to right and Hockney heard the distinct click of each padlock as it was snapped shut. No doubt Weight would make at least one further adjustment when the boy was completely bound to the bed. Weight gave Hockney a pillow for his head and the sub was very grateful. The tutor pulled the chain through the D rings on Hockney's collar and fastened each side of it with a padlock.

Hockney was now bound to the bed, unable to move his arms, since they were chained as well as straitjacketed. His feet were bound in leather ankle cuffs locked to a fairly thick chain at the foot of the bed. Weight made a number of adjustments all aimed at tightening the ensemble of equipment that constrained his slave, thereby making Hockney more uncomfortable. Hockney groaned and remarked that he was bound very tightly. Weight lay beside the sub for a few minutes and told the slave he was still being kind to him, as he could have tightened the restraints even more.

Weight placed his hand over Hockney's hood, covering his mouth and nose, so that it was difficult for the sub to breath. Within fifteen seconds Hockney started writhing around trying to move his head and free himself for a breath of air. Weight let Hockney breathe once or twice then clamped his hand down over his face again. Hockney struggled and begged for air. Weight took his hand away and it was a great relief to the slave to be able to breathe. This was done to remind Hockney of the power Weight held over him. Then the tutor started to slap Hockney's balls through the nappies. Lightly at first, then with increasing strength until Hockney was moaning and struggling on the bed. Weight stopped after a couple of minutes then clamped his hand down over Hockney's mouth and nose. The student was exhausted from his struggles and the lack of air.

Finally Weight got off the bed. Hockney heard him walking over to his closet and the next thing he felt was a leather belt smacking hard against the bottoms of his feet. Hockney yelped in pain but Weight continued to hit each foot on alternative strokes. Then he moved upward to the subs legs and smacked them on the inside a number of times. Hockney wanted to protect his balls, another spot on which Weight liked to punish him. Resistance was futile, the dom whacked Hockney's balls a good few times with the belt but not too harshly. Weight told his charge he'd earned full marks for being in chastity all month and accepting without challenge his tutor's dominance.

Then Weight went off to the bathroom, leaving the door open so that Hockney could hear the sounds of his tutor bathing. Eventually the dom came back to the bedroom. As he dressed he told Hockney he was leaving. Weight informed the young painter he had purposely bound him tighter for this session as he wanted Hockney to think of his master all day. Weight asked the kid if he was alright and the twenty-something replied he wasn't sure if he could withstand the tight restraints for the whole day. Weight checked his bound sub and refused to make any adjustment. He told Hockney he would just have to get used to being tightly wrapped as he really wanted the boy to long for his return and the accompanying release from bondage. Weight made one final adjustment to Hockney's pillow, checked all the padlocks, pocketed the keys and left.

Hockney was so completely restrained he had next to no manoeuvring room on the bed. His arms were bound by the jacket sleeves and chained as well. Hockney felt the padlocked collar around his neck with the chain running through all four D-Rings and secured again on either side of the bed. The chain ran from under the mattress and doubled back, where Weight had added padlocks after tightening the chain so there would be no slack on either side of the sub. Hockney's feet were similarly chained and padlocked through the D-Rings on his leather ankle cuffs. The student's head was totally hooded in tight spandex, with the collar over the material that covered his neck, ensuring that he could not possibly wiggle it upward.

Since Hockney had a cock and ball harness on, rather than a chastity belt, he was able to get a proper boner. As a matter of fact, the harness was now adding to his raging hard-on. The crotch straps of the straitjacket were tightly buckled behind him, up his butt. There was no way Hockney was going anywhere until Weight untied him. The young painter's balls had no room to move at all. Hockney was really tired and wanted to sleep. It was dark in Weight's bedroom and the boy was blindfolded. Sleeping would help pass the time of day.

Hockney slept soundly for three hours. When he awoke he had a stonking erection. It felt good to get a proper boner after his manhood had been locked up in a CB3000 male chastity device for a month and he'd had to turn down dozens of invitations to participate in circle jerks. Hockney wondered whether he would be able to bring himself to orgasm and slowly started bucking his hips up and down, in as far as he was able to do this in his bonds. His cock rubbed against the inside of his nappy and it felt great, but he soon stopped. He was worried that if he continued he would eventually come. He would be severely punished for having an orgasm without permission!

Still Hockney's need to come started to overwhelm him and he decided to give it a try. He would worry about the consequences later. Once more he bucked his hips up and down, slowly at first then gradually picking up his pace. Hockney's dick was hard as a rock and he revelled in it. Twenty-three minutes and nineteen seconds later, Hockney felt that he was getting very close to coming. He longed to stroke his extension but that was impossible. The next thing he knew jism exploded from his plonker and he screamed into his hood. Hockney bucked and writhed around on the bed as much as he could and he didn't stop until every last bit of come had spurted from his length. Luckily for Hockney, it did not leak out of the nappy. Now he was wet and sticky but he didn't care. He was also going to get into a lot of trouble if and when Weight found out. Hockney thought maybe he could hide the fact that he had shot his load. But he was fooling himself, since he knew Weight would figure it out. Hockney lay panting. Eventually he drifted back to sleep. When he awoke an hour later he felt the need to take a piss but he didn't want to further wet his nappy. He knew he had shot a big load of jism after not coming for a month.

Hockney lay bound and helpless thinking about his master. Grateful for the pleasure of being bound to a bed for the day. But Hockney was also annoyed with the dom for tying him up so tightly. The post-grad's stomach felt empty and his bladder was full. His ankles hurt from the tightness of the leather cuffs and the chains he was bound by. Hockney tried moving his head to change its position on the pillow but that was impossible. He felt his neck was starting to chafe from the collar as he tried to move his bonce from side to side. Eventually he gave up and just lay quietly.

Hockney realised he really had to piss. But he didn't want to wet himself yet. About an hour later he couldn't hold on any longer and he peed into the nappy. He started slowly at first, almost hesitantly, feeling ashamed that he was wetting himself. The next thing he knew he was peeing full stream into the nappy and he felt it getting sopping wet. He pissed himself for a solid minute. By the time he stopped his two nappies were really soaked and he was really glad he was wearing extra absorbent ones, with a centre lining of a third that Weight had cut out and placed inside the other two. The tutor obviously wanted to ensure his bed linen wasn't ruined! Even when Hockney followed on his pissing by taking a dump, the nappies he was wearing were able to contain the mess inside them.

The afternoon passed slowly and Hockney's shoulders ached from his arms being in the same position for so long. He was cold from laying on the bed with a thick plastic sheet under him. Weight had not covered his slave before he left.

Hockney was in agony but none the less his love muscle was throbbing again. He tried to ignore this hard-on, but he was lusting for sexual release and relishing his tight bondage, even if it was causing him physical pain. Hockney wanted the rest of the day to pass slowly, so he could savour his discomfort. When he realised that his manhood was still rock hard, he knew he had to have another orgasm. But he also realised he was treading on dangerous ground because Weight had not given him permission to come. Hockney started to buck his hips again, rubbing his pork sword against his wet and soiled nappies, feeling his balls tightly trapped between his legs by the crotch straps of his straitjacket as well as the cock and ball harness snapped over them. He rubbed and rubbed and thrashed around as much as he could and felt himself edging up to the point of no return.

Hockney worked himself into a feverish pitch and then let loose with a scream as he discharged another load of semen into his soiled nappies. He shot spurt after spurt until he was empty and exhausted again. Now his leg muscles hurt from keeping the limbs rigid while trying to get the momentum going to achieve a second climax.

The room darkened as the day came to its natural close. Hockney's stomach was empty and he was getting hunger pangs. His mouth was dry and parched. He drifted off to sleep again and awoke with a start as the door downstairs opened and closed. Hockney's heart was racing and he braced himself for trouble. Weight came straight to the bedroom and silently inspected his prisoner. Hockney could not speak because he was gagged and in any case did not have permission to do so. Finally Weight greeted Hockney warmly and ran his hands over the student's legs and leather covered chest. He checked all the padlocks and chains to see if Hockney was still securely bound. The sub remained still and silent.

Weight was gentle with Hockney and rubbed his crotch before telling the boy that the soiled nappies smelt really sexy. The painting tutor lowered the nappies and started to pump Hockney's love stick. To Hockney's surprise he was erect again. The student started to moan and move around on the bed, so Weight smacked his shit smeared balls. Hockney tried to keep silent but the pain in his balls made him whimper behind his gag and the dom hit him again. Weight did not want his slave to make any noise. He continued to pump Hockney slowly then he picked up the tempo until the sub shot a wad of liquid genetics. That was when Weight noticed that something was wrong. For someone who hadn't come in a month Hockney didn't ejaculate much jism and the dom clocked this right away. He told the young painter to nod his head yes or no as to whether he had managed to come while tied up. Hockney hesitated and Weight prodded him by squeezing his turd encrusted balls. Finally the slave nodded yes and the tutor chuckled before turning serious.

He asked Hockney how many times he had managed to come. Weight said "once" and the sub did not move. He said "twice" and the student nodded his head yes. Again he chuckled and said he was proud of Hockney's determination and endurance. But then he told the boy that he would have to be punished taking pleasures without permission.

Weight unlocked the padlocks around Hockney's collar and the student thought he was being released. Instead, Weight unbuckled the collar and lifted Hockney's spandex hood up to the boy's nose. He then removed the leather penis gag from Hockney's mouth and replaced it with his cock. Hockney groaned and tried to move and for this was whacked with Weight's belt on the inside of his thighs. When Hockney yelped, Weight struck him and again the boy yelped. Weight continued delivering hard strokes to Hockney's inner thighs with his belt. Hockney sucked hard down on the dom's penis and remained silent while Weight who had mounted him 69-style gave his legs a beating.

Finally Weight stopped and cleaned Hockney's bottom and balls, removing both the soiled nappies and the cock and ball harness. Next Hockney felt his master reapply the cuff of the CB3000 male chastity device. The student's blood sausage hurt from coming so much and his master was handling it really roughly, forcing it inside the cage of the CB3000. When Hockney heard the padlock click shut he wanted to yell but he had to remain silent or risk being beaten again.

Weight bent down and whispered to Hockney that he was going back out and didn't know what time he would be home that night. The art student shook his head signalling to his master that he didn't want to be left alone again. The painting tutor simply ignored this silent plea. He told Hockney he had been tied up for eleven hours already. Then Weight put on a single new nappy and made sure to cinch Hockney's crotch straps tighter than before. He smacked the post-grad's balls a few times and Hockney absorbed the pain silently. Weight checked the boy's feet, making sure the chains hadn't come loose. He moved the padlocks on each ankle by a couple of chain links to make them tighter, then left.

Hockney had given in to pleasure's cravings and now he was paying the price. He was fed up with being bound and now all the restraints were tighter and the male chastity device was back on him. Hockney struggled and his cock got semi-hard within the confines of the CB3000. His pork sword felt very sensitive and his bollocks ached. He settled down, tried to ignore his hunger and drifted off to sleep again.

Hockney slept for two hours. The house was quiet and dark. When he awoke, the sub shuffled weakly on the bed, hoping Weight would be home soon to release him from his misery. What a bondage pig Hockney had become!

Hockney's arms and shoulders really hurt and his ankles tingled from being bound for so many hours. The post-grad may have been suffering but he was in a rebellious mood, he had been all day long. He realised that now, he had known he would be punished for coming without permission and still he proceeded to give himself not one but two orgasms. He had worked hard for them and he had paid for them too, no doubt he would pay even more but he had wanted to show Weight that he still had a mind of my own!

Eventually Hockney heard heavy footsteps. Weight was home. He went first into the kitchen, then the toilet. He took his time arriving at the bedroom where Hockney was chained up. What followed next can best be described as a beating. The tutor whacked the bottoms of Hockney's bare feet with his belt again. He received ten whacks on each foot. Then Weight hit Hockney's inner thighs in the same place as he had before. The slave grunted and thrashed around on the bed. Still Weight continued until finally Hockney was broken and the tears started welling from under his hood. The dom could hear Hockney breathing hard and weeping softly. He put down the belt and smacked the boy's coilons (that's old English for balls) five times. Hockney was shaking but still felt defiant. When Weight realised this he stopped beating his sub and lay down beside him stroking his face through the hood.

After Hockney calmed down, Weight unlocked the padlocks. He helped Hockney to his feet but the boy stumbled. The dom sat the slave back down on the bed and held him for a moment or two. Weight told Hockney he had to think of further punishment for his foolish behaviour but that could wait. For now it was enough that he would be sore as hell tomorrow.

The tutor still had made no move to release Hockney from the straitjacket. Instead Weight told Hockney to lay back and rest. Eventually the post-grad was told to stand up and this time he was able to do so unassisted. Weight hugged Hockney tightly then undid the straps to his straitjacket. The dom told the student he was proud of him for his defiance.

Hockney thanked Weight for a great sex session and the painting tutor smiled at him. It was a smile that made Hockney's suffering worthwhile. He left Weight's house and walked home thinking over his day of ecstasies. The post-grad bathed before having a late night bite to eat. He wasn't that hungry anymore. He needed to sleep.

CHAPTER 18

A BOTTLE OF BELL'S UP THE BACKSIDE IS ROUGH SEX HEAVEN!

Hockney rose in the morning with a presentiment that everything would soon be resolved. Determined to take his desires for reality, he decided to beg Kitaj to give him a beating. All he asked was that it be done in a manner that would be most humiliating to him as a sub. He was greatly annoyed, therefore, when Kitaj did not appear in the canteen for an early morning coffee. All day in answer to his inquiries, Kitaj's chums replied that the top was busy. Hockney was quite out of heart at his bad luck and began to be afraid that he would have to sleep on his unhealed psycho-sexual wound another night.

With a heavy heart, Hockney stripped off, put on a slave collar and sat down in an arm-chair. He fell to musing and thought how dreadfully his life had been changed in these few short weeks. He could hardly get back across the gulf which separated him from the self who had come back to London after Easter, full of anticipations of the pleasures and delights of the coming summer term and vacation. While occupied with these thoughts, he heard talking on his stairs, accompanied by a strange lumbering tread. These came nearer, and at last stopped just outside his door, which opened in another moment.

Kitaj walked through the door dressed in a fine suit, he dropped his briefcase to the floor together with his Macintosh coat. The top looked exhausted. With barely a sound, Hockney rose from his chair, naked but for a leather collar around his neck with one single D-ring.

Noting Hockney's state of undresss Kitaj instantly brightened. Smiling down fondly on the sub as Hockney kneeled at his feet, Kitaj instructed him in a manner that was now second nature.

"You may go about your duties slave. I have been told by many today that you have agreed to completely surrender to me."

Hockney rose gracefully, retrieving the discarded mac and case. The slave stowed them in a closet. The sub returned to his master's side and without a word removed the top's jacket and tie, placing them neatly on a nearby chair. Then Hockney removed Kitaj's cufflinks and folded his shirtsleeves up to his elbows with an ease that defied exact precision. He undid two of Kitaj's shirt buttons. Finally Hockney kneeled to remove the dom's shoes and placed them neatly under a chair. Hockney stayed kneeling by his master's feet, eyes downcast, awaiting the next instruction. "BDSM" was what Kitaj croaked through a fit of coughing.

Hockney watched as his master disappeared from the room with a concerned furrow etched across his delicate brow. Hockney put away Kitaj's clothing. In the bedroom he retrieved his clamps from the bedside drawer. These consisted of two nipple clamps and a cock ring all chained together so they met in the centre of Hockney's torso. A lead could either be attached directly or by an additional chain to his collar. This was his BDSM wear.

Standing in front of a mirror, Hockney massaged his nipples into two hard buds, applying the nipple clamps, breathing deeply as he screwed them into place for he relished the pain. He positioned himself on a chair and, aroused by the ache in his nipples, he rubbed his cock frantically while observing himself in the mirror. As his arousal increased, Hockney pulled on the cock ring.

"Good boy," came a voice from the darkness somewhere beyond the door, "now a little extra for my drink tonight."

With that word from his master Hockney increased the tempo with which he was manipulating his cock and he came in his left palm. The sub was careful not to drop the spunk. He stood up and checked himself in the mirror.

"Perfect as always," came the voice from the darkness.

Hockney smiled as he made his way to the bedroom door. Sliding into the second room, Hockney went straight to the drinks cabinet and retrieved a fine crystal tumbler and tipped the spunk into it. When he'd scraped as much as he could of the remaining jizz from his skin on to the rim of the glass, Hockney grabbed a bottle of Bell's Whisky. Ring-a-ding!

"You may bring the bottle," came the deep voice from the leather couch.

Hockney trotted over to his master and presented the tumbler, which Kitaj took. The sub then poured a generous slug of Bell's, stirring the amber liquid with his unwashed spunky fingers. Kitaj grabbed Hockney's cock and pulled him forward, sucking the bottom's fingers seductively at the same time.

"Mmmmm, such a good boy!" Kitaj purred.

Kitaj downed the generous shot in one gulp, spluttering as he switched from the tumbler to the bottle.

"Come sit on daddy's lap," the top instructed.

Hockney obeyed readily, sitting sideways so he could lay back easily as required. With the top of the bottle Kitaj pulled the chain closest to Hockney's right nipple clamp. The sub yelped.

"Relax, little one," Kitaj instructed as his adoring eyes drank in the slave. "Daddy has been thinking of pleasuring you all day, this is for you, just enjoy yourself."

Hockney watched the dom guzzle the last of the whiskey. Using the mouth of the bottle he pulled the left nipple clamp. This time Hockney didn't yelp but it was clear he was suppressing the pain welling up from deep inside him. The slave's eyes had misted but he only broke into a flood of tears when Kitaj pulled his cock ring with great force.

Hockney used a special Japanese breathing technique to control the pain but as his master continued pulling each clamp in turn, he found he was able to enjoy riding the fine line between agony and ecstasy. Breathing deeply and slowly Hockney let out a small moan that acted as a sign for Kitaj to raise the stakes. The top set the empty bottle of Bell's on the floor and retrieved a small paddle from the table. He prised Hockney's legs open and stroked his balls with the handle of the paddle.

"What do you want little one?" Kitaj cooed.

"Pain, daddy," was Hockney's spluttered response.

"Louder!" the dom commanded, sliding the paddle handle into Hockney's anus.

The sub let out a groan and shouted: "Pain daddy!"

As he made small circular motions with the handle of the paddle, Kitaj demanded: "Tell daddy exactly what you want."

"I want you to hit me, to beat me, to make me bleed. I'll be your dog for just one flog. Slap me, cut me, bite me. Bite my cock, drink my come as you drink my blood. Consume me, daddy."

Hockney felt Kitaj's hard-on growing in response to his words and with great confidence he continued: "I want you to own me, rape me, take what's yours. Fill my ass with your big dick and make me come over and over for you. I want to feel alive."

Kitaj slapped Hockney's face hard.

"You forget yourself, boy!" Kitaj said as he rolled the sub off him, unbothered as the slave screamed in excruciating pain. The paddle had jarred, stabbing his anus before falling out.

"Who am I?" Kitaj roared.

"My, my master!" Hockney rejoined.

"Good," Kitaj grunted as he pulled Hockney up by his hair. Looking straight into the slave's eyes, he grabbed his cock. "Who's is this?" Kitaj barked.

"Yours, master!" Hockney replied.

"And these?" Kitaj questioned as he yanked the chain holding Hockney's nipples.

"Yours, master," the sub whimpered.

Kitaj threw Hockney to the floor, so that he landed in a crumpled heap.

"So, who decides what happens to you?" Kitaj demanded.

"You do, master!" the slave affirmed.

Hockney was aware of the coppery smell of blood. Swallowing hard he realised his lip was split. He licked the swelling, cleaning the blood, awakening his senses to the pain that was turning into the delicious stinging ache he coveted so much. Hockney had a throbbing erection and concluded that Kitaj had been intent on arousing him in the quickest possible way, with physical abuse. Hockney shuddered with pleasure.

"Stand and bend over the table!" Kitaj roared.

As he did this Hockney heard tape being ripped from a roll. His chest was pushed hard against the wood as he was taped tightly to it. The pain that surged through the slave's body caused him to come a second time.

Hockney couldn't see what was happening behind him but the anticipation of further abuse sent flutters through his transversus abdominis, pelvic floor, gluts and cock. Hockney felt cold glass pressed against his arse as his legs were forced further apart. Something flat and cold was being rubbed up against his rim of dark pleasures. Hockney felt pressure as the huge object was pushed into his arsehole.

"It's okay baby, daddy's got you," Kitaj sang. "I've put plenty of lube on the empty bottle, so I know you can take it right up your bargain basement!"

"Thank you, daddy," Hockney whispered.

Kitaj was shoving the bottle up Hockney's arse neck first. He kept pushing and adding more lube until only half the bottle was sticking out of Hockney's derrière.

"Mmm baby, you are a good boy," Kitaj spat.

There was a knock at the door and a cloaked figure entered. Kitaj didn't even glance at the new arrival.

"Just pound Hockney with the bottle, I want his mouth," the dom instructed.

The thought of Kitaj's huge member pounding his mouth and throat sent another wave of shudders coarsing through the sub. Pleasure is a natural lubricant and aided the bottle's journey inside him. Hockney could feel the empty Bell's—ring-a-ding—container sliding further in.

Hockney felt Kitaj's strong hands opening his mouth followed by the top pushing his thick dick into his throat. Kitaj pushed and shoved until he was deep inside Hockney. The bottom was relieved when Kitaj suddenly screamed and the pounding ended.

Kitaj's cock filled Hockney's throat with spunk as the glass bottle overwhelmed his sphincter. Waves of pleasure washed through slave. If he'd been able to he would have laughed when Kitaj grabbed his hair and snapped his head back.

"Yes! I knew you would like that, my nasty, dirty little boy. Don't you love it, little slut?" Kitaj crowed.

"Yes daddy, thank you!" Hockney wanted to gasp. But he couldn't because Kitaj was still coming in his throat.

"Now my friend is gonna ejaculate in your tight ass!" Kitaj screeched.

Hockney groaned loudly as he was no longer gagged by Kitaj's cock which had been withdrawn from his mouth. The cloaked stranger attempted to pull the bottle from Hockney's bum but it wouldn't budge. Having gone in neck first, the sub's sphincter muscles had tightened over it, creating a vacuum. The empty bottle of Bell's was now stuck fast in Hockney's arse and wouldn't come out!

"Oh dear me," Kitaj laughed, "I've encountered this problem before. We're going to have to leave you alone Hockney while we go and get a glass drill. The only way to break the vacuum on that bottle you've got in your backside is to drill a little hole in the end. Once we've done that it will come out easily. You'll have to sleep face down on your bed tonight, and I'll come back in the morning to sort it out."

So Hockney was left to spend the night lying face down with a bottle jammed up his shit-chute. When Kitaj came back the next day he told Hockney he'd known putting the bottle in neck first would create a vaccuum causing it to become lodged in the sub's backside. That had been Kitaj's plan all along. Hockney begged Kitaj to take him to a hospital to resolve the problem so that he could be further humiliated by the doctors. Kitaj insisted it wasn't the job of medics to chastise Hockney and drilled a small hole in the bottom of the Bell's bottle to break the seal. After this it was easily removed.

Kitaj and Hockney were back in their old roles. The master/slave dialectic going on between them had resumed its natural course.

CHAPTER 19

LEFT HELPLESS IN A HOGTIE AND THEN FORCED TO VOMIT!

There are moments in the life of even the most self-contained and sober of us all when we fairly bubble over, like a full bottle of champagne with the cork out. This was one of them for Hockney who was neither self-contained nor sober by nature. He hardly knew what to do to give vent to his lightness of heart, and Kitaj, though self-contained and sober enough in general, was on this occasion almost as bad as his friend. They rattled on, talked out the thing which came uppermost, whatever the subject might chance to be. But whether grave or gay, it always ended after a minute or two in jokes and laughter.

The spirits of the two friends seemed inexhaustible. They ate a shit load of food and lasted out the bottle of sherry which Hockney had uncorked, as well as the remains of a bottle of port. Then they went out and wandered the streets, eventually falling asleep on some park benches. They were woken by a couple of drunk women who introduced themselves as Tara and Chloe. The chicks were looking for fun. Kitaj invited them back to his place and they readily agreed. Hockney wasn't much interested in the two girls but Kitaj was desperate for some bicycle action. Once they got to Kitaj's and uncorked a bottle of wine, the conversation quickly became fast and loose and got onto the subject of the puke fetish.

"So what don't you like about vomiting?" Kitaj asked.

The three guests were sitting in one of Kitaj rooms. Their chairs were arranged in a circle and they were all looking at each other wondering if one among them might be the filthiest person alive.

"I don't like the feeling. I hate the sensation of all that food in your stomach trying to come out," Hockney pontificated.

"No one likes feeling sick," Kitaj said. "But why are you afraid of throwing up?"

"I just get so embarrassed." Hockney shrugged. "It's so disgusting losing control like that, people seeing what you ate earlier. It's just so embarrassing."

Tara and Chloe nodded in agreement.

"Have you ever made yourself spew up on purpose?" Kitaj enquired.

"No, of course not," Tara chimed in and Hockney nodded in agreement.

"That's a classic sign of a barfing phobia," Kitaj said. "Hockney, tell me about the last time you did a technicolour yawn?"

"I can't. I don't even want to think about it," the sub said as he shifted in his chair. He looked down at the floor. "It was last year. I got food poisoning from some shrimp. I was out shopping with some friends when I started feeling sick, so I left and hurried home. I was walking as fast as I could despite feeling awful. The chunder started to come up before I got to my pad. I was gagging and burping. I kept swallowing it down until I finally reached my front door. I ran inside and tried to make it to the bathroom but I wasn't fast enough. I just had to get the bile out of my stomach. There was nothing I could do. So I..."

"Come on, Hockney. You have to tell us what happened if you want to get over your fear," Kitaj explained.

"I spewed all over the floor," Hockney admitted while lowering his face in shame. "It was so humiliating even though no one saw. The first wave up was the shrimp that had made me sick. But the bile just kept coming. I couldn't stop until everything inside my stomach was splattered across the walls and lino."

"Why did you hate the sensation so much?" Kitaj pressed.

"I was mortified I'd done something so unladylike and disgusting," Hockney bitterly observed.

"How about a little bondage?" Kitaj suggested.

"Let's do it." Hockney was grinning happily at the change of subject.

"Take your clothes off and lay on your stomach on the bed," Kitaj ordered.

Hockney complied and Kitaj guided the student's arms behind his back, then bound his wrists to his ankles, so he was hogtied.

"What do you have in store for me now?" Hockney was hoping for a beating and a handjob.

He was in for a huge shock.

"Listen, Hockney," Kitaj said seriously. "I think tonight is a good opportunity for you to try to confront your phobia."

"What do you mean?"

"The best way to overcome a fear is to face it. You need to deal with your vomit phobia."

"But I don't need to chuck up. I don't feel sick at all," the student insisted.

"You can't just wait until the next time you feel nauseous and hope that you'll be less afraid then. That's not facing a fear. You need to accept that this terrifying thing is going to happen to you right now and deal with it. I knew you would never do it on your own so I'm going to help you. I'm going to put my fingers down your throat and make you vomit several times and you will see that nothing bad happens. It's not the end of the world."

"No! Please don't. You can't!" Hockney cried in a panic.

"Yes, Hockney. This will help you."

"And it will be fun and educational for us to watch too!" Tara and Chloe chimed in.

"Please! Not tonight! I ate so much at supper. It's going to be disgusting. I can't let you see me do this. Please! I can't do something so repulsive and stomach-turning."

"This is why you have this phobia," Kitaj chided, "you are terrified of doing anything repellant. You wanna boss your guts around and prevent them rebelling against you. Tonight you won't be in control of your bodily functions. You were a complete pig at dinner and that's why I wanna make you throw up now. It's after eating too much that you're most afraid of retching. You'll be stronger once you've spewed and are no longer frightened of chucking up."

"Please!" the student begged. "It's too vile, the food I ate wont be digested..."

"I know, Hockney. I'm gonna force you to do something super-gross and filthy. You're gonna pull your face into extreme expressions of disgust while making super-vile and completely involuntary gurgling and retching noises. All that food churning in your stomach is gonna explode outta your mouth. I put you in the middle of the bed because I want you to vomit all over the quilt. We'll all get to see just what was inside you. You wanna be a beautiful refined angel boy but tonight you're gonna spew and make a putrid mess. When it's done you'll see that you enjoyed it."

Hockney sobbed and clenched his mouth shut.

"I knew you'd try to fight this," Kitaj hissed. "It's to be expected of someone with your phobia."

"C'mon, Hockney, puke for kicks!" Tara and Chloe chorused in unison.

Kitaj gently forced the sub's jaw open and pushed two fingers into his mouth. Hockney tried to struggle but with his arms and legs bound he couldn't resist. Kitaj thrust into the slave's throat.

"Relax and get ready," Kitaj instructed. "This is going to make you throw up. Just accept what your body does."

Hockney coughed and sputtered.

"Good boy," Kitaj said. "Your throat is trying to get my fingers out. Soon your guts will try to clear your throat by vomiting. It may take a while yet. It's always hard to get started."

Kitaj thrust his fingers deeper into the bound boy's moist throat and tears streamed down his face.

Hockney's muscles contracted every time Kitaj's fingers pushed deeper into his gullet. Soon the sub was covered in sweat.

"Are you feeling nauseous?" Kitaj asked.

"Please stop!" the submarine begged.

"No, Hockney. You know I'm not going to stop until your stomach is empty. Just calm down and throw up."

"I'm feeling extremely nauseous," Hockney whimpered.

"That's good," Kitaj affirmed.

He put his fingers back down Hockney's throat. The bottom coughed and gagged violently. Kitaj forced his fingers deeper, then in and out. The dom made his plaything convulse and dry heave. He slid his digits in once more causing the sub to gag and belch loudly.

"See?" Kitaj said. "Look how vile you can be. I stuck my fingers down your gullet and you tried to burp them out. Will you pull any more sick tricks before you empty your stomach?"

"You're ugly, pug ugly!" Tara and Chloe sang together.

Once more Kitaj forced his pinkies down the bottom's throat and Hockney extended his tongue and belched loudly, "URRRRRRRRRRRRP." Then he heaved and retched. Hockney could feel the contents of his stomach being pushed up into his oesophagus.

"Pay attention to your body," Kitaj spat. "Can you feel your guts expelling their contents? You're about to spew. I want you to savour the experience and enjoy it every bit as much as Tara, Chloe and I will enjoy it. Observer yourself as if you were Tara!"

Hockney sputtered again. Kitaj knew one more plunge would be more than the sub could take.

"Ready?" the dom asked. "Here it comes..."

The top stuck his digits deep down into the slave's windpipe, blocking the airway. For a moment Hockney froze, his open mouth stretched around Kitaj's hand, his terrified eyes staring at his tormentor. Then Hockney clenched his pelvic floor muscles, and his transverse abdominis, and his six pack muscles, so that his guts forced up the liquid inside his stomach. The bottom gagged repeatedly, "REPPP... REPPPPP... REEEEPPPP... REEEUUUUUUUURRRRP" And finally the last gag was taken over by a gassy gurgling as he expelled a first wave of semi-digested sludge.

As he spat it out, Hockney cried uncontrollably and tried to speak, unable to beg Kitaj to stop. There was a burning sense of humiliation, since the top had forced Hockney's stomach to do something so vile. Hockney was not in control of his body anymore; Kitaj was. And the top could make Hockney regurgitate all the things he had swallowed that night. Other than cocks of course, since they'd only gone into his throat and come out again. All Kitaj had to do was put his fingers down Hockney's throat, and he could force out everything that was inside his slave's stomach.

"STOPPPPP!" the masochist sobbed.

"But Hockney, you're doing so well," Kitaj coaxed as he wiped a bit of vomit off the boy's lips.

Using his fingers, he gagged the sub again. Hockney made a futile attempt to resist. "Please! URRRRRRR-UGHHHHH."

The slave couldn't even finish his sentence. All that came out of his mouth was a fountain of barf that flowed onto the bed like lava from a volcano.

Kitaj rammed his fingers back into the slave's soft gullet. "BLERRRRRRRRRUGHHHHHHH!" Hockney gasped. The next heave was impressive. The sub kept his lips open and vomit gushed from them like diarrhea from the backside of a poo fetishist after they've swallowed a whole packet of laxatives.

"Doesn't it feel good?" Kitaj was gently teasing Hockney's food passage with his fingers. "Pay attention to your throat closing around my digits and how you gag and retch. Focus on how your stomach muscles tighten. Face your fears!"

"You're so gross! You're so ugly!" Tara and Chloe trilled.

Kitaj gagged Hockney again and the submarine chocked and belched and gasped. The top speared his index and middle fingers into the boy's gullet and the masochist retched without bringing anything up.

"Come on, Hockney," Kitaj chided as he pushed his pinkies into the back of the bottom's throat. "I know you've got more than just air in there. Puke on."

"If you don't put on a decent show for us we're gonna be sick on you!" Tara and Chloe screamed.

"It looks like you need more help," Kitaj announced. The master untied Hockney's legs so that the sub could lie comfortably but he kept the slave's wrists tied behind his back. He slid a hand under the masochist and pressed it against his bulging belly, still packed with the food he'd eaten earlier.

"See how much is still in there!" Kitaj observed as he applied pressure to Hockney's gut. "I know you have more diced carrots and stomach slime for me. I'm gonna get it all out. Open your gob."

Hockney parted his lips. Kitaj stuck his thick masculine digits down the submarine's throat causing the slave boy to heave. As he brought up a wave of vomit, Kitaj pressed his other hand into the kid's belly and forced the post-graduate to spew even more of his half-digested supper. He was literally pushing the puke out of Hockney's tummy.

"Good boy," Kitaj said, clasping Hockney's belly. "That made you barf a lot didn't it? Do you like it when I force you to vomit?"

Hockney sniffled and didn't say anything. He was too exhausted to fight.

"Look how disgusting you are," Kitaj said. "Look at your puke all over the bed. And you're not even done. You're going to make even more of a mess."

"Make a spectacle of yourself. Entertain us by being super-vile and gross!" Tara and Chloe demanded.

Hockney obediently opened his mouth and let Kitaj gag him once more. The masochist sniffled and let out vulgar gagging noises, "ERRRRUP ERRRRRUP ERRRRRUP." It was painful and humiliating. Hockney was actually trying to make himself vomit, pushing with all his might, engaging the pelvic floor from front and back as well as the transverse abdominis and six pack, trying to force out the contents of his gut, effluent that so desperately wanted to escape its fleshy prison. Finally Hockney brought up a decent sized gush with a super-loud belch.

"Gross!" Tara and Chloe shouted together.

"Ugh," Kitaj said. "Disgusting. Look how sick I made you. You don't even care about your appearance anymore, belching on purpose so that you puke! Let's make you really disgusting, give me another 120 decibel burp!"

At the next gag, Hockney made an ear-splitting belch and up came another thick heave of puke.

"Perfect. You're not even ashamed anymore, are you?" Kitaj teased.

"I am," Hockney said quietly. "But I've already done everything embarrassing that I can so what's the point of resisting?"

Kitaj rested his hand on the submarine's belly and said, "Okay, I'm going to make you vomit up a lot this time by pressing on your stomach. Are you ready?"

Hockney complied. Kitaj stuck his digits down the masochist's throat and the sub barfed up a thick gush. When Hockney was almost done, Kitaj gave him a firm push on the belly. Another gush flowed out of the bottom's mouth. Then with a second hard press, Kitaj forced the fine art student to vomit up yet another tidal wave of puke, all without even taking a breath, three continuous projectile vomits.

"Good boy. Chuck up as much as you can. You might almost be done," Kitaj cooed.

"Good," Hockney said weakly, "I can't take much more of this."

Kitaj knelt over Hockney's back, straddling him with one leg on either side of his body, forcing the sub down into the mattress. He inserted his fingers into Hockney's mouth, and the masochist began retching, "ACK... ACK... ACK... ACK..."

"I'm a bug!" Tara and Chloe screamed. Then the two of them fell about laughing.

As Hockney struggled and gagged, Kitaj spoke: "For the last part of the exercise, I want you to completely lose control. I'm going to hold you down and force you to keep vomiting without stopping, until your stomach is empty. Understand?"

Hockney tensed.

"BLERRRRRRRRRRUGHHHHHHH!"

The sub spewed out an enormous stream of vomit. Kitaj kept his fingers lodged in the slave's throat.

"Good boy. Fuck yeah. Keep puking. Spread that vomit all over the quilt."

Hockney struggled for air and when he couldn't get any down into his lungs, he barfed instead.

"ERRRUP ... BLERRRRRRRRUGHHHHHHH-HHH .... BLERRRRUGHHHH."

The sub heaved trying to force out as much puke as he could. Wave after wave of stinking vomit.

"Nice, you're fucking disgusting! Look at you, barfing as hard as you can. You're not embarrassed anymore are you?"

"He's a shameless hussie!" Tara and Chloe giggled.

Still struggling for air, Hockney clenched his guts and braced himself against another geyser of vomit. He choked, swallowed air and struggled to burp it back up "...URRRRRRRP." The belch did the trick and was followed by a forceful, "HERRRRRUUUUUUU-UUUUUUUPPPPPP" as the submarine violently heaved up the remains of his dinner. Hockney knew he was empty but Kitaj made sure by keeping his fingers in place. "HERRRRRRUUP HERRRRUUUPPP," were the sounds the rubber slave emitted as he dry heaved uncontrollably.

Hockney gasped for breath, his face beet red. The bottom gazed at the swamp of vomit in front of him. He was ashamed but not nearly as bashful as he thought he would be before he'd been made to barf it up.

"You see?" Kitaj said. "You're shameless, and you're completely fine. You threw up more than I've ever seen anyone retch before. It's a rare sight to see someone as beautiful as you, tied up with vomit gushing out of their mouth."

Hockney looked completely stunned. He didn't know what to think. He hoped this horrible incident could just be erased from his mind. But it couldn't be because Tara and Chloe had been there to witness it. That was why Kitaj had invited them back and he further humiliated Hockney by indulging in a threesome with the chicks in the pool of vomit the bottom had thrown up!

CHAPTER 20

ON THE PLEASURES OF
ICE BATHS IN BONDAGE AND
PSEUDO-NECROPHILA

The master and slave were a little embarrassed and confused when they first got back together. However, before long Hockney got back into his old familiar way of unbosoming himself to his fuck buddy and Kitaj showed his old desire to meet him half-way with some really hardcore BDSM! This ready and undisguised sex play soon dispersed the remaining clouds which were hanging between them and Hockney found it a groove sensation to try new sexual kicks or revisit old ones with his master.

The approach of summer hung over South Kensington like dirty laundry that had mistakenly been put out to dry without being washed. The air was fetid, hot and stale, sapping the vegetation of moisture and making the grass in Hyde Park grind underfoot like old mouse bones. Clothing stuck to the skin the way that chewing gum sticks to the sole of a shoe. Hockney disliked the feel of the damp fabric as he pried the layers from his body with slick fingers. Bare skin wasn't much better but it was a vast improvement to the stink of sweat that burrowed into the fibres of his clothes. Besides, Kitaj enjoyed looking at him when he was shiny with sweat and would let Hockney lounge on the bed and nap while he sat and watched. It was a little odd, at least at first, but like everything in Hockney's student life at the Republican College of Art, he'd learned to accept it.

Hockney wasn't thinking of any of that—or anything else really—as we catch up with him, because he was immersed to his chin in the over-sized bathtub that dominated Kitaj's large washroom. The water was freezing, magically chilled to exactly replicate the paralyzing cold of freshly melted snow. He'd been there for ten minutes. As always the first 120 seconds had been excruciatingly painful. Kitaj had bound his hands and feet and forcibly held him down in the tub. Kitaj wanted Hockney to feel the pain—intense and unmistakable— his every nerve ending aflame with a cold burn that ripped his thoughts to shreds and became the focus of his world. The process was slow and agonising, the chill of the water sliced into his veins, as sharp as any shard of glass.

Hockney felt as if the cold were slowly crystallizing his blood. It sapped the warmth and strength from his bulk straight through his skin pores and his body reacted violently, jerking as if an icicle had been punched through his chest. Despite this, he wished to experience the pain, just as Kitaj wanted. Hockney loved torment because suffering was both exquisite and necessary to anyone who wished to make great art. The particular brand of BDSM torture the two men were indulging in that day—which would end in pseudo-necrophila— was brutal but wouldn't leave the art student painted in blood and bruises. It was radically different to anything Hockney had ever felt before, each time was like a new experience. It was awful. It was amazing.

The cold froze its memory into the slave's every tendon, lingering with him like a wintry kiss on the back of his neck. And later there would be pleasure as warmth spread through his belly and chest, culminating in the prickle of reawakened nerve-endings in fingers and toes as Kitaj fucked him from corpse-cold to reanimated but submissive zombie. The contrast of immense pain, so keen and rough, with a love that went beyond death, was almost too much to bear. Hockney wasn't really thinking of pleasure, or anything in particular, for his lips were blue and his mind was heavy and sluggish. He felt drowsy and might well have fallen asleep if it wasn't for the press of the leather collar against his throat, a comforting weight that held the glossy threads of his attention as he slid towards total oblivion.

It took a massive effort on Hockney's part to lift his eyes and look up towards Kitaj, who sat on a stool near the tub monitoring him closely.

"B-Kitaj," he stuttered, his voice thick and stupid with cold, "B-brr."

The pervading chill in his veins chased his thoughts away with the snap of icy teeth. His limbs were lead, sunken like anchors below the surface of the water. He had no feeling in his rigid digits. He forgot what having fingers and toes felt like. It was just how Kitaj liked it. Hockney's head lolled back, peaceful drowsiness pushing down hard on his skull. He was ready to submit to it. He was ready to let it seize him. Hockney wanted to purr with contentment, in satisfaction, in acceptance to the offer of eternal death. His eyes were sliding shut. At that moment Kitaj stood and hooked his arms underneath Hockney's own. He lifted him from the tub with little effort and pulled him against his chest—

back-to-pecs, heel-to-toe. Hockney was as yet unable to feel the warmth of Kitaj's bare skin against his back as he was lifted and cradled against his body.

Kitaj was gentle, his touch as soft and caring as a mother cradling her baby. Hockney twitched feebly, his feet dragging unhelpfully on the thick carpeting as Kitaj carried him to the bed. Hockney was dropped carelessly atop the plush covers and he lay motionless where he'd been dumped, still paralysed by the freezing cold that had locked his joints. Hockney let his mind drift as Kitaj arranged him on the bed. The slave was silent as Kitaj placed his limbs in a display that was pleasing to him. It reminded Hockney of times past when Kitaj had trussed him up and fucked him when his head was slippery and his body was thrumming with drugs. He'd been unable to string together a coherent sentence, let alone fight him.

A wave of gratitude engulfed the sub as Kitaj cut the leather bindings on his wrists and ankles. His mouth cracked open as Kitaj rubbed his hands. The blood was slow to return to his mitts, Hockney could barely feel a thing. The warmth in Kitaj's paws felt like a weak ray of sunlight that struggled to break through a thick bank of clouds. Hockney drew in a tight breath, his lungs still uncooperative, as Kitaj blew a hot puff of air onto his scrotum and up his limp, wet length. A dull heat—only dimly felt—began to swelter beneath the submissive's chest. His breath lagged a little faster and his heart beat a little quicker. The blood dripping through his body felt like molasses. There was a tingle in his nether region. Then Kitaj, his skin hot and sleek with sweat, lay his body flush to Hockney's cold, frozen flesh. The dom pressed a kiss to the slave's blue lips, and then the underside of his damp jaw. Hockney felt a brief, pleasant tingle of warmth where Kitaj's mouth brushed over his skin.

As Hockney began to thaw out, he felt like a parasite leeching the warmth from Kitaj's body. A surge of disgust threatened to rise up and consume the sub, who had to force it away. Hockney always had moments like this when Kitaj forced him to play at pseudo-necrophilia—a game where the slave was rendered cold and incapacitated and lay on the bed like a stiff in a mortuary, while Kitaj fucked the warmth back into his body. He'd protested violently the first time Kitaj had wanted to do this, thoroughly repulsed by the idea of role-playing a corpse. Kitaj, of course, got his way because he was the master and stiffs got him stiff. Eventually Hockney had to admit that if he didn't think about the reasons Kitaj liked this fantasy scene, it was immensely erotic. Depraved, yes, but super-sexy just the same.

Hockney felt the pressure of Kitaj's fingers probing his butthole, coated and slick with lubricant. He let go of his disgust, swallowing it down and burying it way beneath his six pack in his pelvic floor muscles. Kitaj pushed into him with scant preparation since the slave's body was still numb. Hockney scarcely registered Kitaj's thick cock inside him, but he knew later he would be sore. At that moment he barely registered he was engaged in sex. The real knowledge of what was being done to him would come later, after he'd thawed out!

CHAPTER 21

DAVID HOCKNEY TRANSFORMED INTO A YUMMY MUMMY BY THAT MASTER OF THE BULLWHIP R. B. KITAJ!

"Are you engaged tonight, Hockney?" Kitaj demanded of his slave through a glory hole in one of the Republican College of Art's male toilets. Hockney answered in the negative.

"Come to me then," Kitaj went on. "I've got something new for you to try and I don't think we'd get away with doing it in one of the studios here. Although it would be very funny to see what was made of it should someone walk in."

What Hockney experienced that night was complete darkness and silence. There was virtually no stimulation of his senses. His entire world was blacked out, he couldn't see, hear, feel, or smell anything. But stranger than that his heart rate was slow and he was at peace. The sub totally trusted Kitaj. Hockney knew his master would not allow any real harm to come to him, just the pleasure of pain that hurt but wouldn't kill him. That night was their first attempt at total sensory deprivation and it proved to be a groove sensation! The trust between the two art students was total. The dom knew his slave would tell him if he felt too much pain and the sub was secure in the knowledge that if he but said the safety word 'merkin' he would be released with no second thoughts or hesitation. If, on the other hand, Hockney merely muttered 'pubic wigs in England are thought to date from the middle of the fifteenth-century' then Kitaj would know things were getting a bit intense for the sub and if the bottom was lucky would ease up a bit!

Hockney lay covered from head to toe in gauze. His hands were encased in thin gloves, both his arms had been individually bound before being swaddled again to his body. Kitaj had been careful not to cut off any circulation by binding the sub too tightly. Before he mummified the slave's face, the dom had dropped a light kiss on his lips and told the masochist how humbled he was to be trusted so much. Kitaj had gently wiped the tears from Hockney's eyes and covered them with cotton patches before wrapping the postgraduate art student's head with bandages. Hockney found this strange at first but he had gradually settled into that special place in his mind where Kitaj taught him to go to when he thought he could handle no more. The sadist was right. Hockney could take a lot more pain than he had ever dreamt of accepting in the dominance and submission game. The sub felt totally safe and secure knowing he was wrapped in Kitaj's twisted love as well as the gauze.

The masochist felt a faint touch to his arm, or at least thought he did, and he found himself straining to meet it. His skin was devoid of sensation so he figured it was a phantom caress. Hockney had no idea how long he'd been lying still wrapped in the gauze. It could have been only moments or it might have been hours. Suddenly he felt scissors cutting a layer of gauze from his lips. Hockney had been able to breath perfectly well, Kitaj had made sure that the bandage was thin there. Feeling a light puff of wind on his lips raised goose bumps on Hockney. He had no idea his lips were so sensitive! Picasso, Duchamp and Malevich! Something brushed across his smackers and they tingled in response. Hockney pursed his lips. When he stuck his tongue out to lick them, it was gently tapped with a rock hard cock and he knew not to do that again.

Hockney desperately wanted to suck the dick but it was whipped away from him. Instead he soon felt Kitaj's lips on his own chops and the dom's tongue sliding across his mouth gave him a raging hard on! It felt wonderful! He wanted to clench his hands because the feeling was so intense but the sub couldn't as they were so tightly bound. More time went by and Hockney's lips were the only part of him that Kitaj was stimulating.

The next thing Hockney knew—and he had no idea if this was hours or seconds later—was that Kitaj was deploying a pair of scissors to cut around the gauze covering his nipples. Hockney's spine arched up when what felt like a feather brushed across his teats. A low moan escaped from his throat as a sexually-induced release of endophins flooded his body. Kitaj's finger brushed across Hockney's lips as the dom's tongue rubbed his nips. The sub knew he was soaking the gauze around his crotch. What he didn't know was whether he was shooting a wad of liquid DNA or pissing himself! There was so much fluid it was hard to believe it was all come! Hockney knew he wasn't in any serious trouble when Kitaj made some comment about nappies. It was urine for sure!

"K. K. Kitaj!" Hockney gasped. There was a pause and then Hockney said his master's name correctly: "R. B. Kitaj!"

The dom paused for a moment before tapping the slave's mouth twice. That was their signal, if Hockney wanted Kitaj to release him now all he had to do was say the safety word 'merkin'. Hockney didn't even give the signal to ease up. He closed his mouth and the dom knew he could proceed with love torture.

For the longest time, or so it seemed to Hockney, the only feeling he had was of something lightly brushing across his nipples. His entire body trembled with desire. He hadn't known that being swaddled like an Egyptian mummy in more bandages than you'd find in a military first aid kit could be so erotic! A jolt that felt like an electric shock shot through Hockney when nipple clamps were placed on him. The pleasure factor went up tenfold when Kitaj lightly pulled on them. The small moans and cries coming from Hockney's throat pleased the dom. As suddenly as the erotic assault began, it stopped and Hockney was once again left to his lonely thoughts. No matter how hard he tried, the swaddled adult baby couldn't get his body to stop shaking. He knew better than to orgasm without Kitaj's consent but he could have easily shot his load. Before giving it his all, Hockney wouldn't have guessed in a billion years that the sensory deprivation kick was so intense!

Some time later the sub felt the scissors slicing between his legs. Once freed, his lower limbs were then spread apart and tied down. Then the scissors went back to work, exposing his cock to the cool air. The instant that his slick dick was bared, Kitaj bent over and ran his tongue along it, licking the sub's length with two short light strokes. As Hockney screamed, a pleased smile lit up the dom's face. He stepped back and admired the slave's body. Hockney couldn't see Kitaj and as long as the dom moved slowly and soundlessly the mummified perv didn't know where his master was or what he was doing. Hockney was beautiful, his big pink nipples bare to Kitaj's eyes, the boy's mouth open and gasping with pleasure, and his cock all flush and erect. It was a dick that was begging to be sucked or wanked off. Kitaj's heart was full to bursting. He knew what it had taken to get Hockney to this point. He was proud to have taken the sub to the outer limits of sex.

With gentle hands Kitaj picked up the thinly woven silver chain that was connected to the nipple clamps and dangled a cock ring over Hockney's throbbing manhood. The master knew that it was cold. He had wrapped it in an icy cloth for an hour before their erotic ceremony. With each pass of the cock ring Hockney's body jerked in response. When Kitaj judged Hockney could take no more, he attached the cock ring to his slave's thrumming length. He stepped back and watched the pork sword swell even more as it turned a light shade of purple. Kitaj knew Hockney was now so excited that all he had to do was touch his staff and it would make the slave come.

Kitaj amused himself for hours, teasing and gently torturing Hockney as he lay bound and helpless. He knew the sub was fighting off his orgasm with all that he had, his body was one quivering mass of nerves beneath the sadist's magic touch. A mere flick of the lash to the slave's nipples was enough to make him cry out more in pleasure than in pain. Kitaj pulled a ten-foot bullwhip from under the bed. After several practice lashes with it, he turned his attention back on Hockney. He knew that if he wasn't careful he'd end up cutting the sub as well as the gauze.

Kitaj carefully flicked the whip over Hockney's body, cutting the bandages at the slave's shoulder down to the skin. At the touch of the whip the masochist jerked and then froze. Hockney felt like jumping up and doing dances that had yet to be invented—like the frug, the twist, the boogaloo, the Boston monkey and even the uncle willie (which in the mid-1960s would briefly be all the rage on Chicago's southside). Hockney knew that the time of his release had nearly come and he was not to move. The subtle kiss of the whip across the gauze made his nerves jump. Kitaj moved his whip all over Hockney's body until the sub lay bare to his touch, all that is apart from the slave's face, hands and feet. The master coiled his whip and picked up his favourite flogger. Kitaj lightly whacked it across Hockney's exposed skin. He knew that the sub's shell was sensitive and that if he lashed him hard it would cause immense pain.

Kitaj played Hockney's body like a finely tuned instrument, like a Fender Precision bass to be exact, bringing him to the brink of orgasm only to pull back over and over and over again, until the sub simply lay there and cried. These tears brought water to Kitaj's own eyes and the dom decided he'd had enough. Using a pair of scissors he cut the bandages hiding Hockney's face. Next he removed the cotton pads from Hockney's eyes and the plugs from his ears. The slave blinked several times. He adjusted to the low light and then stared up at the dom in wonder. Kitaj was kneeling between Hockney's legs and once the sub met the sadist's gaze, the dom bowed and licked the slave's cock, then raised his head.

"Come for art, young David Hockney!" Kitaj announced. "Come for the young idea! Come for Francis Picabia, Wassily Kandinsky and Piet Mondrian! Come for Giacomo Balla, Umberto Boccioni, Carlo Carrà and Gino Severini! Come for Giorgio de Chirico, Marc Chagall, Jean Arp, Max Ernst and Kurt Schwitters!"

Kitaj then got his mouth around Hockney's pork sword and sucked it deep into his throat. The force of Hockney's orgasm was Kitaj's undoing. The love muscle expanded so greatly and so much liquid spurted from it, that the sadist's breath caught in his throat. Hockney sobbed when he came; the pleasure was so hard and intense that he couldn't speak at all. Once he'd got over his coughs and splutters and caught his breath, Kitaj held Hockney tightly in his arms, their bodies pulsating with shared pleasure. Now it was Hockney's turn to wank Kitaj off. The sadist's orgasm giving Hockney a fresh erection. Kitaj told the sub he was exhausted but gave his slave permission to jerk off.

After Hockney came a second time, Kitaj lay back against Hockney,

"Tonight you gave me the greatest gift a submissive could ever give their master, your total trust and your heart. You have mine as well, my own dear Hockney," Kitja whispered.

CHAPTER 22

A REPUBLICAN COLLEGE OF ART
STUDENT GANG BANG!

And so we should turn again briefly to some of the other men who worked alongside Hockney in the Republican College of Art and who were almost as naughty as our BDSM rapscallion. These young gentlemen (of whom we had a glimpse at the outset, but whose company we have carefully avoided ever since, seeing that their sayings and doings were of a kind of which the less said the better) had been steadily going on in their way, getting more and more idle, reckless and perverted. Their doings had already been so scandalous on several occasions as to call for solemn meetings of the college authorities. No vigorous measures having followed, such deliberations had only made matters worse, and given the men a notion that they could do what they pleased with impunity. On the night I'm about to write about the climax had come. It was as if the flood of misrule had at last broken banks and overflowed the whole college like endorphins filling the body with pleasure during orgasm.

For two hours the wine party in Peter Blake's large ground-floor flat was kept up with a wild, reckless mirth, in tune with the host's temper. Blake was on his mettle. He had invited every man with whom he had a speaking acquaintance, as if he wished to face out at once to the whole world. Many of the men came feeling uncomfortable, and would sooner have stayed away had not the lure of free booze swayed their judgement. But Blake knew how he liked to be treated and if he had a fancy for giving away wine, the civilest thing to do was to take it. And so they went and wondered at the brilliant coolness of their host, speculating and doubting nevertheless in their own secret hearts whether it wasn't acting after all. Acting it was, no doubt. But one must make allowances. No two men take a thing just alike, and very few can sit down quietly when they have lost a fall in life's wrestle.

Blake drank freely and urged his guests to binge, which was a superfluous courtesy for the most part. Many of the men left his digs considerably excited. They had dispersed for an hour or so to billiards, or a stroll in the town, and at ten o'clock reassembled at supper parties, of which there were several that evening. Most notable among them a monster one at Sidney Chanter's rooms—a "champagne supper," as he had carefully and ostentatiously announced on the invitation cards.

This flaunting of champagne was resented by Derek Boshier and others, who drank their champagne in tumblers and clamoured for beer in the middle of the supper. Chanter, whose prodigality in some ways was only exceeded by his general meanness, had lost his temper at this demand and insisted that if they wanted beer, they might pay for it themselves. This protest was treated with uproarious contempt and gallons of ale soon made their appearance in jugs and tankards. The tables were cleared and songs (most of them of more than doubtful character), cigars, and all sorts of compounded drinks from claret cup to egg flip succeeded. The company was getting more and more excited every minute. The relics of supper were cleared away and still the revel went on, till by midnight the men were ripe for any mischief or folly which those among them who retained any brains at all could suggest. The signal for group sex in the form of a gang bang was given by the host's falling from his seat.

Chanter was very drunk but not unconscious. His guests used his fall as an excuse to rip the clothes from his body. The host put up a half-hearted defence and was slapped hard across his face for the effort and slammed down on his back on the floor.

He tried to rise but was backhanded again and fell on the floor. Soon student hands were all over the drunk host like a cheap suit. Insistent, frenzied hands. There was drunken laughter and sneered talk. Chanter clearly heard the words "fuck" and "sweet hole" repeated again and again, always meeting with raucous laughter and menacing furtive whispers. He could tell from the jabberings that his fellow postgraduate students were arguing among themselves, but eventually two of the bigger men who he knew only by appearance and not by name, took ascendance. Four others stationed themselves at Chanter's limbs, holding him down and stretching him out in a sacrificial X. Brandy was being poured over Sidney's body and the biggest of his assailants took a mouthful from the bottle, leered, and dipped his head below Chanter's belly. The man's hand was thrust between his legs and the host felt the stinging wetness of the alcohol being spat into his anus. It was stopped there by clamping lips and a searching tongue. There were other men's lips and teeth all over his body, tonguing and nipping the film of brandy, flesh, and especially his nipples and mouth.

Sidney Chanter had never felt so aroused in his life. The very uncertainty and threat of the situation was exhilarating to him. He was trembling with anticipation.

The other bruiser who was not yet known to Sidney by name was above his head, which was arched up and pushed back into a position where he could straddle over Chanter and push a huge dick into the student's throat. He filled Chanter and started to pump his face just as the largest cock of all thrust into the post-grad's shit-chute, taking his mind off all other points of assault with its fury and filling.

Chanter spat out the monstrous cock filling his mouth just long enough to make a plea, borne not from any fear and noncompliance but from his desire to keep his assaulters' alcohol-drenched sense of completely taking him keenly edged.

"Help, help! He is forcing me. Oh, he is so big. No, no, arghhhh. Please, give me time. Please release me. No, no, you're splitting me! Ahhhhhhhhh. Ohhhhhh. Help! Help me."

The only result of this plea was that fat fingers joined the huge tool working Sidney's anus.

"Oh god, not those too. No, no, not that. Ohhhhhh. Help! Help me."

Chanter was crying for help, driving his assailants to a frenzy. He was sure he could be heard by people in the street. But the only response was that someone turned up the radio on which a woman was wailing a rock and roll song about being done wrong by her man.

Chanter lifted his head as the bruiser who had been face fucking him stopped at a signal to take his turn inside Sidney's arse, and Chanter saw Peter Blake, the painter, standing in the shadows. Chanter cried out to Blake for help, since his role play was to pretend he was an unwilling victim. He knew that Blake was beyond intervening. As the biggest dick pulled out of Sidney the sub was able to focus on Blake, who had his cock out of his trousers and was pulling on it as he watched Chanter being taken by the drunken, keyed-up louts.

Chanter cried out as the second cock was thrust inside him, it pumped rapidly in the spunky lubricant left by the first fucker. There must have been fears that Sidney's cries would attract attention even over the wailing of rock and roll tunes because he was roughly backhanded across the face again, and before he could regain his breath, the end of a Union Jack flag was stuffed in his mouth to gag him.

After the second of the assaulters had unloaded inside Chanter, he was roughly turned on his belly and made to service more drunken postgraduate students, two at a time using his mouth and arse. This was a fucking that left him woozy and made his bumhole look like an abstract expressionist painting! As Chanter was slowly blacking out, the one who took him first started his second fucking. He had his fist buried in Sidney's hair, pulling his head back toward him. The top kept repeating the slogan "fuck art I wanna dance" over and over again. Meanwhile the two men holding Chanter's limbs were tyring to outdo each other with the first shouting out that this was better than fucking Paul Klee, to which the second repsonded it was superior to making it with Joseph Albers. The first then retorted it was a bigger turn on than shagging Joan Miro, and so on and so forth! This exchange ended after about ten minutes of boasting with the second student announcing: "I'm gonna take him right up his André Breton!"

In Chanter's room that night, others who were too drunk to fuck took to doing whatever mischief occurred to them. One man mounted on a chair with a cigar in his mouth unsteadily poured the contents of a champagne bottle into a clock on the mantelpiece. Chanter collected antiques and his clock was extremely valuable.

One or two other art students were morally aiding and abetting by physically supporting the experimenter on clocks, who found it difficult to stand to his work by himself. Another knot of young gentlemen continued to shout out scraps of song, sometimes standing on their chairs and sometimes tumbling off them. A further set were employed on the amiable work of pouring beer and sugar into three new pairs of polished leather dress boots, with coloured tops to them. Certainly, as they remarked, Chanter could have no possible use for so many dress boots at once and it was a pity the beer should be wasted but they were too pissed to drink any more.

Others mustered in the street outside, and began playing leap-frog and larking one another. Amongst these last was our BDSM rapscallion Hockney, who had been at Blake's wine party but had not gone inside Chanter's room as it was so crowded. Hockney lent his hearty aid accordingly to swell the noise and tumult, which was becoming something out of the way even for an RCA student party. As the leap-frog was flagging, Derek Boshier suddenly appeared carrying some silver plates which were used on solemn occasions in the senior tutor's dining room. A rush was made towards him.

"Halloa, here's Boshier with lots of swag," shouted one.

"What are you going to do with it?" cried another.

Boshier paused a moment with the peculiarly sapient look of a tipsy man who has suddenly lost the thread of his ideas.

"Hang it! I forgot," Boshier shouted. "But let's play at quoits with them."

The proposal was received with applause and the game began but Boshier soon left it. He evidently had some notion in his head which would not suffer him to turn to anything else till he had carried it out. He disappeared accordingly and the next day could remember nothing of how well fucked he'd been that night. Seven men had been up his arse and each was a horny handed son of toil who worked for London Transport! But we won't linger on that here because we need to move on to our next chapter and get back to David Hockney's high jinx!

CHAPTER 23

DAVID HOCKNEY'S
NYMPHOMANIAC COUSIN KATE

The end of the academic year was at hand and London was beginning to put on her gayest clothing. In one South Kensington lodging Miss Katie Winter and her cousin Mary Millar were sitting. They had been in London for the greater part of the day, having left Yorkshire early that morning. However they had only just come in, for the younger lady was still in her bonnet and Miss Winter's lay on the table. The windows were wide open and Katie was sitting at one of them, while her cousin was busied in examining the furniture and decorations of their temporary home and pouring out praises of London.

"Isn't it too charming? I never dreamt that any town could be so beautiful. Don't you feel wild about it, Katie?"

"It is the queen of cities, dear. But I know it well so I can't be quite as enthusiastic as you."

The RCA rag happened to pass along by Katie and Mary's lodging bearing the soccer eleven home from a triumphant match.

"Now, boys, keep your eyes open, there must be plenty of lionesses about!" Derek Boshier cried out.

"Look up there at that first floor flat."

"By George they're something, a proper pair of minxes!"

"The sitter for choice."

"No, no, the one standing-up! She looks so saucy!"

"Hello, Hockney, do you know them?" the sub was asked since he was pushing a note into the letter box on the door of their building.

"One of them is my cousin," said Hockney.

"What luck! You'll ask to meet them. When shall it be? Tomorrow at breakfast, I vote."

"I don't know that I shall see anything of them," said Hockney. "I was just leaving a note, but I'm not in the humour to be dancing about lionising. Besides and as you know, I prefer men!"

A storm of indignation arose at this speech. The notion that any of the fraternity who had any hold on lionesses, particularly if they were pretty, should not use it to the utmost for the benefit of the rest, and the glory and honour of the RCA, was revolting to the postgraduate mind. So the whole body forced Hockney through the door of the lodgings when it opened to let a tenant out. His chums impressed upon him the necessity of engaging his lionesses for every hour of every day around the RCA, and left him not till they had heard him head upstairs and speak to the young ladies. They need not have taken so much trouble, for in his secret soul he was no little pleased at the appearance of such creditable nymphomaniacs, more or less belonging to him, and would have found his way to see them quickly and surely enough without any urging. Moreover, he had been really fond of his cousin Katie, years before, when they had been boy and girl together.

So they greeted one another very cordially, and looked one another over as they shook hands, to see what changes time had made. He made his changes rapidly enough at that age and mostly for the better, as the two cousins thought. It was nearly three years since they had met, and then he was an undergraduate at art school and she still in her late-teens. They were both conscious of a strange pleasure in meeting again, mixed with a feeling of shyness and wonder whether they should be able to step back into their old relations.

Mary looked on demurely, really watching them, but ostensibly engaged on rosebud trimming. Presently Miss Winter turned to her.

"I don't think you two ever met before, I must introduce you. My cousin David Hockney, my cousin Mary."

"Then we must be cousins, too," said Hockney holding out his hand.

"No, Katie says not," she answered.

"I don't believe her," Hockney blurted. "But what are you doing tonight and where is uncle?"

"Uncle is dining with an old college friend of his."

"You haven't made any engagements yet, I hope?"

"Indeed we have. I can't tell how many. We came in time for luncheon at The Slade. Mary and I made it our dinner, and we have been seeing sights ever since, and have been asked to go to I don't know how many luncheons and breakfasts."

"What, with a lot of stuffed shirts I suppose?" said Hockney, spitefully. "You won't enjoy London, then. The fuddy duddies will bore you to death."

"There now, Katie, that is just what I was afraid of," joined in Mary. "I drew the fact we didn't hear a word about gang bangs or orgies all the afternoon to your attention. It disturbed me. I suspect those whose invitations we accepted are completely aseuxal."

"You haven't got invitations to any sex parties then?" said Hockney, brightening up.

"No, how shall we get them?"

"Oh, I can manage that, I've no doubt."

What Hockney didn't add was that he'd actually been ordered by his top R. B. Kitaj to send a couple of girls along to a regular sex party run by a straight friend of his master. He'd had Pauline Boty and one her chums in mind but Mary and Kate were an even better prospect.

"Get us invited to as many sex parties as you can!" the two women chanted in unison. "We like rubbing our pussies against the bits of other chicks, but we love fucking guys too!"

"I like doing it with men best!" Hockney confessed.

"Well we're not fag hags!" Katie announced. "So maybe you can find us a regular party to go to, while you do your man thing elsewhere."

Hockney claimed to know of several straight sex parties he had no interest in attending, as well as the passwords to get in. This was half-true. The assertion that he knew about the parties was true, the bit about not wanting to go to them wasn't! A few days later he sent Katie and Mary off to an expensive house near Epping Forest. He didn't tell them that he'd be there too.

"Good evening," said Katie, smiling, when her ring on the bell was answered. "I'm Katie and this is Mary.

My cousin David Hockney asked us to come along to this party."

The geezer nodded. "He told us to expect you but I thought you'd be older. No offence but I trust the two of you have proof of age?"

"No offence taken. It's always nice when someone knocks a few years off our age," purred Katie. "Yes, we both have ID."

After checking the passports the girls proffered, the bloke whistled: "Okay. Come along this way."

He led them through the house and into an extensive yard. More a landscaped park than a yard, thought Mary, looking around.

"If you care to wait here," they were told, "things will begin shortly. Actually, if you stop outside that window over there you can hear the gentlemen being given their instructions. Then you'll know exactly when they're coming out. Are you into any weird fantasies?"

"Oh yes!" the two women replied together.

"So you wouldn't mind a fake rape?"

"Well it's not rape as we're consenting to it, so of course we don't mind!" Katie confirmed.

"In my opinion," Mary added, "the only thing better than a fake rape is a fake rape where you pretend it's real! But there has to be consent otherwise it really would be rape!"

"Well," the man said, "to make it seem a bit more real whoever manages to keep their knickers on until midnight will be paid a thousand pounds."

Watching the man return inside, Katie and Mary looked at each other. Katie shrugged.

"Let's go listen," Katie said. "If the only way a girl can get shagged is to indulge rape fantasies then so be it. Men are so sad and weird! Now I'm not sure if I wanna get fucked or I want the money."

"Let's go for the money!" Mary shot back.

The girls crossed over to the window. It was slightly open and they could hear a low buzz of voices. There appeared to be half a dozen men in the room. They'd only been waiting a minute when there was a tapping sound and the voices died away.

"All right, gentlemen," a voice announced, "Hockney has sent a couple of nice young ladies over so the competition can begin. Tonight we are having a fake rape night. The first man to catch one of the girls has her, but only the first man. To lend some realism to this, the girls have been promised a large sum of cash if they can make it through to midnight without getting caught and screwed.

"The bonus is big enough that the sluts who joined us will do whatever it takes to keep their panties on. We're giving the bitches ten minutes to make themselves scarce and after that, good hunting."

"Katie, we've got to get out of here if we're to make a grand each," said Mary.

"You're fucking telling me," Katie confirmed. "Come on."

The two girls dashed along the side of the house to find a tall gate. Locked. One look was enough to tell them that their chances of climbing it were slim. Back to the other side of the house, where they found a similar situation.

"Why don't we knock on the door and lie we were tricked into coming here by your cousin?" Mooned Mary. "Then after midnight we explain this was a ruse and demand our money?"

"And what if whoever answers the door is taking part and promptly jumps one of us?" replied Katie. "If they do that we won't see a grand each. Let's check if there's a back way out. Maybe we can climb the fence."

The yard they found was very large. It took them several minutes to make their way to the back fence. One look and their hearts sank.

"Who the hell puts barbed wire on their fences?" asked Katie with some bitterness. "Totally uncalled for."

The sound of a banging door and male laughter came floating through the air.

"Katie what do we do?" Mary hissed keeping her voice low. "If they catch us we'll lose out on two grand between us."

"Hide," snapped Katie. "It's our only chance. We can't hope to avoid them by just running and dodging. Pick a spot and stay hidden."

The girls split up and headed for different bushes. Katie, in a fit of ingenuity, chose a small shrub standing in a patch of lawn. Lying down, she curled up in a ball around the trunk, the shadows effectively hiding her from sight. She thought she'd be safe. The bush looked too small for anyone to hide behind.

Mary squeezed between two larger bushes and crouched down. Hopefully no one would see her there.

Footsteps passed close to the two girls and they could see the flash of torches. In Mary's opinion that was cheating but then again, no one had explained the rules of the fake rape game to her before she'd consented to taking part in it.

From where she crouched, Mary could see Katie's little bush. Several times men passed close to it, a couple of them running their torches over it without seeing Katie.

After a while the search drifted away to other parts of the grounds, with much grumbling from some of the men, who had apparently expected an easy catch.

Even knowing where Katie was, Mary couldn't spot her. She gave a sigh of relief. It looked as though they might just get clean away with two grand between them.

R. B. Kitaj had been standing quietly, torch off, listening. He was fairly certain that the paler patch between the bushes was one of the girls, but he'd waited for a little privacy before acting. Now hearing the faint sigh, he smiled and moved forward.

The first indication Mary had that she was not alone was when a hand closed over her mouth and she was pulled out of the bushes.

"I suggest you don't scream," said a quiet voice. "You don't really want the rest of the men coming to watch now do you?"

Mary did but she figured she'd indulge the man who'd caught her with the fake rape fantasy of his choice. Besides, perhaps she could talk her way out of it and still make the money.

"Listen," she said as soon as the hand was removed from her mouth and she was able to speak. "There's been a mistake. I was sent here by the cousin of my friend Katie. He's a raging faggot and was upset we didn't wanna go to one of his male sex parties. He must have done it as a prank."

There was a snort of cynical laughter.

"You didn't know what sort of party this was and just came along because someone suggested it?"

"Yes," gasped Mary. "Honest. We thought it'd be fun."

"The bonus for not getting shafted can't be very large if that's the best you can come up with," was Kitaj's reply.

With that Mary felt her dress being pulled up. She didn't bother struggling coz she wanted the money but she also really wanted to be fucked. Kitaj ruthlessly stripped off her dress and tossed it to the side.

"You want to take the rest off?" he asked. Mary didn't reply. "Prefer me to do it, I guess," Kitaj laughed and Mary's bra and panties were deftly removed before she was pushed down onto the grass.

Kitaj was appalled at the ease with which he was able to handle Mary. He knew she wanted to be balled but she was supposed to pretend she was unwilling. He relaxed his hold on her for a moment, to undo and drop his trousers. But he could have relaxed his hold at any point and she wouldn't have run away.

"Please resist just a little bit!" Kitaj pleaded.

Mary held her legs together to please him, so he slipped his foot between her ankles and gently moved them apart. Why was she acting so willing? Couldn't she pretend to resist him? She should be able to keep her legs together, damn it. Not so it appeared. He eased her legs further apart and she just let him do it.

Then Kitaj was slowly lowering himself onto Mary. She felt his erection pressing against her, then it slid smoothly into her hot creamy slit while he cursed her for not fighting and instead just lying back enjoying it.

This was supposed to be a fake rape, damn it. But Mary just lay there and let Kitaj pleasure her without pleasing him back. She even pushed up to meet him. She wasn't even pretending to be a rape victim since no one being sexually assaulted would do that! Didn't she know how to fake resisting him?

Kitaj, who Mary didn't know from Adam, started driving into her hard and fast. He moved smoothly and Mary found herself following his lead as though they'd done this a thousand times before. Perhaps they had since the people at the sex parties she attended were often masked. She certainly knew what she was doing and she was enjoying every second of it. But Kitaj was disappointed his fake rape fantasies weren't being indulged.

Mary gasped, her body happily meeting the strange cock and taking control of it. When Kitaj pushed into her it sent exciting vibrations racing through her body. He hammered her, going on and on, taking her, pumping her, giving her fun. And Mary went with him, pushing eagerly to meet him, refusing to give him the resistance and scratches all over his body from her nails he so desired.

Kitaj was moving faster now. Mary could feel her heart beating quickly, trying to keep up with the rhythm she was forcing upon a man she otherwise refused to resist. She felt hot and her breaths were rushed. Rational thought had deserted Kitaj, leaving him at the mercy of his instincts and these were all screaming yes, ride her like the big dipper at the fun fair, or better yet like a jockey determined to win the Grand National—even if she refused to indulge his fake rape fantasies!

Kitaj's climax when it came was not a surprise but an immense relief. He imagined he'd have died if he hadn't seen the fucking through to orgasm. As it was, it merely felt like he'd died and risen again on the third day like some mythical god, his fake rape fantasies entirely abandoned.

"What now?" Mary asked when she had finally gathered her wits.

"Now we go inside and wait until your friend gets caught or midnight comes," Kitaj told her.

The time passed interminably slowly.

"It looks like your friend was lucky or skilled," Kitaj informed Mary. "No one has found her. Do you know where she is?"

Mary nodded. "Then why don't we go out there and break the happy news. She scores her bonus." Relieved on Katie's behalf that she at least would see a grand, Mary returned to the yard.

"Katie is under that small bush," Mary said pointing. "You can come out now, Katie. It's gone midnight."

There was a muffled groan and Katie writhed out from under the bush. Soon she was in an upright position, rubbing cramped muscles.

"I saw you get caught, Mary," she muttered. "I'm sorry. It was all my fault."

Mary shrugged. "These things happen. I just want to get out of here. But I did enjoy the shag even if I didn't make any dough!"

Turning to her escort, Mary asked Kitaj if he could show them out.

"Well, I would," he said, "but it appears that I've made a slight mistake with the time. It's still fifteen minutes to midnight. Hello, Katie. I'm very pleased to meet you."

"I can see that from your erection!" Katie snapped. "Let's go inside to fuck, it will be so much more comfortable."

There were two beds in the room Kitaj led the girls into. Our rapscallion David Hockney was already in one stark naked and grinning from ear to ear. Katie got into the other bed. Hockney slid over to his cousin's bearth and started to kiss her as Kitaj had instructed him to do. He was hot and hard, it wasn't long before her T-shirt was gone and Hockney was whispering in her ear how badly he wanted to fuck her.

Kitaj watched the kissing cousins get it on from the shadows in the doorway. Katie wondered whether Mary would observe her and Hockney doing the shag nasty, or if she'd rather just rest on the other bed with her back turned. Just then Katie felt something brush her hand. Before she knew what was happening Mary was in the bed with the two cousins whispering dirty things in both their ears.

The erection which was still pushing between Katie's legs wasn't wasted.

Miss Winter lent in and told Hockney to kiss Miss Millar. At the same time she put her hand in Mary's silky hair and guided her head towards Hockney's face. As soon as they'd finished snogging, Mary lent in to kiss Katie, letting the sub know the girls were going to enjoy each other, not just him.

Mary was soon rolled gently onto her back so that Katie could help Hockney undress her, pulling her satin shorts off while he kissed her breasts and pulled the top over her head. They both gasped at the sight of Mary lying there naked, her full round breasts, her skin as smooth as silk, her pussy neatly shaved with just a thin strip marking out the pleasure hole they now knew they were both going to enjoy.

And then they both turned their attention to Katie. Mary struggled up and got on top of her, kissing her hard, pulling back just far enough for Hockney and Kitaj to see their tongues exploring each other's mouths. Katie felt Hockney pull at the black lace that held her tits in, gently exposing her D cup breasts which now sat right under Mary's. Mary slid to the side so Hockney and Kitaj could see Katie's boobs. Millar was kissing Winter's neck and teasing her nipples with her fingers, as Hockney's tongue found the same place. Then Katie felt Mary's hands take over her slow strip, her last shred of modesty removed as Millar tugged at the lace between her legs before gently pushing them open to show Hockney her pussy.

Mary got Katie's legs all the way apart, making sure Hockney could see what she had exposed for him, as if this throbbing pussy was a gift from her. Katie found it amazingly sexy to be lying there with her shaven pussy completely exposed, being offered to a relative she'd known all her life. Hockney licked Katie's love button and before long she felt a new tongue lapping gently at her clit, fresh fingers pushing slowly into her. Katie looked down and sure enough it was Mary who was now sucking and kissing her for Hockney and Kitaj's viewing pleasure. Hockney was behind and above her, clearly enjoying the sight of Mary giving Katie girl-on-girl action, but at the same time slowly sliding his fingers in and out of her cunt.

Katie's pussy was on fire and she wanted more than slim digits inside her. Gently Katie pulled Mary away from her and sat up, kissing her deeply on the mouth and licking around her lips seductively so she would know she wasn't finished with her. Hockney was rock hard after going down on Katie and watching Mary do the same, while Kitaj was standing in the shadows flogging himself off.

The two girls pushed Hockney onto his back and Katie slid all the way down onto his hard cock. As she began rocking back and forth, taking him ball-deep into her smoothly shaved pussy, Mary knelt with one leg either side of his head and lent forward to kiss Katie, rubbing her nipples at the same time. The view from where Hockney lay must have been incredible.

Hockney stiffened even more as he pumped a load of come deep into Katie, crying out loudly as he did so and sounding for all the world like a cock frantically attempting to outrun a fox in a chicken coup. Mary came up behind Katie and lifted her from Hockney's still-hard member, pulling her down to give Hockney a full view of two soaking wet pussies.

Mary reached down and placed her fingers into Katie's cunt. Winter started to stroke Millar's tits, drawing slow circles around her nipples, both for her own pleasure and that of the three pairs of eyes watching her. Moments later she felt her pussy tighten around Mary's fingers and the world slid out of focus as DNA scrambled and unscrambled itself across the muscular structure of her bulk. Katie really dug the feeling of letting herself disappear completely into the throes of her own orgasm. The fact that Hockney and Kitaj were looking on as she did so made the pleasure even more intense!

Hockney kissed the girls, ending up in a three way snog with all their tongues lapping at each other, and with the taste of Katie's cunt in all their mouths. Katie decided it was time to use Mary's beautiful body to give Hockney and her more pleasure. She pulled the tie Hockney had been wearing from the back of the chair and bound Mary's wrists tightly together above her head, then she kissed her cousin's beautiful round tits.

When Hockney bent over to get a good look at Mary's pussy, Katie knelt underneath him and pulled Mary up onto her knees so they could both slide their tongues down the shaft of his cock, carrying on into an all-girl kiss as they reached the tip. They continued to share Hockney's length until the pre-come dripping from their mouths told them it was time to fight over his erection, and he lay down to fully enjoy the blow job.

The girls greedily sucked Hockney's pork sword one after the other, competing to get closest to the bottom of his shaft. Then Katie left Mary pulling him deep into her throat while she sucked his balls into her gob and began to nibble them, running her tongue around in circles and moaning gently, knowing the vibration would drive him wild.

When Hockney had enjoyed these oral attentions for as long as he could take it, he pushed both girls back onto the bed, laying them out next to each other, legs open, and knelt back to choose a love hole. It was no surprise that he decided to try Mary first, he'd already had Katie once and the other girl's sopping wet beef curtains were still new to his throbbing dick.

Hockney's hand found its way to the back of Katie's head, pushing her towards Mary's slit to prepare her for him, although Millar was already dripping with cunt juice. Katie obliged anyway, since she loved the taste of pussy and was keen to please Hockney and Kitaj. As Mary started to moan under Katie's tongue, Hockney moved his cousin away from Millar's fun hole and took up position between her satin smooth legs.

Katie guided Hockney all the way in and he gasped with pleasure. Hockney was soon pumping his shaft deep into Mary, his cock disappearing into her and reappearing covered in her love juice. He cried out. Even Kitaj could see Hockney's legs trembling as he drove down into Mary again and again.

Then Hockney guided Katie down on top of Mary, face up so she was spread out for his visual pleasure while he was pumping Mary's quim. He pulled out of Millar and thrust quickly into Katie, then after a few strokes inside his cousin he yanked his manhood outta her and drove his cock back inside Mary.

Hockney carried on like that, going from one to the other whenever he felt the urge, keeping both girls on the brink of orgasm. Katie could feel Mary's breasts pushing against her back while Hockney fucked first one and then the other of them. Before long Katie reached down and rubbed Mary's clit until she came again, even harder than the first time. Every inch of Katie's skin tingled as she and her cousin basked in being Hockney's filthy little fuck sluts.

Mary put her still-bound hands on Katie's breasts and began to knead them, holding on tight as Hockney drove her towards release. After a little more shagging she went rigid as the tidal wave of orgasm hit her like a storm tossed sea breaching land defences. Katie turned her head to kiss Mary and the girl came on Hockney's pork sword, her body wracked by a tsunami of spasms.

All of this felt amazing to Hockney and he was putting maximum effort into holding back his own orgasm. As soon as Mary stopped shaking he pulled out of her and made both girls get on their knees, heads together, mouths open. He shot hot wet semen over both their faces, into their open gobs, rubbing it into them as they kissed each other. He wiped his cock on each of their tongues when he was finished. The nympho cousins licked him clean, fighting over his cock one last time, as Kitaj also brought himself off, shooting his load on the floor!

CHAPTER 24

BDSM ALL SUMMER LONG!

Hockney decided being submissive to Kitaj all summer was a more exciting prospect than returning home to Yorkshire. So he stayed in London with his master despite the Republican College of Art being closed for a long holiday. The sex was great with day after day of bondage, spankings and cock sucking. What follows is just one of the more unusual examples of the rumpy-pumpy from that long hot summer!

Kitaj was in a spanking mood when he arrived at Hockney's pad one sunny Sunday. He had a corporal punishment look playing around his eyes, mouth and Adam's apple. As soon as Hockney opened the door there was Kitaj, standing on the other side of the portal with a lusty look of anticipation on his face and a huge bulge wriggling like a glow-worm beneath his tight black trousers.

This was the Kitaj that Hockney had come to adore and respect. If the dom had arrived minus the proverbial bulge, then Hockney would have been concerned that the rubber freak was going soft or suffering from erectile dysfunction, or just possibly had been diagnosed with cancer of the bowel, or some rare tropical disease that no one at the Republican College of Art had ever heard of.

But Kitaj showed all the usual signs of expectancy and it wasn't long before the whip master was freshening himself up by splashing on some really high class eau de toilette labelled as being made in France. In reality the liquid fragrance was made in the east end of London and sold on dodgy market stalls as having been imported from the continent. Once in Hockney's boudoir Kitaj had dressed down and was wearing only his very sexy tight blue briefs, which revealed the raging monster of his throbbing manhood lurking beneath his panties.

Kitaj had everything Hockney wanted and more, a blue veined 8-inch cock beneath those oh so sexy knickers. The sub hoped he was going to receive a good beating before getting his mouth around Kitaj's glorious pork sword. Beneath a thin veneer of civilisation Hockney knew he and all those around him were little different from cavemen—identical really apart from the fact they lived in bedsits, studied art, wore mass-produced clothing, went to the cinema, used public transport, rode bicycles, ate processed foods, &c. &c…

Hockney found spanking incredibly stimulating and if taken to an extreme—as he liked—a tad painful too. As a sex act spanking was decidedly pleasant and fun. Hockney loved the way Kitaj liked to role-play and experiment with fresh forms of perversion. He was already wondering what new sex kick he might be hit with that day. Things didn't pan out quite the way Hockney expected that particular Sunday. Kitaj showed the sub his erect length, presenting it to him in such a way as to indicate that he wanted Hockney to play with it and then suck it dry.

"Here it is, David!" Kitaj said.

Hockney instinctively knelt down between his master's open thighs. Kitaj sat neatly on the edge of an armchair so that his huge bollocks gorgeously slopped over the edge while his lovely length stood up to attention awaiting an excitable tongue. Hockney licked it from the tip downwards and then took Kitaj's balls— one at a time—in his mouth. Eventually Kitaj told Hockney to end the oral stimulation.

"Get down baby on your hands and knees!" Kitaj instructed.

Puffing and panting like Thomas the Tank Engine— as voiced by the hippest and most talented Beatle Ringo Starr—Kitaj drilled his fuck stick right up Hockney's arse, making the sub go limp like a rag doll. And not just like any old rag doll, but like Looby Loo from the kid's TV show *Andy Pandy*. Just before he climaxed, Kitaj unplugged Hockney's butt and drove his shit smeared manhood into the slave's mouth, then pulled it out again, so that the bottom was able to experience Kitaj's hot spunk spurting into his face.

Kitaj then pulled a half-switch on his slave and before you could say "Ringo Starr is an English musician, singer, songwriter and actor who gained worldwide fame as the drummer for the Beatles," the dom had gone down 69-style on his very favourite bondage boy. Hockney's face was already sticky with Kitaj's spunk and before long he was in a sexual frenzy that would have done the Marquis de Sade proud. Hockney felt the tension rise in his groin and seconds later his own honest and warming Yorkshire love juice spurted into Kitaj's open and welcoming gob.

The two men aimed to be as deliberately filthy and polymorphously perverse in their sexual exploits as they could manage. Hockney loved the kinkiness of it all. Kitaj could say what he liked and do what he liked as far as Hockney was concerned, and the top certainly liked to take advantage of this. Hockney was shocked by the tenderness of Kitaj's lips indulging in a heated French kiss before the dom thrillingly spread the bottom's arse cheeks apart so that his master's mouth connected to his unworthy bumhole. For Hockney this was anal sex with a difference, rather than being brutal it was kind and tender! What a shock!

There was no messing, or rather there was plenty of mess up Hockney's shit-chute, but that didn't stop Kitaj going the whole hog and really giving his boyfriend's bumhole a thorough working out with his tongue. For Hockney the day's 'tenderness experience' was simply out of this world. When the sub was with Kitaj all his passion exploded and he became whatever his master wanted him to be. But the rim job was totally blowing Hockney's mind. Surely a master should not be shoving several inches of tongue up a slave's fun-hole! Wasn't that role reversal? But this was exactly what Kitaj was doing and by breaking all the BDSM rules to boot, he was truly turning Hockney on! Hockney knew how to be all arse when Kitaj wanted arse (in fact he was a bit of an arse most of the time), and David also knew how to be all fingers and mouth when Kitaj wanted a deep-throated blow job.

But having turned Hockney's world upside down by doing a switch, Kitaj soon reverted to form and decided that after too much tenderness the bottom needed a bloody good spanking. Kitaj told Hockney he had been thinking about his slave's butt a lot. It was obvious that Hockney had a backside that had been made for punishment, and that Kitaj could make their booty sessions the talk of the London BDSM scene.

Hockney shifted to one side, to give Kitaj access to his arse. The top stroked and lightly scratched both cheeks, then indulged in a little more rimming which Hockney loved, it stirred him up for a good fist fucking later!

Kitaj and Hockney had spoken a lot about how pain and sex can combine to make for a really passionate kink session. Kitaj told Hockney to get on his lap and then push his arse up in the air—making his tail bone rise and arching his spine at the same time. It felt nice and Hockney touched the floor with his hands, his head hanging downwards—almost as if he was performing yoga or perhaps pilates—as he awaited the first slap across his taut buttocks.

After a hard slap, Kitaj paused before hitting his target again. Then the tempo of the beating slowly increased. Hockney's arse tingled and felt very tender as Kitaj carefully spanked one cheek and then the other alternately and occasionally both together—almost as if he was hammering out a rock and roll monster beat. Sometimes Kitaj firmed his slap, at others he was looser and less careful, and this gave a flexibility to his rhythm that could be found in the blues but not in western classical music. Hockney closed his eyes and took each sting of pain across his wonderful booty as a perverse pleasure that turned on both himself and his master Kitaj.

CHAPTER 25

A FIGGING FOR HOCKNEY TEACHES THIS BDSM FREAK THE VALUE OF THINKING WITH HIS DICK!

At the start of their second year Kitaj was doing very well at the Republican College of Art. Hockney wanted to see whether he could make a better fist of the new term at the RCA than he had of the last. He began with a good chance of doing so, for he was thoroughly humbled. The discovery that he was not altogether such a hero as he had fancied himself had dawned upon him very distinctly by the end of his first year as the full depths of his masochism had been revealed. The events of the long vacation had confirmed the impression, and pretty well taken all the conceit out of him for the time being. The impotency of his own will, even when he was bent on doing the right thing, his want of insight and foresight in whatever matter he took in hand, the unruliness of his temper and passions just at the moments when it behooved him to have them most thoroughly in check and under control, were a set of agreeable facts which had been driven well home to him. The results, being even such as we have seen, he did not much repine at, for he felt he had deserved them. There was a sort of grim satisfaction, dreary as the prospect was, in facing the facts, and taking his punishment like a worm. Or at least like a girl since he most enjoyed bondage scenes

243

in which he was made to put on dresses and act like a member of the 'weaker' sex.

Kitaj was so fully occupied with painting and a muscle-building regime that he'd taken up, that Hockney had scruples about demanding much of his spare time in the evenings. Nevertheless, the two men still wanted to enjoy some kinky sex together, and were able to do so both at the RCA and in their rooms. On the first day of term Hockney checked out the new students and had even sucked one of them off in the men's toilet at lunchtime. He hoped Kitaj would hear about this and punish him severely for it. And that was precisely what happened towards the end of that first day back at college.

Hockney stood in the corner of a lecture room, his hands firmly planted on the top of his head, muttering at the injustice of it all. He knew that Kitaj was strict but he was in his early twenties for fuck's sake, a post-graduate art student, and he had been standing with a view of nothing but peeling paintwork for the last forty-five minutes. Hockney heard Kitaj step back into the room and the blinds of the lecture hall fell, leaving only the glow of the lights.

"What did you think you were doing?" Kitaj's voice was harsher than before, Hockney could tell this time he was in for it.

The sub's response came out as a mutter: "Nothing, it was just a bit of fun..."

"Just what? A joke? I'm sure that fresher's orgasm wasn't a sarcastic orgasm, was it?"

"No," Hockney was sulking by this time. He was being spoken to like a child, it had just been guys messing around in the john, a quick blow job, and now he was taking a heavy rap for it.

"No, sir, is how you shall address me, Hockney! I see it is not just your submissive peers you treat with such disrespect but even your master. Come over to the lecture desk."

Hockney walked over to the most imposing piece of furniture in the room. He lowered his arms from his head and gave them a little rub to improve their numbed circulation.

"They tried punishing you with lines when you were at school I presume?" Kitaj snapped.

Hockney rummaged in his bag with one hand, thinking how cruel it was that his position in the corner had made his arms ache.

"And writing lines didn't make an impact on you I see," Kitaj continued as he sat down in a chair behind the lecture desk. "So instead of getting you to write out 'I must not suck fresher cock' a thousand times, I want you to bend over this desk and we will see if I can't beat some discipline into you."

Hockney jerked his head up to look at Kitaj and was shocked to see he was done up like a tranny. Kitaj was wearing make-up and a low cut dress, not to mention a sick but stern kind of smile that made it clear he was on some strict school-mistress trip. Kitaj even had on long false nails that had been painted with purple varnish! The dom hadn't looked anything like this when he'd left the room. It was sick, in anyone else the way Kitaj was done up would have looked like forced feminisation, but the dom was able to carry it off and retain his aura of authority and masculinity. Still being beaten by a top wearing a dress was a new level of humiliation for Hockney.

Hockney took his time bending over the desk, taking in Kitaj's female scent, a perfume he was unable to name. Kitaj stood and walked round the desk and out of Hockney's line of sight. The apprehension the sub felt was nearly unbearable and although it could only have been a few seconds it felt like minutes had passed before Kitaj spoke.

"Hockney, earlier today you seemed to think it amusing to suck some boy's cock without my permission." This was clearly a statement, not a question, so Hockney kept his mouth shut. "I think it is fair that you shall drop your trousers for your caning."

Before Hockney had time to refuse to comply, Kitaj pinned the sub to the desk with one hand. Hockney felt Kitaj's body against his own and a strange sense of arousal came over him as he once again took in his master's feminine scent. Hockney was thinking he shouldn't be turned on by this, a master who has dressed himself up in a frock, plastered make-up over his face and drenched himself in cheap perfume. It was a new low in Hockney's sexual fetishism.

Kitaj practically assaulted Hockney. The sub felt one hand undoing his belt. The dom used a length of rope to tie Hockney's hands to hooks on the other side of the desk, stretching him across the wood and pressing his cock against it. Hockney clenched his legs together determined that Kitaj would not remove his trousers but his master's strength was astounding, probably the result of all the weight training he'd been doing. Hockney's overpants were at his ankles, and Kitaj ordered him to step out of them, his smalls did little to preserve his dignity. Hockney snapped his legs back together, determined that Kitaj wouldn't see through to his cock, which was rock hard. Hockney clenched his butt cheeks tightly in anticipation of the cane.

"I am going to give you eight strokes for your cock sucking antics. You are to count them and if you miss one I will start again. If you try to avoid your punishment by squirming, I will start again. Don't give me a reason to make this worse."

Hockney heard the cane before he felt it. A swoosh through the air then a thwack as it landed on his clenched buttocks. The pain took a few seconds to register in his brain, being felt as a tingle before it became a sting, and by the time the sub fully appreciated its full agony it was nonetheless every bit as bad as he was expecting. Hockney clenched his gluteus muscles to help him control himself and stay still.

"One, sir."

Hockney wasn't ready for the second stroke, he tensed up just as the cane hit. Hockney and Kitaj knew the gluts are a group of four muscles. Three of these muscles make up the buttocks: the gluteus maximus muscle, gluteus medius muscle and gluteus minimus muscle. The fourth and smallest of the muscles is the tensor fasciae latae muscle, which is located anterior and lateral to the rest. Without Hockney even thinking about it all of his gluts had tensed. Even Hockney's hamstrings had contracted.

"Hockney, why are you clenching your buttocks like that? Does the caning hurt too much or are you daydreaming that you are performing squats with a heavy barbell across your shoulders?" The sub wasn't fooled by the mock sympathy in Kitaj's voice and didn't answer. "Do you know what they did to naughty boys who clenched their buttocks during a caning in the ancient world?"

"No, sir."

"Let us have a little history lesson then…"

Hockney felt Kitaj getting up close and personal with him, before pulling down his skidmarked knickers. The slave tried to struggle against his master but it was useless. The top already knew Hockney didn't have the best hygiene habits in the world and was often reduced to boiling his shit and piss stained underpants in a pan to get them clean. When he did this, Hockney always feared a knock on the door from his landlady Mrs Long. She would scream at him and yell that she ran a Christian house in which no man was allowed to boil his underpants on a hot plate since the smell was an affront to the dignity of upright and moral women of all classes.

Just as he tried to hide his underpant boiling activities from Mrs Long, Hockney hoped to hide the fact that he now had a raging hard on from Kitaj. The top's false nails scraped against Hockney's cock as Kitaj pulled the sub's skidmarked underwear down. But the dom didn't mention the state of extreme sexual arousal the slave just happened to be in.

Hockney wobbled as Kitaj pulled one of his ankles towards the leg of the desk and tied them securely together—the operation was then repeated on the other side. Hockney was trussed up like a turkey at Christmas and was hoping he'd end up just as well stuffed. The bottom was unable to move his arms or his legs, but he could still clench his butt cheeks. He heard the clink of Kitaj's high heels on the floor and the door opening but not shutting. He was tied to a desk, naked from the waist down with the door open whilst Kitaj went out for what Hockney wrongly imagined to be a wank in the john.

Hockney had no idea how much time passed before Kitaj returned with what looked like a carved vegetable that had been shaped into a buttplug. The dom stood behind the sub and fondled his butt cheeks, spreading them apart.

"Relax, it will be worse if you don't."

Worse? Hockney wondered what the hell Kitaj was going to do with him. With one hand holding Hockney's arse cheeks apart, the top slipped something cold and wet into the sub's anus. Why was Kitaj doing that, Hockney wondered? Then his bum started tingling and the sub tried to clench his anal rim to stop Kitaj pushing the unknown thing in any further. Despite Hockney's pitiful attempt to struggle against it, the strangely carved vegetable kept going in deeper and deeper. And while this was happening the tingling had progressed into a burning.

"This Hockney is called figging, the tighter you clench, the more it hurts and burns."

"What is it sir?"

"Ginger, four inches of it, freshly cut and shaped for your naughty little bumhole."

Hockney winced as Kitaj stepped back to retrieve his cane. The sub had no choice now but to relax because the more he tightened his gluts and pelvic core the more the ginger burned him. He wondered how much the caning would hurt? Determined to stay relaxed, Hockney awaited the third stroke of his punishment. And it came.

Harder than the last two on his now bare and figged bottom.

"Ahh shit, fuck, oahh, th-three sir." Hockney had been relaxed for the stroke but then clenched on the ginger once he felt the pain of it, getting the worst of all worlds. And yet through it all his cock was throbbing. For a moment sexual desire took over from the agony.

"That was not three, boy, we have to start again and your appalling language has done little to help you. Counting is clearly too difficult for your hormone crazed brain to handle. That's right, I have seen how hard your little dick has got from me punishing you. Let's try it again, eight more strokes."

Kitaj walked around to the desk and shoved Hockney's filthy skidmarked drawers into the sub's gob. The smalls were wet with piss and shit and tasted dirty in Hockney's mouth. Before Hockney could consider using his tongue to push the underwear out of his north and south, they were taped firmly in place and he was instructed to remain silent.

The next three strokes came in quick succession, one after the other on the delicate fold between the leg and the cheek. That is to say he was being whacked on the gluteal sulcus, also known as the gluteal fold, the horizontal gluteal crease, or the fold of the buttocks. It is an area found on the body of both humans and great apes. The gluteal sulcus is formed by the posterior horizontal skin crease of the hip joint and overlying fat, and is not formed by the lower border of gluteus maximus, which crosses the fold obliquely. It is one of the major defining features of the buttocks in both great apes and humans.

But Hockney was not giving much thought to anatomy. The sting of the cane mixed with the burn of the ginger left him in a state of sexual agony. His anticipation of the next stroke forced his buttocks to clench hard around the ginger, intensifying the burning sensation and immediately making him relax in an attempt to dull the pain. Kitaj waited for that moment before he struck. This stroke came firmer than the previous three and was immediately followed by another swift blow.

As the sixth stroke came, Hockney's body thrust forward by the three millimetres available to it. The sub's knob, trapped between his body and the desk, rubbed pleasurably against the tough oak. Hockney let out a low moan despite the shit-smeared gag in his mouth. This cry articulated both pain and sexual arousal. Kitaj heard it and let out a disapproving chuckle. Hockney, meanwhile, thrust his cock against the desk in an attempt to gain some release from that hard and sexy surface.

As the seventh stroke smashed into Hockney's reddened backside, it greatly added to his sense of extreme sexual arousal, and all pain was washed away by the genetic urges coursing through his core. Hockney awaited stroke eight. The sub was unable to see his master but he felt his hand, cold against his burning bumhole, making its way towards the ginger plug. And then the pain intensified. Kitaj was fucking Hockney's arse with the ginger, renewing the sensations that had begun to subside.

Then it finally came! The eighth and last stroke of the cane. It was, in fact, the eleventh stroke—and Hockney's arse burnt and stung as if it had been attacked by a swarm of angry bees who believed their queen to be imprisoned in the sub's guts. The bottom's cock was hard and pressed against the art school desk.

Then Kitaj spoke. "Well done. You coped well with that in the end. Was it really worth making such a fuss over a little corporal punishment?"

Hockney tried to speak, but through the shitty gag his words came out as an incomprehensible murmur. He wasn't going to argue. His love muscle was too hard and his bulk ached for release too much for him to do anything. He simply found himself grateful for the restraints. They kept him from falling to the floor.

"However, I am disappointed at this." As he spoke Kitaj reached underneath Hockney and cruelly prodded his throbbing member. "It seems I have done little to teach you in the long term about the consequences of unauthorised cock sucking. It seems that no matter what I do you are only able to think with your dick..."

After the figging Hockney was convinced that thinking with his dick wasn't such a bad idea—since it opened up so many orgasmic possibilities. He even made a student painting on the theme entitled *Be A Man, Think With Your Dick* but sadly it has been lost to posterity.

CHAPTER 26

NOSE PLAY, FIRE PLAY, ANIMAL PLAY

Hockney sat next to Kitaj on the bed. His hands shook as his body responded to his master even though the dom had yet to touch him. Hockney kept his hands beside him and turned his head towards the floor. He desperately wanted to touch Kitaj's length. However he knew that if he did anything now without his master's permission, he'd pay for it later.

Kitaj could see that Hockney was growing nervous under his glance and laughed at him.

"You should relax a little bit. I'm not going to hurt you just yet. Did you finish your tasks for today, pig?"

"Yes, Master." Hockney took a deep breath and tried to calm himself. His mouth was dry and his palms were sweaty.

"Good." Kitaj stood up. "I would hate to have to punish you before you have a little fun."

Kitaj had instructed Hockney to do several things before his visit. He'd had to bathe himself. Kitaj would be inspecting him later for cleanliness. Hockney had been told to give himself an enema and clean out his arse. When the sub had arrived, Kitaj had instructed him to clean the bath. Hockney had a feeling it might be dirty again before the day's end. He'd been ordered to make himself extra doll-like. As he'd painted his face in the mirror, Hockney thought of what he would look

253

like once his makeup was smeared from trails of tears running down his face.

Kitaj placed his hand under Hockney's chin, raising the slave's face and looking him in the eye.

"You're very pretty today, piggy." Kitaj stroked Hockney's cheeks and ran his fingers through the sub's pigtails. Hockney's instructions had included wearing a wig.

Kitaj bent down and put his arms around Hockney's waist, and pulled the sub up to standing.

"Open your mouth and stick out your tongue."

Kitaj grabbed Hockney by the throat and squeezed, then spat onto Hockney's tongue.

The sub swallowed the phlegm.

"Take off your clothes," Kitaj instructed.

Hockney stood before his master and took off his dress, bra and panties. Then the slave put on his piggy ears and nose, and waited.

"It's time to look you over now, slut. Spread your legs," the dom instructed.

Hockney stood before Kitaj and simultaneously spread his legs and raised his hands over his head. The master looked into Hockney's arse, then carefully inspected his cock and balls, before sticking a finger in his backside. Hockney moaned. The dom pulled his finger out of the sub's sphincter and put it in the sub's mouth to be licked clean. Then he made Hockney turn around and bend over, to show that he was clean and ready.

Hockney was so worked up by this point that it took a huge effort not to grab Kitaj's cock. All Hockney wanted was to have his master inside him, fucking his arse and satiating the hunger he had to be sexually used and abused.

"Now get on your knees like a good pig."

Kitaj put a collar and cuffs on Hockney. The sub was beaming from ear to ear as he let out his first oink of the day.

"Good girl. Now listen because I'm only going to say this once. I don't want to hear a fucking word from you today. If you want to tell me something, figure out a way to do it without words. You will only speak if I ask you to answer a specific question, and you must ask my permission to spunk up. Other than that, I don't want any human-like noises coming from you at all. Do you understand me?"

Hockney nodded and let out a grunt.

"We need to get you warmed up. I like my pig meat nice and soft. I know you're a pain slut and can't wait for me to hurt you. Isn't that right?"

Hockney resisted the urge to say, "Yes, Daddy," and oinked a few times instead. He did not want Kitaj to hurt him. There had been a time when the bondage boy cringed at the term pain slut, he hadn't thought it applied to him. But now that Hockney's ultra-masochism had been released from deep inside him, he couldn't get away from these cravings. The sub could only think of how much he needed to be hurt by his master, and transformed completely into the animal he was. Hockney was a slave to these desires.

"Come over and bend over my knee. Don't wiggle. If it hurts, squeal. If you try to get away from me, you'll regret it."

Hockney hobbled over to Kitaj and desperately tried to focus his attention on anything other than his throbbing erection. All the sub could think about was how desperately he wanted to be bum-fucked by his master.

"Before you service my cock, go to the kitchen and bring me a glass of water. When you get back, grab your big pink plug and bring it to me."

Hockney oinked, anticipating anal action as he set the water down and then grabbed his butt plug and lube.

"This is going up inside your arse in one push and you're going to hold it there the whole time I spank you."

Kitaj lubbed up Hockney's bumhole and then pushed hard and fast. The slave screamed. Then when his arse clenched around the plug, he savored the feeling.

"This won't work if you're wailing like a banshee. You're supposed to be a pig today! You must behave like a porker or I won't be making bacon with you! And if I don't get to sink my sausage between your firm round arse cheeks, I'm going to be very angry."

The master grabbed a gag and pushed it into the sub's mouth. He pulled it tight around the slave's head.

"Bend over," the dom hissed.

Kitaj lightly stroked Hockney's porky arse cheeks, then suddenly hit hard with all the force he could muster. No warm up. It took a lot of effort on Hockney's part not to squirm. The sub was doing his best to oink after every hit. He didn't scream. He oinked and squealed and acted like a pig. With each smack he gasped and closed his eyes, trembling and breathing deeply, knowing he couldn't escape the pain. Every time Hockney was hit his arse clenched tighter around the plug, and the combined sensations of pleasure and pain made him go crazy. As he oinked he was becoming pig.

"Get up, and put yourself down on the bed."

Hockney buried his head in the blankets but from the corner of his eye, he could see Kitaj sipping from a glass of water. When the top was satiated he threw half the fluid on Hockney's red hot arse. The dom grabbed a wooden spoon and hit the masochist harder than before. Hockney had to clench his fists in his efforts to keep still. The wet wood really stung and the slave moaned and resisted the urge to fight the blows. Kitaj redirected his efforts from Hockney's arse to his thighs, focusing on a delightful little spot just under the butt cheeks, Each stroke was harsher than the last, the snap of the spoon and Hockney's cries were the only sound in the room. Kitaj stopped and thrust his hand between Hockney's legs. The slave groaned as the dom's fingers twisted around his cock. The bottom couldn't hide how aroused he was. Kitaj grabbed the plug that sat securely in Hockney's arse and twisted it.

"You are such a pain whore. Thank me for beating your porky ass."

Hockney turned his head and snorted.

"Good piggy. Keep your face buried in the bed." Kitaj hit Hockney over and over until the slave felt dizzy from pain.

"Don't think I'm going to spend all day pleasing you! You're not my only fuck. If you forget that you're in trouble. Look at you all wet and red. Get up now!"

Hockney slowly pulled himself up, his arse hurt as it pressed against the bed. Kitaj grabbed him by his collar and pulled him to his feet.

"You're fucking slow! When I tell you to get up, do it! I don't care if it hurts."

Kitaj put his hands on Hockney's shoulders and pushed him to the ground. The sub fell on his knees and bowed his head.

"A pig's place is on her knees. Don't move until I get back."

Hockney contemplated reaching for the zipper on Kitaj's jeans but didn't want to risk another punishment. Kitaj walked out of the room and, rather than making himself more comfortable, Hockney stayed still and waited. The gag he was wearing made his jaw ache, his arse and back were throbbing too.

Kitaj returned and set a bowl on the table.

"I'm glad to see that you haven't moved. I've brought you something but you're only going to get it if you show me what a good little pig you can be."

Hockney oinked.

"I want you to walk around the room on all fours showing off your porky bits and making all your best piggy noises. Understand?"

Hockney let out a big oink. He was happy to act like a porker!

Kitaj sat while Hockney crawled around the room, oinking, snorting and grunting like a pretty piglet. He waggled his porky ass and jiggled his pig meat. He nuzzled at Kitaj's cock but was pushed away away.

"I didn't say stop, did I?"

Hockney snorted, he wasn't really fat enough to be a pig but neither he nor Kitaj let that get in the way of their fantasy play.

"Good little piglet." Kitaj patted Hockney's head.

Then he bent down and cuffed the sub's wrists and took the gag out of his mouth.

"Piglet, if you want your prize, you're going to have to come and get it."

Kitaj grabbed the bowl and walked out of the room. Hockney followed on all fours.

"Crawl over here."

Hockney's knees hurt as he made his way across the hard floor. His jaw still throbbed from being stretched and the butt plug was still up his arse.

"You're a hungry little bitch and I think you've been good enough to get something to eat."

The dom placed the bowl on the floor and Hockney saw it was filled with oatmeal.

"If you're good, I'll feed you from my hands. For now, eat from the bowl on the floor. Slurp it all up like a good piggy."

Kitaj knew Hockney was hungry for his cock and there was an unspoken understanding between the two men that if the slave ate the oatmeal right he'd get to deep throat his master. Hockney put his mouth to the bowl and snorted as he consumed its contents.

"You're such a messy slut."

Hockney looked up at Kitaj. The top pulled him hard by the hair and slapped his face.

"Just because I'm talking to you, it doesn't mean you can stop eating!"

Hockney bent his head back down to the bowl and chowed on the oatmeal.

"Good piggy. Lick the bowl clean and I might feed you something else."

Hockney bolted down what was left, oinking and snorting at the same time. Before long his face was plastered with food.

"Follow me back to the other room."

Hockney's wrists were still cuffed together as he crawled behind his master.

"I know you're still starving. Show me how hungry you are, swine."

Hockney clawed at Kitaj's crotch and pulled out his master's cock.

"You can suckle on this like the little pig you are, but don't move your mouth. Just suckle."

Hockney did as he was told. He wanted to deep throat Kitaj but resisted the urge. He kept his neck still until Kitaj put his hands on the pig's head and pulled it up until the dom's dick was buried in the sub's mouth. The slave let out a happy snort.

"Show me you are a cock sucking whore."

Hockney slid the dick out of his mouth and grabbed it with his hands.

"I'm your shameless cock sucking slut, Kitaj."

Without a second's hesitation, the master struck the slave across the face with an open hand. Hockney's cheek throbbed but he obediently swallowed Kitaj's length again.

"Are you stupid?" Kitaj yelled. "You're acting like a dumb whore. You can't obey the simplest of orders. I told you not to speak. You don't even deserve my time but today you're lucky that I need a hole to service my cock."

Hockney pumped his porky head up and down, loving the taste. He was gagging and grunting.

Kitaj bent down and squeezed Hockney's nipples HARD. The slave let out a yelp but carried right on sucking. The sub fought through the pain and didn't let up with the deep throating until the dom pulled his dick out of his mouth and pushed him down on the floor.

"Get on all fours and stay there."

Kitaj reached forward, grabbed Hockney's hair and pulled his head backwards. Then he tied a bandana around the sub's eyes. The slave whimpered. Next the gag was forced back in his mouth.

"Don't move."

Kitaj walked around Hockney and yanked the buttplug out of his arse. The sub screamed through the gag and collapsed forward.

"Bad shit happens to nasty pig sluts that disobey orders. You're getting arse fucked now!"

Hockney felt lube being rubbed into his bum. This was followed by Kitaj pushing a big dildo into the slave's arse. The sub screamed through the gag once again.

"Squeal like a pig if you wanna me to fuck your arse."

Hockney squealed as best as he could with a gag in his mouth. Next he felt Kitaj's cock push into his bumhole. It felt so good Hockney thought it might kill him if he didn't come, and he simultaneously realised that with the gag in his mouth he couldn't ask for permission. As the arse fucking proceeded his g-spot was hit time and again and he felt himself inching up towards orgasm.

He tried to push the gag out of his mouth. It was too big and too tight to dislodge. The sensations were all too much. Hockney oinked frantically.

"What's that slut? Are you asking to come?"

Hockney oinked three times. Kitaj pulled out of his bumhole as the slave was about to orgasm. The sub screamed because ecstasy had been snatched from him. Kitaj was laughing at him.

"You really are a dumb bitch. If you come, you're not getting near this cock again. You have to learn how to wait you fucking whore. Get up."

Kitaj grabbed Hockney by his dog collar and threw him on the bed. The next thing the slave felt was a cane thwacking against the back of his thighs. He squealed. The strokes rained down against his arse and thighs, they seemed to get harder. Hockney's bum felt like it was on fire and he'd been stung by a thousand hornets. He wriggled, Kitaj pushed his hand into the sub's back to hold him down.

"Don't fucking move."

Kitaj got on top of Hockney, sat on his arse and punched his back. The sub buried his head in the sheets and screamed into his gag. Kitaj stopped briefly to take the slave's gag off. The pain in Hockney's jaw felt worse when he tried to close his mouth.

"Go ahead and scream."

Kitaj punched Hockney repeatedly between his shoulders. He got up and the punishment shifted from spanks to caning and back to punching. Hockney oinked after each hit and tried to be a perfect pain pig by staying still. Eventually Kitaj got up and stood over his victim.

"You took that well pig. But don't think I'm done with you. I know you're hurting but get down on the floor."

Hockney threw himself down despite the lingering pain that almost incapacitated him. The slave crawled to his master's feet and awaited the next order.

"I know you've suffered a lot of pain today, pig. I also know that you're gagging for me to fuck you. I'm going to make you beg for sex. Now get up. Put yourself in the bathtub. Be on your knees when I get there."

Hockney did as he was told. When Kitaj walked in he began to shake. The dom stepped in the tub.

"I know you want my dick. I'm only going to give this to you if you show me you really want it. You're allowed to fight for it now."

Kitaj placed both his hands on Hockney's shoulders. The slave tried to reach forward with his head but his master was stronger. The sub's desire made him angry, he hated not getting the meat in his mouth. After a struggle, Kitaj uncuffed the slave and positioned himself to fuck the sub's throat. Hockney braced himself against the base of the tub as Kitaj thrusted the full length of his cock into his gullett. The dom tilted the sub's head so that he could get his length all the way down. Hockney couldn't breathe. Kitaj face fucked his grinding partner, and when he pulled out made the sub lick his balls. He repeatedly slapped Hockney's face and held him by his hair as he pushed back into his mush. After the deepest thrust, Hockney vomited on Kitaj's cock and ended up covered in the spew too. He was choking and yet the only thing on his mind was more cock and more punishment. Kitaj got out of the bath and Hockney started crying.

"Stay there, don't fucking move. Keep your mouth open. Don't even think about cleaning yourself up. You'll wallow in your own shit."

Standing at the edge of the tub, Kitaj started pissing. The urine splashed all over Hockney until his master got a firm aim into the slave's open mouth. The dom sat on the toilet and looked at the slave. Hockney oinked.

"You're a fucking animal with a one-track mind. Now clean yourself up. I'll wait for you in the living room."

Once Hockney was clean, Kitaj put his hands on his shoulders and stroked them, then he pushed the sub so hard he fell flat on his face.

"You know what, Hockney?" Kitaj said rhetorically, "you've been having too much BDSM fun and your work is suffering. I'm not going to give you another beating until you've made 100 new paintings. So I doubt you're going to have sex again this term!"

CHAPTER 27

DESPERATE FOR COCK,
HUNGRY FOR FAME

Kitaj simply refused to indulge Hockney with BDSM sessions until the slave produced more art. Suffering from not suffering, Hockney poured all of this suffering and non-suffering into his painting. He was burning the candle at both ends, getting up early and staying late into the night at his RCA studio. He was producing pictures at a prodigious rate and while he might have satiated his desire for dick by deep-throating men he encountered in public toilets, his was a muscular masochism and he would endure the pain of no pain until Kitaj finally consented to give him a beating.

One evening Peter Blake wanted to drag Hockney from his studio, he hoped to take him to a party. He insisted a break from making art would be good for him and his painting would be even better if he returned to it refreshed.

"You know the press are interested in us as something new, as representing pop. But I think there's too much expressionism in what you do. I can still see the influence of Francis Bacon in your pictures, slowly that's disappearing but it's still there!" Blake offered.

"If I still need to overcome my influences then I should stay here and work on that. I promised Kitaj I'd make 100 painting before Christmas and I'm going to stick at that."

"The party will do you good and a break from painting will better enable you to move forward with your art."

"But I said I'd do no socialising until I'd completed that task Kitaj set me."

"So you did. But you can change your mind. What's the good of having a mind if you can't change it?"

"People will laugh and sneer at me if I go to a party when I've only completed 69 paintings out of 100."

"They'll laugh at you twice as much if you don't. Fancy they're just beginning pool now, on that stunning table. Come along, Hockney, don't miss your chance. We shall be sure to divide the pools, as we've missed the claret. Cool hands and cool heads, you know. A bit of fun will do you more good than squinting at a damp canvas all night."

"Very likely."

"But you won't? Do be reasonable. Will you come if I stop with you another half-hour?"

"No."

"An hour then? Say till ten o'clock?"

"If I went at all I would go at once."

"Then you won't come?"

"No."

"I'll bet you a sovereign you don't even complete one picture that shows no trace of your influences if you don't take a break, and then how sad you will be at Christmas! It will be much worse failing to make a breakthrough with your painting because you didn't take a break when you needed one."

"I shan't go to a party until I've completed 100 paintings."

Hockney's interlocutor put his hands in the pockets of his heather mixture shooting coat, and took a turn or two, pacing backwards and forwards around the canvas our rapscallion was working on. He didn't like going in and facing the pool players by himself, so he stopped once more and reopened the conversation.

"What do you think you'll achieve by painting all night, Hockney?"

"I'll show Kitaj and all those fellows at the party that I mean what I say. I said I wouldn't socialise until I'd competed 100 canvases and I won't."

"You don't want to overcome your influences then?"

"I don't much care. I just want to paint 100 pictures this term and if I keep on painting eventually I'll leave art history and the art world trailing in my wake. One day I'll achieve the highest ever sale price for a living artist. You'll see."

"I say, Hockney, I like that. For someone whose painting is about 5 years behind mine you have a very high opinion of yourself. I'm trying to help you but I'm not going to turn my head and gaze back, on the lookout for you and Boshier and some other fellows trailing behind me."

"I admit that right now I'm behind you but you're not going to have to look back. You'll see me in front of you before long!"

"You ought to have more fellow-feeling. I suppose you go on the principle of art being 99% persperation and 1% inspiration?"

Hockney made no answer and his companion went on.

"Come along like a good fellow. If you'll come in now we can come out again in an hour all fresh and do better painting."

"Not we. I'm not going. But you can come out again if you like. You'll find me here in my studio."

The man in the heather mixture had now shot his last bolt and took himself off to the party, leaving Hockney by his canvas. November was over and Hockney carried on in this way through the first half of December. Kitaj visited Hockney in his studio on the last day of term, after which the college would be locked up for the holidays. Hockney was working on his final painting. Canvas 99 was barely dry but it was a triumph!

"By Sacher-Masoch!" Kitaj exclaimed. "Hockney you've done it. Your penultimate picture shows no influence of the past. You've created a new way forward in art. By Restif de la Bretone I'm going to reward you for this!

CHAPTER 28

THE MATTER OF BRITAIN

On the evening Hockney completed his hundredth painting there was a sex party at 13 Hyde Park Square. It was the start of the holiday season and celebrations of all kinds were going on across Great Babylon, but the entertainment in question was the event of that evening, as well as evidence that select parts of London were already swinging in the early sixties. If you'd talked to a hipster in the previous ten days you'd have been told that 13 Hyde Park Square was where all the groovers would swing on this particular night. If you did not happen to be going there, you had better stay quietly at your club, or your home, and admit you were as plain as vanilla. Later some called it the Man in the Mask party and others The Feast of the Peacocks.

A great awning had sprung up in the course of the day over the pavement in front of the door. Then came the lighting up of the rooms and the blaze of pure white light spread into the street until the curtains were drawn. Musicians passed in with their instruments. Then the intimate friends, who came early at the hostess's express command, began to arrive. Mariella Novotny threw the orgy in her husband's London flat. There may have been a porter at the door but that was because this was an apartment block, the shindig was in Hob's basement pad. Novotny had been Stella Marie Capes a topless dancer at The Windmill until at the age of 17, she married a man nearly 40 years older than she was and who put out the appearance of being wealthier than he was. Now she was 21 and her husband Horace Dibben at 60 could almost claim to be the oldest swinger in town. Among his many business interests, Hob had a club in Mayfair's Shepherd Market that attracted the likes of the Kray Twins, Lord Astor and The Duke of Kent. Through her other half, Novotny met entertainment impresario and Soviet agent Harry Alan Towers. Hob made money selling any state secret he could glean through his social contacts, so it wasn't surprising he was in cahoots with Towers.

Novotny and Towers soon became lovers and with Hob's blessing off they went to New York, where the man who would marry Eurocult star Maria Rohm in 1964 and work alongside legendary Spanish director Jess Franco, pimped his married lover out to the likes of JFK. Alongside sex film star Suzy Chang, Novotny had played nurse to the president-elect's horny patient in a three-way sex game. The American establishment was not amused and although Novotny and Towers were only charged with running a vice ring, the FBI understood this to be a front for Cold War espionage. Partially protected by the fact they'd compromised JFK, rather than being clapped in jail, Towers was allowed to skip bail and return to Europe. Novotny, being a minor according to American law, got back to London even faster, where she was able to tell the press she was the niece of the hardline Stalinist President of Czechoslovakia Antonín Josef Novotný. The FBI and others in the USA power elite really did not want it to get out that when JFK had made the beast with two backs with Novotny, she'd been fucking for Soviet-style state capitalism and authoritarianism.

There were 24 people invited to dine at 13 Hyde Park Square but more present, mostly women. The evening had started with drinks and card playing. The winner of each hand got to disappear into the master bedroom with a girl. Hockney tried his hardest to make sure he lost and was admirably successful in this. The post-grad was now seated at table. The emphasis was on so called 'characters' and fine food served over eight courses, with a different wine for each. Hockney was tricked out as Helen of Troy in a gown of gold that revealed all of his back and left little to the imagination on the other side since his dress was short and he wasn't wearing panties. Another man-woman was pimped up as Juno in a silver mask. There was a man masquerading as the last head of the Knights Templar Jacques de Molay, with a large red cross over his chest. His companion was a crippled looking elderly lord encased in silk and wearing a turban held together with a ruby broach. Like Novotny, these two men were well aware that Jacques de Molay had been burned at the stake after being found guilty of worshiping Satan in the form of Baphomet, a corruption of the name of Prophet Muhammad. The man in silks carried a sultan's magic wand made from a dildo and topped with a crescent moon cut from card. Novotny was naked but held a pair of handled spectacles in her right hand.

There were girls in blackface and grass skirts who were present for the benefit of the straight men, but they weren't to sit at table. Hod had on a pea green hussar's jacket and a pair of pink women's tights. Derek Boshier came as a Viking in a bronze helmet with horns. Other couples were wearing evening clothes, their identities concealed by sequined masks. Aside from our artist friends, those present were showbiz celebrities, diplomats, lawyers and politicians. Tethered between two pillars and naked except for a masonic apron and a leather mask was the son of former prime minister Anthony Asquith. There was a whip placed before the man in the mask and every guest—including Hockney—was expected to flog him upon arrival at the party.

As Hockney was seated, Asquith Junior was released and ordered under the table. There were twelve guests down each row with the hosts at either end. Asquith was ordered to sit at Novotny's feet, from where she slipped a dog collar around his neck and held the lead. There were two bowls on the floor by her chair, one filled with water and the other dog food which Asquith was expected to eat. After starters came the main course. Novotny had prepared two young peafowls, a male and a female, which she'd skewered in place and decorated with feathers from an older masculine bird. Hockney and many other men present were crossdressing, so the youthful peahen they ate served to swing things the other way. Novotny told everyone they were attending 'the feast of the peacocks'. A 19 year-old dressed as Joan of Arc cried out that the peacock symbolised death. The teenager was told to pull herself together and provided with a choice, either gangbang all the men present or go home. She decided to go home.

To revive the spoilt atmosphere, Novotny ordered Asquith to crawl along to Hockney and give him a blow job. The spectacle of the young art student getting his jollies was met with much laughter and warm applause.

Stephen Ward was particularly effusive and so his host asked him if he'd like some oral action too. Ward quietly explained that he did some spying work for MI5 and while his bosses there didn't mind him attending sex parties with participants who swung both ways, they might look as askance at homosexual activity on his own part since it was a criminal offence.

"Do you tell your security friends all the details of any gay sex you witness?' Hob asked.

"Of course," Ward replied, "they need to know about that sort of thing so they can blackmail the culprit into doing some dirty work for British intelligence. MI5 consider knowledge of this sort terribly useful, they want all the details."

"Do you know what's in my file?" Novotny enquired.

"Sheffield," Ward replied.

"Of course," his hostess laughed, "I'm made of steel."

At this point Hockney made a faux pas, he sprinkled his food with salt rather than place some on the side of his plate.

"Good God, Hockney," Hod boomed, "you're acting like a working-class barbarian! Haven't you learned any social graces since you arrived in London?"

"Don't worry," Boshier put in, "I'm going to take him home now and punish him."

"There's no need," Hod said. "Flog him later, let's finish the meal and have an orgy before you leave!"

"I am his master and I must beat him immediately!" Boshier insisted.

In fact, Hockney had been instructed to sprinkle salt on his food in this way when it was time for them to leave, Del-Boy could then insist on taking him home for punishment. It was a cunning ploy on Boshier's part to get them out of Novotny's bargain-basement-sex-party-cum-dangerous-occult-rite once they'd caught and internalised the vibe. Let's not forget this was but sixteen years after the end of WWII and many of the staff at the RCA were ex-military men who maintained their links to the armed forces. Ward might have connections to MI5, as well as the Russians to whom he sold compromising pictures of politically influential guests at sex parties, but at the behest of one of their tutors with some serious war connections, Hockney and Boshier were on a mission for British Military Intelligence. M15 and M16 be damned, everyone above a certain rank in the forces knew they were riddled with Soviet moles!

Hockney and Boshier didn't go home, they went upstairs to the flat above Novotny's. The owner had been persuaded to vacate it for a dinner date with a young actress he lusted after called Fenella Fielding, she lived at number 15 in the same street. He'd only agreed after being reassured that her flatmate Albert Finney was treading the boards that night and that they'd get to eat in candlelight.

Hockney and Boshier knew that between them and a dozen well muscled young soldiers the fate of Britain hung in the balance. Novotny's feast of the peacocks was merely the prelude to a Satanic ritual in which a cone of power would be raised and then directed right into the heart of the British establishment. In the upstairs flat, an army hypnotist Major Edwards, who was an expert in psychic warfare, put Hockney into a trance. Hockney was then stripped naked and taken into the bedroom where twelve very well hung squaddies awaited him.

While Hockney enjoyed being gangbanged, in his mesmerised state as one cock after another plunged into his arse he drew the cone of power being generated beneath him into his anus. His earlier attendance at that soon to be notorious sex party had created a sympathetic bond between his backside and its participants. Many of Novotny's guests had little idea of what they were doing as she tricked them into conjuring up a deadly and hostile occult current of Soviet authoritarianism directed at the heart of the British establishment. Novotny's guests thought they were playing sex games, they didn't realise they were performing sex magic. What Novotny didn't know was that rather than going where she directed it, the malevolent force she'd created was being sucked directly into Hockney's sphincter!

"Quick," Major Edward's barked as Hockney's breathing became irregular, "he's absorbed the entire Satanic force magicked up by the Soviets! Get him on the toilet and make sure one of you is standing by to flush the second he shits it out!"

To get to the sewers the turd radiating the evil Satanic force had to pass through basement pipes, and as it did so those down there were exposed to its putrid might. Five of the men present, including Stephen Ward, would die within a very short time. Not even Novotny who thought she could control the current that had been absorbed by Hockney's shit would live to old age. Twenty years later she would get up in the middle of the night after swallowing a heavy dose of sleeping pills, grab a plate of jelly from her fridge, fall asleep again and drown in this midnight snack.

As always, Mandy Rice-Davies and Christine Keeler arrived late. They were lucky because by this time

Hockney's evil ordure was well on its way to a sewage treatment plant. Stephen Ward answered the door wearing nothing more than a smile and one sock. Most of the guests were naked. Novotny had six men in bed with her, two of whom got whipped for failing to perform cunnilingus enthusiastically enough. Ward was already in disgrace because during her ritual Novotny had caught him sniffing the shoes in her bedroom cupboard with one of her dirty socks stuffed in his mouth. Knowing nothing of Hockney's role in saving the British establishment, Novotny came to blame Ward for the failure of her occult shenanigans. To get her own back because as soon as it was completed she realised the rite had been a flop, Novotny put on a pair of ultra-high heels and stood on Ward's crotch.

Keeler watched in fascination as Novotny made half a dozen men pleasure her. Rice-Davies found a plate of tangerines and consumed the lot, then she stuffed chocolates in her mouth until she felt sick. Hockney, meanwhile, was rushed in a military ambulance to an army hospital on the outskirts of London, where he was given colonic irrigation. In the space of a few days he made an excellent recovery and was soon back home in his student digs. The disposal of the water from Hockney's colonic irrigation had to be carefully handled. It was dropped on a field just outside Prague, where it did a lot of damage to Czechoslovakia's authoritarian government.

CHAPTER 29

HOCKNEY THE BROWNSHIRT

Hockney's few days in hospital had brought him into closer contact with some military men, who in their turn introduced him to those RCA students whose politics were to their taste. In particular they recommended the company of one Jonathan Bowden. Thus Hockney came into more intimate relations with a set of whom he had, as yet, seen little. For want of a better name we may call them "fascists." There were few practical jokes at their parties and little boisterous mirth, or talk of canvases and sculptures and BDSM. Instead patriotism, racial purity and metaphysics were discussed and ranted over with an enthusiasm that would utterly bore those who are not unreconstructed neo-nazi fanatics.

With this set Hockney fraternised and drank in many new ideas. As a result he took up many new crotchets besides those with which he was already weighted down. All his new acquaintances were far-Right in their politics, but only a few were ready to go the full length with him. They were the Hitler boys and Hockney, of course, followed the fashion and soon propounded theories that at the RCA gained him the name of Brownshirt Hockney.

There was a strong mixture of self-conceit in it all. He had the notion that he had discovered something which it was creditable to know and that it was a very fine thing to have all these feelings for, and sympathies with, "your country," and to believe in dictatorship, and "racial pride," and "saving the British nation," and I know not what other absurd matters. It startled and pained him at first to hear himself called ugly names, which he had hated and despised from his youth up, and to know that many of his old acquaintances looked upon him not simply as a madman but as a madman with nasty proclivities. Yet when the first plunge was over there was a good deal on the other hand which tickled his vanity and was far from being unpleasant.

The disagreeables were such that had there not been some genuine belief at the bottom of it, he would certainly have headed back very speedily into the fold of political and social orthodoxy. However, amidst the cloud of sophisms, platitudes and half-mastered one-sided ideas which filled his head and overflowed into his talk, there was growing in him a true and broad sympathy for the English as English. He especially saw Yorkshire men as English as opposed to soft southerners. He developed a righteous and burning hatred against all notions which according to him seemed to be setting aside or putting anything else in the place of his England. It was with him the natural outgrowth of the child's training and the instincts of those early days were now getting rapidly set into habits and faiths, and becoming a part of himself.

In this stage of his college life, as in so many former ones, Hockney got great help from his intercourse with Kitaj, who became increasingly concerned at his friend's slide into anti-Semitism. Kitaj was travelling much the same road of self-discovery himself as our rapscallion but was somewhat further on, having come into it from a different country and through quite other obstacles. Their early lives had been very different and both by nature and from long and severe self-restraint and discipline, Kitaj was much the less impetuous and demonstrative of the two. Therefore he did not rush out the moment he had seized hold of the end of a new idea that he felt to be good for him and tell the world about it. Kitaj, on the contrary, would test his new ideas, turn them over and prove them as far as he could, and try to get hold of the whole of them, and ruthlessly strip off any tinsel or rose-pink sentiment with which they might happen to be mixed up.

Hockney often suffered under Kitaj's severe critical methods and rebelled against them. He'd accuse his friend of coldness, want of faith and all manner of other sins of omission and commission—the worst being that he wasn't English, which he wasn't. In the end Hockney generally came round, with more or less resentment depending on the severity of the argument, to acknowledge that when Kitaj brought him down from riding the high horse, it was not without good reason. The dust in which the American was rolled was a most wholesome dust.

For instance, there was no phrase more frequently in the mouths of the party of RCA fascists than "patriotism." It was a fine big-sounding phrase which could be used with great effect in perorations of speeches at the student union, and was sufficiently indefinite to be easily defended from ordinary attacks, while it saved those who used it the trouble of ascertaining accurately for themselves, or settling for their listeners, what it really meant. But however satisfactory it might be before promiscuous audiences and so long as vehement assertion or declaration was all that was required to uphold it, this same "patriotism" was liable to come to much grief when attempts were made to define it. Kitaj was particularly given to persecution on this subject when he could get Hockney and one or two others in a quiet room by themselves. While professing the utmost sympathy for "patriotism" and a hope as strong as theirs that all England's enemies might find themselves suspended by their necks from lamp-posts as soon as possible, he would pursue it into corners from which escape was most difficult, asking it and its supporters what exactly England was and who were its enemies? He'd drive them from one cloudland to another, and from "patriotism" to fascist authoritarianism, the holocaust and other troublesome historical facts, until the great idea seemed to have no shape or existence any longer even in their own brains.

But Kitaj's persecution, provoking as it was, never succeeded in fully undermining the convictions in the minds of his juniors, it only helped them to clear their ideas and brains as to what they were talking and thinking about, and gave them glimpses—soon clouded over again, but most useful, nevertheless—of the truth. There were a good many knotty questions to be solved before a man could be quite sure that he had found out how to set the world thoroughly to rights, and heal all the ills that 'Aryan' blood is heir to.

After hearing about the glories of fascism from Hockney one time too often, Kitaj cunningly lured the sub to his digs on the pretence of talking over the prospects of overthrowing democracy and then, having seated him by the radiator, propounded suddenly to him the question:

"Hockney, I should like to know what you mean by ignoring the bidding of your master?"

Hockney at once saw the trap into which he had fallen but made no effort to break away.

"I try to be a good slave," Hockney replied. "You take care of me and treat me well, you only use cruelty for sexual kicks. The biggest rule I have broken is that when I go out I do not flirt with other men. I am meant for you alone and will not fuck anyone else unless you directly order me to do so."

Kitaj did not say anything but his strong jaw was tensed more than Hockney had ever seen it tightened and that meant he was pissed off and the slave was in for it. When Hockney reflected on the matter he could see why. Kitaj had not ordered him to save the British establishment by letting a bunch of squaddies gang bang him in an occult ritual. On top of that Kitaj's Jewish roots meant he had good reason to have given Hockney's flirtation with neo-nazism short shift.

"Strip," Kitaj commanded.

"Yes, Master," Hockney replied.

"Strip and hand me each piece of clothing. You'll be allowed to dress once I am satisfied you have learned your lesson."

Hockney pulled off his jumper first and handed it over. Kitaj reached into a drawer and pulled out several zip up bags. He put the top inside one of them and shut it, impatiently gesturing for Hockney to keep going. The slave shimmied out of his shirt, trousers, panties, all of which Kitaj put into separate bags. Each of Hockney's socks was put in a different bag too. Once Hockney was standing naked before his master, Kitaj picked up all the bags containing his garments and put them in a cabinet, then locked its door and put the key in his pocket. He reached into a drawer and produced a black, silk blindfold. Hockney turned around and Kitaj put the blindfold over his eyes.

"Go through to the bedroom," the dom ordered.

Hockney moved tentatively forward, trying not to trip or crash into anything. Kitaj gave him a big shove, slamming the slave into a wall.

"I don't have all fucking night," Kitaj hissed into Hockney's ear.

"I'm sorry, master," Hockney apologised.

The slave walked forward at a clip so as not to anger Kitaj any further. Then his ankle caught the leg of a table and he crashed to the ground. The slave positioned himself on his hands and knees to get back up, but felt his master's foot on his back, pushing him down to the floor.

"I want you to crawl, you clumsy whore."

"Yes, master."

Eventually the slave made it to the bedroom. His tormentor was right behind him. Kitaj told Hockney to lie on the bed, with his legs spread like the slut he clearly was. Hockney could hear the sounds of Kitaj rifling around in his night table drawers, eventually there was the clanking of handcuffs. Kitaj grabbed Hockney's right wrist and clamped cold metal tightly around it. He attached the other part of the cuff to the bedpost and then did the same to the slave's other arm with a second pair of handcuffs. Next Hockney felt the rubbery taste of a ball gag in his mouth. Kitaj fastened it tightly. The slave heard his master leave the room. He lay in fear and anticipation of what would come next.

It seemed like Kitaj was gone for hours. Hockney tried to stay awake but failed to do so. A loud, sharp sound jolted him back to consciousness.

Hockney heard another smack. It was the sound of a paddle being beaten against the doorframe. Kitaj walked over to him. The sub felt the cool leather of the paddle tickle his balls and immediately got a hard on. Before Hockney had time to fantasise about a second occult-rite-cum-gang-bang to save what remained of the British Empire, he heard a loud swish and the paddle came down hard on his bollocks. He tried to cry out but the ball gag prevented this.

Kitaj snatched the blindfold from Hockney's eyes.

"So, Hockney, have I not told you time and again that you are my slave? If you are a slave you are to submit to me and give up your fantasies of belonging to a master race!"

"Yes, master," Hockney replied as trickles of saliva dribbled down his chin.

"But you continue to disobey me and act like a nazi slut. That is unacceptable. You will have to be punished."

Kitaj held up his paddle, big and leathery, with holes in it to make it less wind-resistant. The holes were arranged to spell SLUT, so whenever Hockney was whacked this was etched into the part of his body receiving the punishment. If Kitaj hit hard enough, the letters didn't go away for days.

A devilish smile crept across Kitaj's face as he crawled on top of Hockney and got into a straddle. The slave could feel Kitaj's stiffy through his pants. The gag in the slave's mouth muffled his orgasmic moans. Despite the beating his balls had received, Hockney was still erect. Kitaj raised the paddle above his head and brought it down hard onto Hockney's left pectoral muscle. Smack! A stifled scream escaped the slave. Smack! Smack! Smack! The dom paddled Hockney's nipples over and over. Tears of pain came to Hockney's face, his screams were stifled by the gag. With a strong grip, Kitaj grabbed the ball gag and yanked it out of Hockney's mouth by snapping the leather. Now the slave's cries were ear-piercing.

"I love to hear you scream like this," Kitaj informed Hockney as he simultaneously rubbed his hard-on against the slave's body.

The dom raised the paddle again and continued to go to town on the sub's chest. The word SLUT was written every which way across Hockney's upper body. Small bruises were also starting to form. The slave was numb from the pain. After what seemed like an eternity, Kitaj finally relented.

Hockney's rapid breathing slowed. The beating was over. It was customary after punishments that Hockney thank Kitaj for setting him straight.

"Thank you, master."

Kitaj shook his head and stroked Hockney's hair.

"It is so sweet that you think that was your punishment. It is far from over," the dom said as he hopped off the bed and flipped Hockney onto his side.

"Now slave, how many squaddies gang banged you during that occult ritual two months back?" Kitaj queried, running the warm paddle over Hockney's ass.

"Twelve, master."

"Correct. That is twelve more than there should have been. You are not here to save the British establishment. You are here to serve me. Your whorish actions were beyond unacceptable, so I think it is appropriate for me to give you twelve paddlings, one for each squaddie who had you."

"Yes, master."

Hockney closed his eyes and braced himself. He heard the paddle go into the air and anticipated a blow that didn't come when he expected it. He waited and waited. Finally, smack! The echo reverberated throughout the room, as did the slave's cry.

"One," Hockney whispered, knowing that he was to count every blow or else Kitaj would start again.

"Two, three, four, five."

Hockney was in agony, but this was also when he got the most horny, as Kitaj asserted his dominance over him, punishing him mercilessly for his slutty infractions. It made no difference that Kitaj had ordered him to get down and dirty with the squaddies. Hockney had an absolutely stonking erection.

"Seven, eight." Hockney wanted Kitaj, he needed his master to take him...

"You missed number nine," Kitaj announced.

"Yes, master."

Kitaj began again, this time harder. Hockney marvelled at the fact his master was able to hit so hard. He changed paces, sometimes going so slowly that it felt torturous, as Hockney just wanted him to finish. Sometimes he went fast, trying to catch Hockney out on the count, so he could start over again. The slave's arse burned. It was as red as a tomato. His cock was quivering with pleasure. Finally…

"Twelve."

Kitaj dropped the paddle on the floor and looked at Hockney expectantly.

"Thank you for my punishment, master."

Kitaj sat down on the bed beside the slave and put his hand between his legs.

"You have one hell of a hard-on. What kind of a slut gets this turned on by a paddling like that, huh?"

"A slut like me." Hockney knew the correct answer.

"That's right. A slut like you."

Kitaj flipped Hockney over and began stroking his cock, his fingers softly caressing, making the slave moan with desire. He sped up and Hockney could feel an orgasm building. Then Kitaj stopped.

He stood up, rubbed Hockney's sore chest, began to strip. When he was naked, Kitaj rolled the slave over and climbed on top of him. He slathered lubricant on his big wide cock and rammed it inside the sub. As he thrust Kitaj stroked Hockney's pecs, feeling all the SLUTs displayed across them. Then the stroking became rougher and rougher, until the dom started smacking Hockney's nipples. The slave yelped in pain.

"You know you love it."

Hockney did love it. He felt like he was floating on a sea of pleasure. His and Kitaj's bodies made the sexiest smacking noise as they collided. The dom was hitting his g-spot. Hockney was in danger of coming without permission.

"Please may I come, master?"

"I need to hear you beg." Kitaj increased his pace, going deeper and deeper.

"Please master, will you please let me come? I am nothing but your slave and I live to make you happy. The only pleasure I have is when you fuck me like the horny bitch I am. Please master!"

"Yes, my slave, you may come if you renounce racism and fascism."

"I renounce racism and fascism!" Hockney screamed.

The sub shrieked with pleasure. His entire body was shaking and trembling in exquisite ecstasy. He almost passed out from the orgasmic sensations. Hockney could feel Kitaj start to come too. The dom pulled out, flipped Hockney over and rammed his cock into the slut's mouth. Hockney greedily swallowed Kitaj's come. It was good when Kitaj's spunk was mixed with just a taste of the sub's bum juice. When Kitaj was finished, Hockney cleaned him off with his tongue. The dom then batted his semi-hard dick lightly against that slave's face, which was a sign of his complete satisfaction. The master got up and began to dress.

"Good night, Hockney," Kitaj said as he turned out the lights, leaving the slave still tied to the bed, tired and spent from pleasure. "I'm going out for a drink with some friends."

And it was in this way that the spring term was passed. Hockney put neo-nazism and his army contacts behind him and instead set his mind to making art and serving his master Kitaj. He spent much of the Easter holidays in Bradford and was glad to get back to London and Kitaj for his last term as a postgraduate at the Republican College of Art.

CHAPTER 30

HOCKNEY THE SLAVE BECOMES
A MASTERLESS MAN WITH
A MASTERS DEGREE

We will have one last look at the RCA where we have already had so much kinky fun. Our rapscallion was in his last term, soon to be the proud possessor of an MA degree. He was sitting in Kitaj's rooms. Tea was over, candles lighted and silence reigning, except when distant sounds of mirth came from some drunk postgraduates cavorting in the street.

"Who will you fuck when I set you free at the end of term?" Kitaj asked.

"It's fun to go down on the men you meet in Bradford's public toilets."

"Don't talk about going down on any Tom, Dick or Harry." Kitaj chided. "To make your mark in the art world you need to stay in London and be selective about who you fellate. Don't waste your blow jobs, give them to people who matter and who can further your career."

"Just give me a week in Bradford. I could suck a hundred men off in a week. I'll have them come in my mouth coz their sperm is full of nutrients. The spunk I swallow will keep me looking young and healthy"

"You ungrateful dog! Do you mean to say my come isn't good enough for you?"

"I'm very glad when you spunk up in my mouth, old fellow, but variety is the spice of life!"

"You make a very poor slave, Hockney, and you might regret both your words and what you're forcing me to do this evening, rather than waiting until after you are presented with your MA. But first you are to shave your legs and pubes for me. I want the skin baby soft. I don't often watch you but tonight is special. Tonight is the night I'll remove my collar from you."

Hockney smiled as he touched his beautiful collar and bathed his body in a deep, sudsy, perfumed wash. Everything down to his toes must be soft, deliciously scented. Satisfied that he was clean and smooth for Kitaj's pleasure, Hockney rose from the bathtub. His nipples hardened at the rush of cool air and he saw his master smile. Hockney took a towel, wrapped it around his body and stepped out onto the bathmat. The slave left the bathroom and as he approached Kitaj in the next room, he dropped the towel. The sub's body was damp, still warm from the steamy water, scented lightly from the soap. The slave dropped to his knees and back onto his heels, legs spread and hands palm down on the tops of his thighs. Hockney bowed his head and waited for Kitaj. He sensed his master move and felt Kitaj's hand caressing his hair, letting the loose strands slip through his fingertips. The dom's hand slipped lower, tilting the sub's chin so that their eyes meet. Love, adoration and pride showed brightly and Hockney smiled, shyly, at the loving approval of his master.

"Have I pleased you, my master?" Hockney asked quietly.

"You have pleased me very much, my own." Kitaj's voice was hushed. "Rise, mine."

As Hockney rose, Kitaj stood up too. The master pulled the slave towards him and claimed a heated kiss, his hands holding the sub tightly. Hockney could feel Kitja's arousal growing against him. The dom gripped Hockney's hair tightly, tugging it and causing the slave to whimper as they snogged.

"Please me, pet," Kitaj growled.

Hockney dropped to his knees, untying Kitaj's drawstring pants, letting them pool around his ankles before helping the dom step out of them. The slave slid his hands up his master's thighs, the skin soft yet the texture of his hair making it rough. His scent was fresh, he'd showered before Hockney arrived. His cock was beautiful and Hockney took it in his hand, lightly running his fingers up and down its length. The sub leant forward and lightly flicked the head with his tongue, tasting the shiny drop of pre-come that had already begun to form. He ran his tongue along the ridge to the base of Kitaj's cock, licking and sucking his balls. The master sighed and his hands gripped the slave's hair, twining his fingers in the strands. Hockney traced back to the head of Kitaj's cock with light kisses and took it full into his mouth, tasting the velvety salty-sweetness.

"Mmmmmm..." he groaned around the cock as it jumped in his mouth.

The taste was so sweet. Hockney couldn't get enough of it and he sucked the swelling member deeper into his throat, feeling the throbbing gristle bounce back against his tonsils. He felt the John Thomas go deeper. Kitaj moaned. Hockney pulled back so that he might worship the cock with his tongue, licking, sucking, tasting, teasing. Kitaj grew harder as his length was worked over and his breathing became more and more laboured. The master pulled Hockney up and off his cock, he didn't want to come just yet.

"No, pet... not now." Kitaj's breathing was uneven and his voice was strained.

He'd been on the brink of orgasm and there was disappointment on Hockney's face.

"Please, Master... I wish to please you..." Hockney began but he was cut off.

"You do please me. I am very proud of my sweet, submissive girl. You have learned everything you need to know to make a huge name for yourself in the art world. In a few weeks you will have your MA."

As he spoke, Kitaj undid the dog collar around Hockney's neck.

"So I am uncollaring you. You are now a masterless man. We will never have sex again but I expect you to become an art world sensation. You must fuck your way to the top, and perhaps whenever you and another man rut, you will imagine that other man is me."

Denizen of the Dead
The Horrors of Clarendon Court
edited by Stewart Home

On the border between the City's Cripplegate ward and south Islington's Bone Hill district stands Clarendon Court AKA The Denizen - an elite and newly built luxury apartment block of 99 flats marketed to property investors.

Exclusive? Yes. Reassuringly expensive? Yes. Safe? Undoubtedly not!

There were stories, just rumours, about what went on there. Rumours about perversion, orgies, ghosts, bad feng shui and shockingly unpleasant deaths. When a gorgeous young nymphomaniac bursts into a Clarendon Court apartment, the whole story of depravity and corruption is revealed.

In this collection of short fiction by today's top writers the Clarendon Court investment flats really are haunted by the ghosts of Cripplegate's wild past, when the hood was notorious for its brothels and the ultra-violent criminals who frequented them.

On top of this there's a problem with the spirits of hundreds of thousands of unhappy souls whose corpses were dumped in both local plague pits and the more recent Golden Lane mega-morgue, a huge Victorian Palace of the Dead.

This anthology is a protest against property speculation and a new take on the genre of haunted house horror fiction. The book itself is a talisman that defends our communities against developers and inside it also features Spell Series by the w.o.n.d.e.r. coven. The symbols of this living spell are a lock and key designed to dismantle the neoliberal project and overdevelopment as represented by Clarendon Court.

Featuring Paul Ewen, Tariq Goddard, Iphigenia Baal, Chris Petit, Steve Finbow, John King, Chloe Aridjis, Tom McArthy, Liz Rever, Katrina Palmer, Michael Hampton Bridget Penney and many more!

ISBN: 978-1527261549